THE WALKING BOY

THE SECOND NOVEL IN THE
CHUANQI 傳奇 TRILOGY

LYDIA KWA

ARSENAL PULP PRESS
VANCOUVER

ARSENAL PULP PRESS
Suite 202 – 211 East Georgia St.
Vancouver, BC V6A 1Z6
Canada
arsenalpulp.com

The publisher gratefully acknowledges the support of the Canada Council for the Arts and the British Columbia Arts Council for its publishing program, and the Government of Canada (through the Canada Book Fund), and the Government of British Columbia (through the Book Publishing Tax Credit Program) for its publishing activities.

Arsenal Pulp Press acknowledges the xʷməθkʷəy̓əm (Musqueam), Sḵwx̱wú7mesh (Squamish), and səl̓ílwəta?ł (Tsleil-Waututh) Nations, speakers of Hul'q'umi'num'/Halq'eméylem/ hən̓q̓əmin̓əm̓ and custodians of the traditional, ancestral, and unceded territories where our office is located. We pay respect to their histories, traditions, and continuous living cultures and commit to accountability, respectful relations, and friendship.

This is a work of fiction. Any resemblance of characters to persons either living or deceased is purely coincidental.

Cover and text design by Oliver McPartlin
Tang Empire map by Malcolm Cullen
Edited by Susan Safyan
Proofead by Shirarose Wilensky

Printed and bound in Canada

Library and Archives Canada Cataloguing in Publication:
Kwa, Lydia, 1959–, author
    The walking boy / Lydia Kwa.
Originally published: Toronto: Key Porter Books, 2005.
Issued in print and electronic formats.
ISBN 978-1-55152-763-5 (softcover).–ISBN 978-1-55152-764-2 (HTML)

    I. Title.

PS8571.W3W24 2019   C813'.54   C2018-906222-3

C2018-906223-1

In loving memory of
my mother, Audrey Hee
(1934–2017)
and
To all who nurture others

PREFACE

The Walking Boy was first published by Key Porter Books in 2005. Janie Yoon was the editor who championed the work, and for that, I will always be grateful. She was also the one who suggested that I write a trilogy. It seemed a wild and wildly unfathomable notion at the time.

The Walking Boy was met with warm enthusiasm in some quarters of literary publishing and also nominated for the Ethel Wilson Fiction Prize.

It took about a decade—after writing two other books—before I felt inspired to create *Oracle Bone*, a novel set some forty years before *The Walking Boy.*

Thanks to Arsenal Pulp Press, *The Walking Boy* now has a second life. It has been transformed from the original, with traces of *Oracle Bone*, the second book in the trilogy, evident between the pages. As a result of numerous subtle changes and additions, this new version is critically different from the original.

While completing *Oracle Bone*, I fell in love with the notion of a trilogy. Two down, one more to go—this sounds possible and not unfathomable, after all. I hope to complete the last book in the trilogy within the next few years. I call these three novels a *chuanqi* 傳奇 trilogy. The term means "to transmit the strange," a once-popular narrative tradition in Chinese literature. My interest in writing the trilogy is to acknowledge that tradition, while conducting experiments in literary subversion.

—Lydia Kwa, August 2018

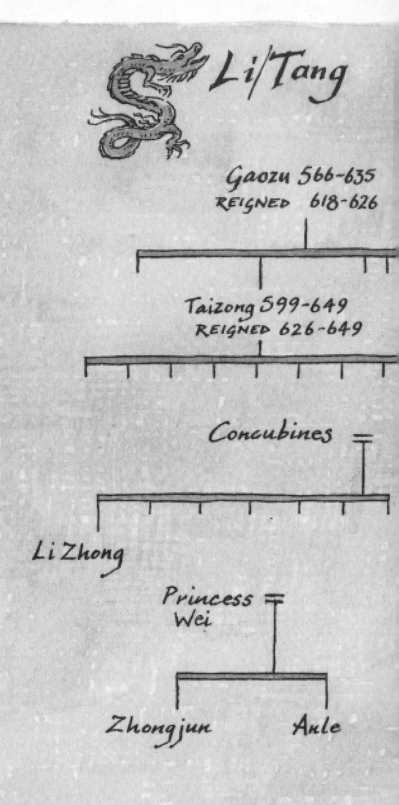

Li/Tang

Gaozu 566-635
REIGNED 618-626

Taizong 599-649
REIGNED 626-649

Concubines =

Li Zhong

Princess = Wei

Zhongjun   Anle

Imperial Family

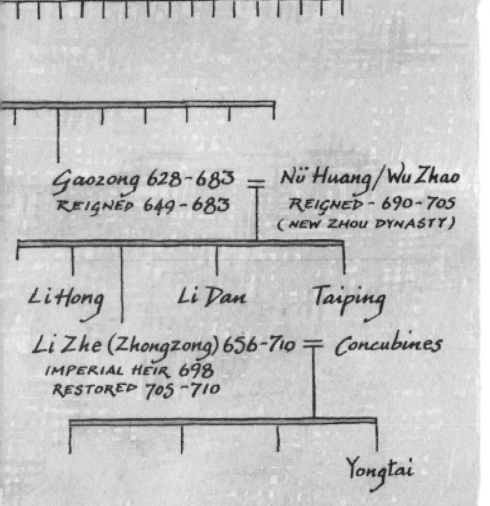

Gaozong 628-683 = Nü Huang/Wu Zhao
REIGNED 649-683   REIGNED - 690-705
(NEW ZHOU DYNASTY)

Li Hong   Li Dan   Taiping

Li Zhe (Zhongzong) 656-710 = Concubines
IMPERIAL HEIR 698
RESTORED 705-710

Yongtai

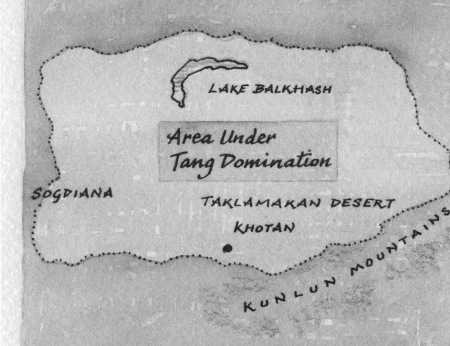

LAKE BALKHASH

Area Under
Tang Domination

SOGDIANA

TAKLAMAKAN DESERT

KHOTAN

KUNLUN MOUNTAINS

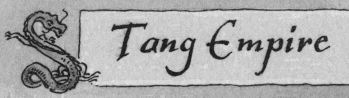

Tang Empire

TUFAN

ARABIAN
SEA

HIMALAYAS

BAY OF
BENGAL

INDIA

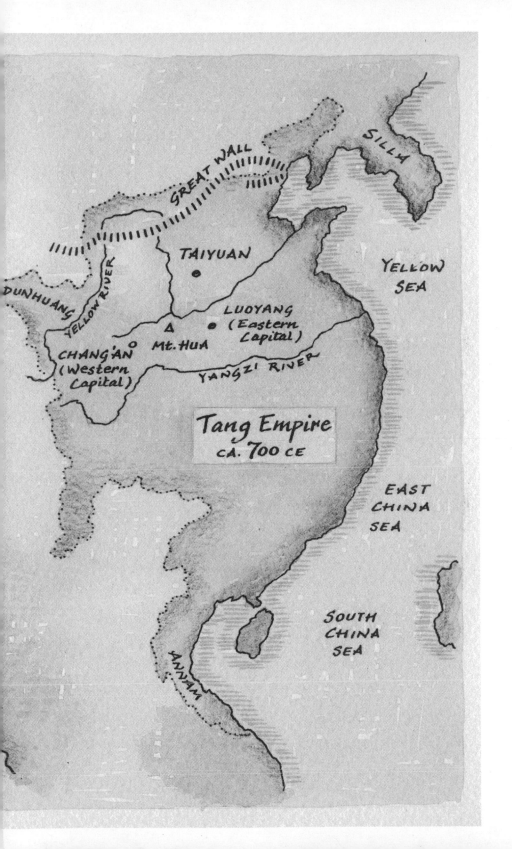

TAIJIGONG
THE PALACE CITY

IMPERIAL PARK

Black Tortoise Gate

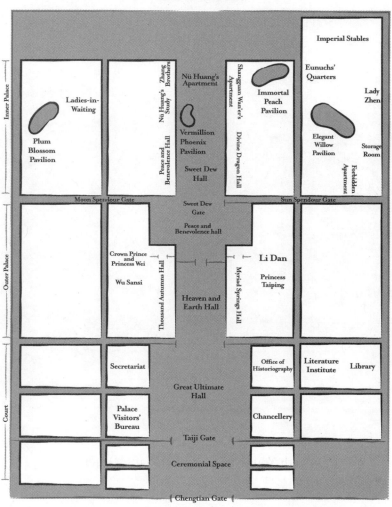

Imperial Stables

Inner Palace

Ladies-in-
Waiting

Nü Huang's
Apartment

Zhang Brothers

Nü Huang's Study

Shangguan Wan'er's Apartment

Immortal
Peach
Pavilion

Eunuchs'
Quarters

Lady
Zhen

Plum
Blossom
Pavilion

Peace and Benevolence Hall

Vermillion
Phoenix
Pavilion

Divine Dragon Hall

Sweet Dew
Hall

Elegant
Willow
Pavilion

Storage
Room

Forbidden Apartment

Moon Spendour Gate

Sweet Dew
Gate

Sun Spendour Gate

Peace and
Benevolence hall

Outer Palace

Crown Prince
and
Princess Wei

Wu Sansi

Thousand Autumns Hall

Myriad Springs Hall

Li Dan

Princess
Taiping

Heaven and
Earth Hall

Secretariat

Office of
Historiography

Literature
Institute

Library

Court

Great Ultimate
Hall

Palace
Visitors'
Bureau

Chancellery

Taiji Gate

Ceremonial Space

Chengtian Gate

THE MAIN CHARACTERS

BAOSHI
The walking boy

SHANGGUAN WAN'ER
Imperial Secretary to Nü Huang

HARELIP
Hermit monk, Mount Hua

ARDHANARI
Sculptor in Chang'an and the Mogao Caves

NÜ HUANG
Female Emperor, Wu Zhao

LING
Abbess of Da Fa Temple

LADY ZHEN
Shangguan Wan'er's mother

WU SANSI
Minister of the court, Nü Huang's nephew

ZHANG YIZHI
Fifth Young Master, Nü Huang's lover

ZHANG CHANGZONG
Sixth Young Master, Nü Huang's lover

OLD GECKO
Ardhanari's uncle

PRONUNCIATION GUIDE FOR SOME CHINESE NAMES

This is meant to be a rough guide to pronunciation. I've transliterated the names according to common ways of sounding vowels and consonants in English; this is not at all related to the Pinyin system, the basis for how the names have been spelled in the novel. The all-important tones have not been indicated here either.

Baoshi is pronounced "Bao Shir."

Shangguan Wan'er is pronounced "Shanh kwan Wanher."

Wu Zhao is pronounced "Woo Chow."

Zhen is pronounced "Tzehng."

Wu Sansi is pronounced "Woo Saanh see."

Zhang Yizhi is pronounced "Tzang Yee Tzeh."

Zhang Changzong is pronounced "Tzang Chanhg song."

Without intuiting the sublime,
You will not experience freedom.
—Nagarjuna

PROLOGUE

The dream began one quiet summer afternoon. With no pressing duties left to perform, I had lain down alone in my private chamber and became quickly ensnared. The story that was revealed to me seemed unnatural, strange, and filled with superstitions. A year has passed, yet the dream still breathes and insists. I preserve it here for my own pleasure, neither dictated by another's whim nor to fulfil any of my obligations to transcribe the thoughts of others. I have been wracked with indecision concerning the future of this document. We will be returning to the Eastern Capital in time for the Autumn Equinox celebrations. I must decide soon. For the time being, this will be safe in the secret compartment. To quell my anxiety, I prepared a concoction of chrysanthemum petals infused in wine. I think of Tao Yuanming, that philosophical poet recluse of the early fifth century who found it painful to exist within the contradictions and political dilemmas of his time. Although I am no direct relation of his, I am a poet and a woman acquainted with dilemmas. I respectfully adopt as my sobriquet a description he was fond of using. Why not raise a few cups to such a soul? This elixir of chrysanthemum, a flower that blooms in the cold season and whose tonic abilities to confer long life can be released only through an intoxicating trance.

"Cold Flower"

*H*arelip wasn't easily convinced. Burrowing under the quilt, the old man argued with himself or, rather, his dream. His mind relived the story countless times, the scenes occupying his attention with stinging clarity. His heart fluttered in awkward, irregular spurts. He turned toward the window. No light from the sliver of moon concealed by clouds. He shivered with dread as he gazed at Baoshi, sleeping undisturbed next to him.

In the dream, he was the incredulous onlooker. Watching Baoshi descend Mount Hua, watching another face instantly recognizable to him draw closer and closer. Man and boy shed copious tears. Was it joy? Grief? He couldn't hear what they were saying. He wanted to move toward Ardhanari, to beg him for forgiveness.

He woke up, throat parched. The dream was a beast whose claws dug deep into him. When he rose from the kang, his lungs were seized by spasms of pain. He stumbled outside the shack and coughed into his hand. The blood-tinged phlegm sat resolutely in the well of his palm.

Jinzhe 驚蟄 Jieqi
Waking of Insects
Second Lunar Month
New Moon
702 CE

Mount Hua

270 Li East of the Western Capital Chang'an

At this time of the early morning, just as the perpetual lamp indicates the Hour of the Rabbit, everything exists in the bluish shadows before dawn, suspended between life and annihilation. The candles on the altar to Harelip's left flicker in the draft. His upright torso vibrates, swayed to and fro by an invisible wind. The sensations from the dream are still with him—the raspy dryness in the throat and the fickle heart rhythms. His hands clasped in his lap break out into a sweat. Last night he washed off the blood immediately after coughing it up, but the memory hasn't disappeared. He checks the height of the incense stick on the altar. Barely half. Why is time passing so slowly? He directs his gaze back to the ground. A dull ache spreads across his shoulders and he stifles a sigh. The jade pendant rests against his chest with the weight of regret. Ardhanari has probably spent all these years wondering what has become of him. Last night's dream took him by surprise, seeing his friend's face just as he had looked so many years ago.

A narrow beam of light through the one window in the wooden shack caresses Baoshi's left cheek and tickles the fine hairs of his nostrils.

He twitches his face then sneaks a look at Harelip sitting directly across from him. His Master is deep in concentration, head bowed and body showing no signs of slackening since they both began to sit before sunrise. Dust motes suspended in that beam of light are rushing toward him with news of recent adventures in the magic realms. He smiles with pleasure.

Harelip's mind wanders through various incidents in his early life in the Chang'an monastery, learning from both Buddhist and Daoist medical texts. The meeting with Xuanzang, who brought the sutras back from India. Then Xuanzang's death shortly after his translation project was completed. Two years later, preparations by his superiors to recommend him to the court, where Daoist influence was threatening to overshadow Buddhist sympathies. He was the perfect gambit, a young, intelligent monk who was a gifted healer. Oh, yes, a bit of a renegade but absolutely suited to his superiors' plans to increase their influence with Emperor Gaozong. That recommendation to the court was to happen at the same time as Gaozong and Wu Zhao's ascent up Mount Tai for the Feng and Shan rituals. That was the reign year Qianfeng. Well, he turned his back on all that when he didn't join the procession up the sacred mountain.

He even knows more about the world of Wu Zhao since she has become Nü Huang, Female Emperor. He hears news about the intrigues at court from the villagers below. When they make the trek up the mountain to see him with their ailments, they rattle off what they've heard without any suspicion that their hermit healer has his own secrets. Twelve years ago, Wu Zhao usurped the throne from her son Li Zhe 李哲—successor to the throne after Li Zhi 李治 died and was given the posthumous name Gaozong 高宗—and proclaimed herself Holy and Divine Emperor. That fact has been repeated to Harelip countless times, the tone of incredulity surprisingly fresh. These days, the villagers are harping on Nü Huang's affair with those two half-brothers. "Imagine," they say in hushed tones, "in her seventies." Harelip often feels tempted to say to them, "Just how exciting can that be?" The villagers have been especially nervous ever since Nü Huang moved the court back from Luoyang to Chang'an last winter. Rumours are circulating that her health is failing.

Harelip clears his throat uneasily. He shouldn't let his mind drift aimlessly through such troublesome reminiscences. He looks up and notices that the incense stick has completely burned down, leaving a pile of grey ash. The perpetual lamp confirms the time. The Hour of the Dragon. He's surprised by growling sounds emanating from Baoshi's belly. That boy! He bends forward to gather up the pair of tiny bronze cymbals in front of his feet, strikes them together, and waits for the sound to fade away before striking the cymbals together a second time, then a third.

Baoshi raises his head at the sound of the cymbals and frowns. His loud stomach embarrasses him. These days, he never seems to go for very long before feeling gripped by monstrous hunger pangs. Only moments before, his mind had started to fantasize about a pig roasting above hot coals. He listens as Harelip recites the Heart Sutra.

"... whatever is form is emptiness, whatever is emptiness is form ..."

Baoshi's attention drifts back to the idea of the roast pig. When was the last time he had eaten suckling pig? Or any kind of pork for that matter? When he was still with his parents. Sadness lodges in his chest. Before too long, the final words of the sutra penetrate his daydreaming.

Their eyes meet. Together they emit sighs as if one were prompting the other, yet their furrowed brows are plagued with vastly different concerns. Harelip uncrosses his legs from the lotus position and groans. The two small hours of sitting were painstakingly slow this morning.

Curse of old age! Wooden screws coming undone! How could a creaky wheel reach immortality? Will my body be nimble in that Pure Land?

He and Baoshi rise up from their tattered cushions and turn their bodies to face the altar. They make their prostrations before the figure of Buddha, a modest wooden sculpture only two hands high whose sensuous red and gold robes are faded and chipped in places. Even Buddha is in need of repair, Harelip notes. He turns to face Baoshi and rests his gnarled fingers lightly on the boy's shoulders.

"Baoshi, I've taken care of you all these years."

"Yes, Master, I remember, and I'm always grateful." He blushes, the memory still able to flood him with shame. He fidgets under Harelip's hands. That tone of voice is what Harelip uses when he's about to launch into a speech or a teaching. How much longer before their morning meal?

"My dear Baoshi, do you remember what I told you about my reason for coming to this mountain?"

"Yes, Master. You said you were fleeing for your life."

Harelip's cheeks flush red-hot. Would Wu Zhao have become so enraged by his absence at the Mount Tai ritual that she would have had him imprisoned or killed? Or exiled to Lingnan to the south? He'll never know for sure.

He nods to Baoshi, appreciating the firm jawline and elegant cheekbones. What bright, curious eyes! And those lips, as yet untainted by carnal pleasures.

"I had a troubling dream last night. When I woke up, I knew I couldn't ignore it." He notices that Baoshi looks somewhat distracted.

Harelip chokes back the rush of feelings and hobbles over to the window to peer outside. A sparrow pecks at seeds on the ground, its hopping movements swift and urgent. He thinks to himself, he's nothing like this sparrow, utterly focused on picking out everything edible in its path. Instead, his mind is distracted by misgivings about the past. Had he made a mistake, fleeing to Mount Hua, without any consideration of Ardhanari's feelings?

He can't answer his own question. He turns around to find Baoshi replenishing the oil in the perpetual lamp.

"Do you know what a novice on a pilgrimage is called?"

"No." Baoshi shakes his head vigorously.

"A walking boy."

Baoshi looks at his Master quizzically.

"I dreamt that you left the mountain and found your way to Chang'an. And you met this man, Ardhanari. He was a special friend of mine before I fled the city." Harelip pauses before continuing. "You must become a walking boy for my sake. Leave this mountain, find Ardhanari, and bring him back to Mount Hua to see me." He means to sound firm, even confident, but his voice wavers.

"When?" Baoshi sits down, elbows on their small table, his hands cupped against his forehead.

"Not for another two or three months. When the ice on the paths has completely melted, and it's warm enough for easier travelling." As he finishes speaking, he shudders at the memory of his harrowing journey up the mountain in winter. To think that had been half a lifetime ago, and he has never left since then.

He joins Baoshi at the table and leans toward him. "Do you remember what I called you that first day we met?"

"You said that I'm a miracle of Heaven. I shall never forget." His ears burning with upset, he asks, "How long do I have to be away then?"

"Until you find Ardhanari and convince him to return with you. Can you accept this, my son? That I would ask you to set off on this pilgrimage based on a single dream? A dream I find so compelling I would sacrifice having you at my side." Harelip's body trembles with all the emotions he's holding in check.

"Master, I owe you my life. I will do what you ask, even though I'll be very sad to be away from you."

Harelip inhales loudly, sucking back his own urge to cry. "If you decide to assume a hermit's life on Mount Hua at the end of the pilgrimage, you'll be doing so of your own volition. You had no choice when you were placed in my care. You were a boy. You are still a boy, really. When you go out into the world below, you'll be exposed to all kinds of possibilities, and that will allow you to discover your true path. I must stay on the mountain for the sake of the villagers. Besides, in the dream, you were the one who met Ardhanari, not me."

Baoshi's belly offers another long growl. Harelip laughs. "Come, miracle of Heaven! We're taking up too much time talking about a pilgrimage that will begin many weeks from now, and here I am ignoring your hunger. Let's fill your belly before you faint from starvation."

Nü Huang's Apartment
The Inner Palace at Taijigong
North Central Chang'an

The eagle-owl launches herself from the top branches of a cypress, swooping down into the clearing. *Wu-wu, wu-hu-huhu,* the raptor announces, as her wings slap the cold night air. Small creatures scurry into hiding, burrowing under piles of leaves or escaping into the crevices of tree trunks.

Not enough time. A hare moves too slowly, too late, the scent of fear betraying his presence. The eagle-owl grips the hare with her claws and lifts him up into the darkness.

In the middle of the Hour of the Tiger, Nü Huang moans while still asleep. The owl's stare entraps her as she fidgets and squirms, struggling out of sleep. She sits up abruptly between Changzong and Yizhi on the heated kang, her heart pounding violently in her chest. She glances down at their curled-up bodies to reassure herself where she is.

"Heaven help me! It cannot be true," she exclaims.

Ah Pu, the Ordinary One, emerges drowsily from the antechamber, stumbles once as she hurries across the room toward her sovereign in her padded slippers. This is all too familiar to the maid. She lights the lantern on the side table next to Changzong and averts her eyes from the brothers' naked bodies, partially concealed by the quilt. She places her hands on Nü Huang's shoulders.

"Your Majesty, come back. You are only having a dream," her seasoned voice coos gently, keenly aware she must be careful not to startle her mistress. She studies Nü Huang's eyes. Not quite returned to this waking realm yet. How sad it is to see the crinkly old woman still plagued by these horrible nightmares.

Ah Pu touches Nü Huang's forehead with the back of her own hand. Clammy and cold, despite the fact that the coals inside the kang are still simmering with white heat. Nü Huang's skin is a shocking contrast to her own warmth. The wind rattles against the wooden latticed windows and doors, insulated with translucent rice paper, and leaks through the minuscule gaps between the panels. A storm is building. Ah Pu can feel it in her old bones.

She massages Nü Huang's shoulders gently with her hands. No matter what she has heard of Nü Huang's misdeeds, beginning in the days when she was Wu Zhao, the concubine, to when she became Gaozong's Empress, to the days since she proclaimed herself Nü Huang, Female Emperor, Ah Pu feels pity for her mistress. She, more than all the other maids and the younger ladies-in-waiting, has known the full extent of Nü Huang's growing dependency on her, especially since Her Majesty's health has been deteriorating in the last two years.

Nü Huang doesn't respond to Ah Pu's touch at first, her eyes engaged by a vision. The women laugh at her from behind their unkempt, blood-soaked hair. She can't understand what they're saying. The sounds resemble gurgling more than words. The gurgling of brooks or of infants? She can't be sure. They flail against the darkness, their protesting limbs whipping up turbulence in her.

The warmth of Ah Pu's skilful hands eventually rouses Nü Huang from her dazed state. Nü Huang's eyelids flutter rapidly and she looks up, relieved, finally able to focus her attention on Ah Pu. Treading quietly out of the room, Ah Pu soon returns with a tray. She places it down on the side table and deftly removes the red cork of the miniature jade flask, taps its narrow neck until enough of the Sleeping Comfort powder spills into the waiting spoonful of warm honeyed water. She extends the spoon toward Nü Huang, who meekly accepts the medicine.

After the maid has returned to her own kang in the antechamber, Nü Huang lies back down. The coals glow reddish-white in the brazier across from the bed. She stares at the lantern.

Nü Huang ponders, mesmerized by the light, that forty years have not made enough of a difference. Have they returned only in her imagination, or are they still here roaming the Inner Palace? Those virulent demon souls! Not deterred by zigzagged bridges or lang, the covered arcades that extend from the forbidden lou apartment in the southeastern section of the Inner Palace to her own lou in the north wing. Nor has their presence been diminished by the most fanciful of exorcism ceremonies. What is the point of that large ornate screen placed right inside the main doors of her apartment when it fails to block them? Demon souls with not even a liang of respect for the passage of time. Are they planting fears of the owl in her dreams now? She pushes her tongue against the roof of her mouth, feeling annoyed.

When Changzong and Yizhi came to lie down beside her last night, nothing seemed out of the ordinary. They had set out their collection of objects on a square of golden embroidered cloth at the foot of the bed and then surrendered themselves to playing the usual games. She penetrated each one through his rear heavenly gate with her ivory implement, and they both responded with abundant gratitude as always. Then they smeared their jade stalks and her jade gate generously with lust ointment before thrusting gleefully into her. She was again pleased to see that the half-brothers competed with each other to enter her. She clutched at their lithe, muscled forms, giggled with delight at their shifting chameleon selves, and felt gratified by the infusion of their life force. Afterwards, she sunk rapidly into a deep slumber.

So why the dream? There had been no signs in those first few months back in the Western Capital. Are the former Empress Wang and concubine Xiao still keen to distress her? She had thought that calling the former Empress "Snake" and the concubine "Owl" would banish them to the far reaches of the forest. Yet they return, entering the wilderness of her dream. Yizhi turns toward her and his head falls against her neck. He emits a single, loud snort before starting to snore, a continuous wheezing sound.

Nü Huang studies Changzong's face. What exquisite eyebrows. Like the wings of a crane in flight. She tries to keep her eyes open. Despite the loud clattering of the doors and lattices, the magic powder is working. *Why am I falling asleep,* she wonders, *when those demon souls are still eager to penetrate the doors and walls?* She shifts her body again, this time to lie on her back. Her eyelids close tightly as the rain breaks through the clouds, striking the roof tiles.

THE CEREMONIAL SPACE, TAIJIGONG
NORTH CENTRAL CHANG'AN

The musicians on either side of the Taiji Gate raise the long dahao brass trumpets to their lips and sound the fanfare as the royal procession enters the courtyard from north of the gate. Standard-bearers lead the way, moving down the length of the courtyard in two rows. They plant their banners firmly in bronze rings attached to their waist belts. The yellow silk fabric with violet trim hangs down from the angled standards elegantly. Against the terracotta eastern wall, the first pink buds of peach trees are just starting to open, masses of solitary, delicate blossoms, while along the western wall, plum blossoms are in their glory, white with red eyes set against the thin, naked branches.

Nü Huang, in her yellow gown trimmed with gold thread and wearing a crown encrusted with rubies and emeralds, enters the courtyard borne on a palanquin by four Imperial guards. Walking behind, her son Crown Prince Li Zhe and his consort, Princess Wei, with their entourage of concubines and children, followed by Nü Huang's youngest son, Li Dan, the Imperial Heir, and his family. Then her daughter, Princess Taiping, and her second husband, Wu Youzhi; her nephew the Minister Wu Sansi; the Imperial Secretary Shangguan

Wan'er; and the brothers Zhang Changzong and Zhang Yizhi, with the retinue of zaixiang senior ministers and other lesser officials close behind. The zaixiang are dressed in their wide-sleeved, round-collared ceremonial gowns of bright crimson with orange-trimmed front aprons and pale green hems. The black ribbons of their fu tou headdresses flap in time with their slow yet exaggerated strides. At the end of the long retinue are the remaining members of the Imperial household, the ladies-in-waiting and the eunuch guards.

Nü Huang's palanquin is set down at the foot of the steps. She is helped by two ladies-in-waiting as she ascends the steps to the Great Ultimate Hall and occupies the south-facing throne chair, which is draped with a tiger pelt. She places her feet on the dainty footstool embroidered with the forms of dragons. The retinue file into the Hall and take their appointed places on either side of the throne.

"Light the fire!" commands Nü Huang to the head of the eunuch guards, who runs down the steps and dips a lit torch into the ceremonial urn. Its insides flare up immediately.

After a long silence, Nü Huang signals to Shangguan Wan'er to assume her place at the left of the throne, where a low table with brushes, ink, and blank scroll await her. Wan'er bows to Nü Huang and sits on the cushion, preparing to record Nü Huang's words.

Whenever Wan'er faces a large ceremonial gathering such as this, her heart quickens and her hands chill. After many years of being Imperial Secretary, she still can't escape this feeling of anxiety. Her thoughts turn briefly to the quiet solace of her own study. How she wishes she could be there instead. Nü Huang's voice pulls her back into the present moment and she begins to write, recording every word.

"I, the woman Wu Zhao, born the very same year Taizong succeeded his father Gaozu as second Emperor of the Tang Dynasty, at thirteen sui was the girl who entered the Inner Palace to serve as a cairen, Person of Talents, and Fifth Grade concubine to Taizong. I have enjoyed an illustrious history at court, rising to become Empress to Gaozong, then to rule in his stead when he was stricken with illness, and finally to gloriously fulfil the prophecy of becoming Nü Huang, Female Emperor of my Zhou Dynasty.

"On this auspicious occasion we once again remember that it is the time of the year when the growing yang first achieves its equality with the diminishing yin, when these forces in our world meet and have intercourse. From now until the Summer Solstice, yang begins to gain strength and prominence in the universe."

Nü Huang pauses and smiles at her retinue, several of whom are nodding their heads or smiling in appreciation. The burning wood in the urn crackles loudly as the flames leap upward. Nü Huang signals a lady-in-waiting for a cup of tea before continuing. "Now, the whipping of the bull."

The head guard shouts out the order, whereupon four of his eunuchs proceed through the Chengtian Gate to drag in a cart with a bull in a wooden cage. Two eunuchs hit at the sides of the cage, distracting him, while the other two open the top of the cage. The guards direct their clubs at the animal's head, taking care not to spill any blood. The bull grunts, struggling helplessly against each blow until he collapses.

"May the life force of the bull pass into the land and bring about an abundant yield of crops!" shouts the head eunuch, as his guards leave the courtyard, towing the carcass away.

Nü Huang leans forward and scrutinizes the audience in the Hall. In a surprisingly intimate tone of voice, she says, "You all know how it is at this time of year. The swallows return from the south to nest and we must take heed of the need to reconcile the male and the female energies, and seek to be fertile in our lives, whether to create offspring or to honour the life force in our elders. We must pay attention to the forces of transformation. As recorded in Mozhu, *Transformation, as when a frog becomes a quail.* Heaven, the progenitor of us all, and the proclaimer of my sovereignty, continues to guide us. I have seen fit to return from Luoyang to Chang'an to assert my commitment to the people's needs. The Emperor does not ignore their wishes. At this first Spring Equinox since the court's return to the Western Capital, it is opportune and auspicious to declare amnesty to all who had been implicated in plots against my reign. Your Emperor acknowledges the will and grace of Heaven."

The guards in the courtyard cheer, "Long live the Holy and Maternal Emperor, long live Her Majesty!"

Nü Huang clears her throat loudly. "With this return to Chang'an, I will begin a Palace Diary to record my private thoughts concerning key events.

"The Veritable Record is going to be written much later by a host of men from the Office of Historiography once I am dead. I have no doubt that the administrative duties of the court, daily noted in the Court Diary and the Administrative Record, will be accurately replicated in the Veritable Record. But what about the subtle, internal realities? The thoughts and desires left unexpressed? A Veritable Record ignores such details. A woman on the throne cannot assume that her truths and interpretations will be obvious to others, especially to those who are concerned only with how a formalized Veritable Record advances their version of history."

At this last comment, some ministers raise their eyebrows in con-sternation, while others strive to conceal their surprise or discomfort. Wan'er's upper lip curls up in an expression of delight. Although her head is bowed, her eyes looking down at the scroll, her smile is clearly visible to those who are watching. Wu Sansi is alarmed and embarrassed by the Imperial Secretary's lack of restraint. He frowns and presses his lips tightly together, averting his gaze. Changzong and Yizhi giggle loudly as they raise their sleeves to cover their mouths.

Nü Huang pauses for another sip of tea before continuing. "This Palace Diary will be the most intimate version of my rise to power as the unusual and gifted woman Wu Zhao. It will surpass the official records in revealing my deepest secrets. Only within its pages will I receive the fullest acknowledgment as Nü Huang. The pathetic title of huanghou, Empress, imparts a sour taste to my mouth. She who sits behind the Emperor. Thirty years of sitting behind the ailing Li Zhi, behind a veil no less, calling out decisions and judgments in his stead during those times when he could barely blink his eyelids or move his mouth. When he finally died, I emerged from behind that veil, that mantle of illusion, to proclaim myself Female Emperor. For the sake of our empire Zhongguo I have sought to recreate the absolute perfection of that first Zhou reign. As Emperor of the new Zhou, I urge all to be reminded of the generative forces of this season, of how life is constantly being renewed and transformed. Bring forth the doves now."

The herald calls out, "Send for the Imperial Netter of Birds," a command that is echoed down the line of guards and repeated until this most unusual of men, accompanied by his two sons on either side of him, appears through Chengtian Gate and passes through the Ceremonial Space before finally ascending the steps to the Great Ultimate Hall. His sons kneel just inside the entrance. The Netter, a mere husk of a man, perhaps weighing not much more than a fatted goat, might be hunched over, but he makes his way nimbly toward the throne in his new soft-soled cloth boots, his twisted body jerking forward in his plain, unembellished blue robe, a linen fu tou askew on his head. The robe brushes the ground more heavily on the right, yet his footsteps hardly make sounds on the marbled floor. He has learned to walk lightly so as not to startle the birds he seeks to capture. He kneels twenty paces from the throne on a silk cushion, which emits a soft hissing sound.

"You have been in the service of our court since the time of the former Emperor Gaozong. You come here at every Spring Equinox to complete your duties. I commend you for your long-standing service to us."

He prostrates himself so that his forehead touches the ground in acknowledgment of Nü Huang's remark. He's relieved that he and his sons have accomplished their task. Not only to capture a thousand doves but also to ensure they've remained undamaged and flawless while in captivity.

The Netter announces, "Your Majesty, the doves are ready."

"Distribute them to the aged as gifts."

The Netter of Birds rises from the cushion and bows, once again moving swiftly down the hall in that uneven gait. He and his sons descend the steps of the Hall, leaving the courtyard through the Chengtian Gate to distribute the doves to the elderly among the throngs of people eagerly waiting outside the Court at Taijigong.

Nü Huang, satisfied at the completion of the rites, gestures to Shangguan Wan'er to stop recording. Wan'er lowers her brush onto the porcelain rest and folds her hands in her lap in compliance.

The head of the Imperial guards shouts, "All rise and bow!"

The ministers and the Imperial household rise from their seats to bow as their Emperor descends into the courtyard and is borne up on the palanquin once again. The procession exits, heading north.

Qingming清明 Jieqi
Pure Brightness
Third Lunar Month
New Moon

THE FOREIGN QUARTER
WEST CENTRAL CHANG'AN

What an odd development after all these years, thinks Ardhanari. The letter from his uncle Old Gecko was entirely unexpected. After almost forty years away, with only a rare word heard now and then about the Mogao Caves from people they know in common, he has never received a direct letter from his uncle. Until now. Old Gecko and his sons, Ram and Arun, have remained rooted to the caves, while he has been living in Chang'an, over three thousand li away.

Did he imagine the tone, read something of his own unexpressed wish into the letter? Surely not. If a relative bothers to seek you out after years of silence, that singular act is weighted with all that hasn't been said, as far as he's concerned. *Nephew, we've toiled in these beloved Caves for such a long time. I'm reaching the end of my days here, and I'm not sure how much longer I might have. Please spare some kindness for your uncle and return for the summer to work alongside us.*

Ever since he arrived at this overpowering metropolis, he has never questioned that Chang'an is the place he wants to live in. Yes, he had grown up in Khotan, and he apprenticed at the Mogao Caves for a few years. But Chang'an he has chosen, unlike the other places. He hears from travellers that this is the largest city on the face of the earth. That might be true, but what does it matter? *I am a humble sculptor, and I concentrate on one figure at a time, not masses of people.* He shuts the door to his room, runs down the creaky stairs, clasping the cloth bundle in front of him, and heads across the street. The sun is barely up, and the cool air causes him to shiver, even though he's wearing long woollen trousers and has wrapped a swathe of his favourite vermillion muslin around his torso. He glances up at the rooms above. Could she still be asleep? He told her last night when he would come by. He can't wait for very long. He'll have to set off for the market soon to meet the caravan driver who will take him to Dunhuang, the town nearest to the Mogao Caves.

Sita is angry that he's leaving. He cannot fathom her lack of sympathy. She had said to him, "The man can't be that ill since he plans to work through the summer."

He stares longingly up at the window, hoping she'll show her face. But she doesn't. Ardhanari slips the key under a clay pot outside the entrance of the tea shop for the man who will use his room while he's away. Time has run out, so he heads toward the market. He does understand Sita—after all, who likes to be left, even temporarily? There was that lover years ago who left without any explanation and never came back. Harelip had disappeared without leaving the slightest clue as to where he had gone. This departure is different, he reassures himself. He had discussed this with Sita; there is no sudden, inexplicable disappearance.

It's difficult to be the one left behind. He supposes that's partly why he feels this sudden tug to respond to his uncle's letter by setting out for the Mogao Caves. People are very strange, he muses. They won't say anything for years and years, and then when they feel close to the end of their lives, they'll make the most surprising gestures.

He licks his lips, chapped and dry. How will he get used to the extreme temperatures at the Mogao Caves? As he walks along the winding alley, he smiles and nods at neighbours emerging from their houses.

Sita's words ring in his head: *You are trying to flee your disappointments.* Despite his protests, waving the letter in front of her face, reading it aloud countless times, she insists there must be more than the letter that motivates his decision to leave.

It's true, the letter had arrived at the peak of his exasperation, and so it seemed particularly timely. His recent sculptures lack vitality. He has felt a growing despair. How could he be doing such stale and dismal work? Something else nags at him, but he isn't sure what to make of it.

The market looms ahead. At this time of the morning, most of the sellers are already set up. The early customers are eagerly procuring the freshest vegetables and the best cuts of meat before the market throngs with crowds. Ardhanari heads toward the caravans and horses. When he finds the owner of the caravan he is to travel with, he instantly drops his cloth bundle down on the sand in front of him. For a few miao, he stares blankly at his hands. What is causing them to fail him so? He winces at the baying sound of the camel behind him. It's as if the animal has read his mind and is now exposing his secrets to the rest of the world.

Mount Hua

"Step into the light so that the monk can see you," Baoshi's father instructs him.

The chill bites into Baoshi's skin. His naked thighs shiver with cold. He steps reluctantly into the light.

Dissatisfied, Baoshi's father lifts him onto the table and pries open his legs. Harelip draws close to Baoshi and stares down at his private parts.

"Miracle of Heaven!" he exclaims. "Another uncommon one."

"Will you take him?" asks the father, his whole body trembling. He fishes out a pouch of silver coins from the inside pocket of his well-padded winter coat and drops it onto the table next to Baoshi.

Harelip lifts up the pouch from the table and places it back into the man's hand. He moves to the far corner and gestures to Baoshi. "Boy, come over here."

Baoshi slips off the table and wipes away the tears with the back of his hand. He pulls up his pants, ties the drawstrings securely at the waist before he walks toward Harelip, his eyes downcast.

Harelip bends slightly forward and touches Baoshi's chin, tilting his face up. He addresses the distraught boy in a barely audible whisper. "Do you understand what is being asked of me?"

"My father wants you to take me in as your burden, and relieve my family of their shame."

"I have been alone on this mountain twenty-eight years now. It seems that fate would have me change that."

Baoshi is remembering that day eight years ago as if it has just happened. The chill of shame, the burning glare of his father's eyes. He is nearly seventeen sui, yet he sometimes feels as if he is no older than that confused boy he had been. *You don't know how hard it is for your mother and me now that we must give you up, our only child so far. But we have hopes for another son, as your mother is with child again.* Shame once again washes over him. Perhaps the lunar eclipse is causing him to feel more agitated tonight. The light of the full moon has diminished gradually over the hours until it is now completely gone, eaten up by the darkness.

He lies down on the straw mat, wide awake while Harelip sleeps. Here he is, faced with his Master's conviction that he is to set off alone on a pilgrimage to the Western Capital. What choice does he have? If he wants to make his Master happy and to eventually return to him, he must not break that vow. Six weeks have passed since the day Harelip first told him about the imminent pilgrimage. How much longer before he has to leave?

I have to remember what he said to me that first day, Baoshi reflects. How had Harelip put it?

"Remember this: You are truly a manifestation of the Buddha! Two in One! How apt your parents named you Precious Stone."

"It was my mother who gave me the name." Baoshi's lips quivered with anguish, thinking of how he had been taken away in the night while she slept.

"When I came here, I discovered it was my destiny to leave the world behind, to live peacefully with mountain spirits and magical creatures. Yet this mountain, this place I call home now, frightened me terribly in the beginning. One cannot merely rely on the five senses to survive here. I'll teach you. You have nothing to fear. What makes one man flee in fright or go mad is the very elixir for another's soul."

"What kind of magical creatures? What do you mean?"

"Answers arrive through experience, or through intuition."

"What is intuition?"

"You'll know the meaning of that in time, Baoshi. The same goes for your questions about magic. Your destiny is to learn Two-in-Oneness, to embrace the marvellous contradictions of your whole person—your body, your essence, and your soul."

Baoshi turns his body toward Harelip's slumbering presence. He wonders if the pilgrimage will sharpen his intuition. What if he meets others who won't accept him the way Harelip does? When Harelip said to him that he was a miracle of Heaven, he retorted, "If I am such a miracle, why did my father give me away?"

"Why? Because your father is a lesser being than you!" Harelip banged the table with a tightly closed fist, startling Baoshi. When he calmed down, he said, "He fails to appreciate the wonder that you are. He cares too much for what others might think. I know this cannot make any sense to you now, but years from today you'll remember these words, and their meaning will penetrate your mind."

In a more subdued tone, Harelip said, "You've been raised to think of yourself as a boy, and then shown by your father that you're not enough of a boy according to his estimation. But 'boy' is what you make of it. Only a word, meaningless until we impart meaning to it. We are away from others' judgments on this mountain, so you're free to be whatever kind of person you are. I merely call you 'boy' because that is what you're used to hearing, but know that you are like no one else, and like everyone else."

Baoshi had been puzzled and confused by what Harelip said, but he listened and remembered, the conversations returning to him vividly now. He sighs. Perhaps Harelip was right. His father cared too much about what others would think. *He couldn't bear to look at my body. Why was my body so reprehensible to him? Just because it carries both male and female within it?* Baoshi wondered what his father would say if he could see him now. He caresses his growing left breast, a fleshy bud. He likes the feel of it, the way he's soothed when he strokes it. He squints at his Master's sleeping face, more wrinkled with the years, especially around the eyes, now shut in a restful sleep. But he can see those eyes clearly in his mind, recall the first time he looked into them. Full of such lively warmth that he knew then, despite his deep distress, that he had nothing to hide anymore, not even his shame.

Shangguan Wan'er's Apartment
The Inner Palace at Taijigong
North Central Chang'an

"Her Majesty is quite preoccupied with presenting her version of historical events. She wants to regale readers with personal anecdotes. The entries are far from straightforward. Some topics must be too sensitive for her to address, and she thus steers clear of them. There are times during her delivery when she stops midsentence and drifts off. Maybe it has to do with her anxieties about the Jin Dan elixir. The hand tremors have gotten worse, so she seems pleased that I do the writing on her behalf. But then she gets very easily annoyed at my slowness. A mass of contradictions. One moment very focused, another quite confused. I don't know whether to feel exasperated or awed by her sheer tenacity. I sit at her side day after day in her study, recording whatever she tells me. Then she checks what I've written.

It's mostly tedious work, but I will admit there are some witty moments and remarkable insights."

Shangguan Wan'er speaks confidently and without pause. She is seated on the edge of the kang to cool down after vigorous exertion. It might appear that she's being entirely spontaneous, but she has chosen her words carefully, having rehearsed beforehand what to say. She doesn't want to disclose to her listener some of her other observations, especially concerning the expressions on their sovereign's face as she dictates her Palace Diary entries. That last entry on the importance of prophecies, for instance. Nü Huang licked her lips rather lasciviously as she talked about her father's oracle bone, and Yuan the fortune teller's prophecy about her. And what about that narrowing of the eyes as she made the comment about her sister Lady Helan? *Infamous meddling* was how she put it. Spitting out her words with that dismissive wave of her hand.

The Imperial Secretary notes privately to herself that these physical gestures speak more loudly of the true character of the Emperor than her well-fashioned phrases. While others in the court may on occasion glimpse such signs, she's the one who notes them privately while her hand has to remain faithful to every word Nü Huang utters. Wan'er stares at the curtain hanging at one corner of the kang for a while longer before turning back to look at her lover, who's resting his head on the square pillow.

"You know how adamant my aunt is. She must have her intellectual challenges, and she detests being bored. Just like you." Wu Sansi returns her warmth with a restrained upward turn of his lips. He listens to her comments with some dissatisfaction. She has said a lot and still gives him little that he doesn't already know. She seems reluctant to disclose. He believes that Wan'er is impatient with his rambling aunt, so why this hesitation to tell him? The scrolls that form the Palace Diary are stored in an unspecified location, and he has no access to them—a secret project that only his aunt and his lover can have any direct knowledge of.

"Sansi, it's simply ridiculous, isn't it, that Nü Huang would move the whole court from Luoyang to Chang'an all because she desperately wants to try the version of the Jin Dan elixir made by the alchemists here. She couldn't even risk entrusting our very best horsemen to ensure the safe delivery of this most elusive elixir? All this upheaval for the sake of immortality!" Wan'er can't conceal her exasperation.

He doesn't feel the need to answer. Instead, he strokes the inside of Wan'er's arm while his eyes savour the curve from waist to hip, then travel along her thighs, which she has drawn close together, blocking the view of her celestial valley. What a pity. Pleasure always ends too soon.

He tilts his head slyly at her, wondering if he can convince her to lie down again. There's enough time. Princess Wei in her apartment in the Outer Palace doesn't expect him until after the Hour of the Sheep. Sansi enjoys dividing his attention between Princess Wei and Wan'er. A fruitful pastime replete with rewards of praise and appreciation. Different from his accomplishments at court. He would be tremendously unhappy if deprived of these affairs.

"You must go now," Wan'er places her hands on Sansi's chest and pushes lightly, trying to encourage him out of his comfortable reclining posture.

"How can you kick me out so soon? I just got here!" He frowns, then flashes her another suggestive look.

"You're not afraid? Although Her Majesty chooses to turn a blind eye to your visits to the Inner Palace when it serves her interests, do you think she would be so kindly toward you if she knew you were exhausting the Imperial Secretary and interfering with her Palace duties?" She flings this mock threat at him while leaping out of bed.

At the wash basin, Wan'er splashes her face and neck with water and wipes her body down quickly. Gazing into the vanity mirror, she sees that her cheeks are too flushed to go unnoticed by the palace gossips. Even the scar in the middle of her forehead, floating like two stick figures between her eyes, seems slightly aggravated by her present state of excitement. Doesn't really matter. She will rely on Nü Huang's poor eyesight. She slips the linen tunic undergarment over her head. Next, the light yellow long-sleeved cotton jacket, followed by the long red skirt woven through with the dancing shapes of butterflies, which she fastens high up, just under the armpits, winding the ribbons twice around her body before tying them securely in front.

Sansi watches Wan'er, musing to himself that she moves swiftly like a deer. He would like to tie up this wild animal and exhaust her further with his ardour. His jade member hardens once again, raising the sheet and causing a wet spot to appear.

Wan'er bends forward so that she can brush her long thick hair. When she straightens up, she sweeps her hair away from her face to form a bun at the back. She keeps her hair in place with three large combs made of rhinoceros horn and several pearl-studded hairpins. She hears a flurry of soft moans coming from the bed. Must he be so brazen and shameless? She ignores the sounds, applying the white powder over her face. When she covers the scar with powder, she feels that familiar twinge of awkwardness, wishing she could completely obliterate the slightly raised, wrinkled anomaly on her otherwise smooth skin.

She colours her cheeks with rouge, then dramatizes the slope of her eyebrows with blue-black pigment. After she applies the reddish tint of pomegranate on her lips, she turns around to catch Sansi satisfying himself, his eyes shut tight in concentration. The ecstasy on his face reminds her of the first time he admired some poems hidden under a stack of official scrolls on her long table.

She dabs some scented oil on her wrists before striding back to the bed to stroke the side of Sansi's neck with one finger, light as a feather, inducing shivering waves of release. She laughs, delighted at her effect on him, then smacks him hard on the shoulder.

"You can't get away with that, beating up on your lover." He nonchalantly pulls her toward him.

"Oh, yes I can!" She exclaims, slapping both hands down on his chest and pinching his nipples between her fingers.

He grins warmly. "You should tell me more about the contents of that Palace Diary, my love."

"Why would you need to know? The Palace Diary has no impact on our plans."

"I just want to make sure there are no surprises. If there's anything Her Majesty says to you that might affect our plans, you will let me know, won't you?"

"Of course."

"In the meantime, it's very useful that she is being kept preoccupied with it."

"This obsession of hers is taking up a great deal of my time. A whole double hour in the morning, and sometimes, like today, a small hour in the afternoon. I could be organizing the archives in the Imperial library, writing more poetry, organizing literary evenings for our poets and scholars, instead of almost exclusively concentrating on her pet project."

"This isn't going to last much longer," he reassures her.

She keeps silent. A comment like that could be interpreted in many ways. How much longer will Nü Huang live? Will the plot to remove her favourites, the Zhang brothers, succeed? Sansi hasn't told her any of the details yet and keeps saying he'll inform her when the plans are more definite.

Wan'er turns her head away from Sansi, staring at the porcelain dish on the side table. The tiny white blossoms of the narcissus are withering away. They remind her of crushed, fine paper.

Sansi pushes back one of Wan'er's sleeves and lets his gaze sink into the crease of her elbow. He wraps his hand firmly around her arm, as if that would provide some temporary solace from his dilemma. That's right, he wants Her Majesty to be engrossed by her Palace Diary as much as possible. That will give him some room to make plans. And possibly spare her life. Poor aunt, thinks Sansi as he closes his eyes, savouring the relaxation that's settling in. He doesn't want her to suffer, but there's no guarantee he can protect her once the plot is carried out. There are just too many things that can happen in the heat of palace rebellions. The more she indulges those Zhang half-brothers, the more threatened the Tang loyalists are. If she can dispose of her own grandchildren simply because they criticize her foolish lovers, then what else could the Zhang brothers persuade her to do?

He shakes his head. To think that Wu Zhao had been that callous, shrewd beauty who had outwitted so many men and women, and had Gaozong completely in her grip. At first only a minor concubine of Taizong's, then she rose in power to become Gaozong's Empress. What a feat. And what is she now? A cantankerous woman deluded by her infatuation with her pretty boys.

He lifts Wan'er's left wrist to his nose and takes a whiff of the frankincense, then on impulse, licks the spot.

"My love ..." She's tempted to tell him about the poems she plans to write, but she hesitates.

"Hmm?" He looks sleepy. Any moment now he'll doze off into his usual nap.

"Never mind. I'll tell you another time. I am expected in Her Majesty's study shortly."

The drums from the central tower signal the Hour of the Sheep. She smooths the wrinkles on her gown, slips on her brocade shoes, and leaves the room, closing the door softly behind her.

Heading along the covered arcades toward Nü Huang's study, Wan'er passes by the Vermillion Phoenix pavilion. Peach blossoms fall from the trees, scattered by the wind along pebbled paths. The light pink petals are adrift, tiny boats on the surface of the pond.

The breeze cools Wan'er's face. That heat from her rendezvous with Sansi is already dissipating. She shakes her head and brushes the petals off her lips and hair. Beauty is lost too quickly, she reflects.

Under the roof of the pavilion, two familiar figures lean over the balustrade admiring the view, their backs to her. The Crown Prince and his daughter Anle.

Anle's singing voice with its gentle inflections floats through the air. Wan'er quickens her steps as she walks down the covered arcade behind them, hoping that they don't see her. The Crown Prince isn't a happy man, especially now that he has lost his son Zhongjun and his favourite daughter Yongtai. They and Yongtai's husband were just three immature members of the Imperial household, carelessly gossiping about the Zhang brothers. Wan'er shudders, remembering Nü Huang's rage. It wasn't too long after the execution of the three youths that Nü Huang decided on the move back to Chang'an.

Sansi is right. She must humour Nü Huang and be patient about her work on the Palace Diary. As Wan'er approaches Nü Huang's study, she nods to herself, lost in deep thought. She and her mother could have died along with her father and grandfather, but Nü Huang spared them. It isn't a thirst for revenge that plagues her. Instead, there lingers in her some discomforting mix of gratitude and bitterness.

Lixia 立夏 Jieqi
Start of Summer
Fourth Lunar Month
Three Days past New Moon

Mogao Caves near Dunhuang

The journey to Dunhuang took a little more than four weeks. Then Ardhanari rested a night at the local inn before coming here. Now he's finally arrived, southeast of the town, standing outside the Mogao Caves. He looks up at the two rows of caverns—dark entrances that hint at inner mysteries. Where could his uncle be? The man with the donkey cart who gave him a ride here from town had told him a bit about the patronage of the wealthy Cui family from Dunhuang, that they have sustained Old Gecko and his sons in this work for all these years. His uncle continues to design and supervise the proper execution of murals and sculptures in the new caves and to see to the repair of the older ones. "Devoted Buddhist family," the man whispered, as he tapped his donkey's hindquarters with the bamboo rod and rode off.

Ardhanari stares at the stretch of caves dotting the cliff face and begins to imagine the creation of the very first cave.

The three monks, having passed the last outpost several days prior, were relying on directions given by others. A few animal skulls whose horns pointed the way disconcerted them as they trudged through the desert in the searing heat of day. Through the chilly nights, the constellations in the sky were their compass. The travellers slept little, making the most of whatever time they had before their water supplies ran out. In the early hours after dawn, the air still cool enough for a comfortable trek, they spotted the grove of elm trees in the distance and began to do prostrations in gratitude as they stumbled toward the grove.

The pilgrims shouted with relief when they discovered a stream winding its way next to the grove. They wept invisible tears of gratitude, their bodies so parched that no water escaped from their eyes. They led their one donkey to the stream, then lowered their mouths to the water. The faster they drank, the thirstier they felt. They filled their gourds, then walked until knee-deep in the stream, scooping water over their bodies to clean off the dust and despair of the past few days. They knew that if they followed the stream north until it met the river, then headed west, they would reach Dunhuang within a day.

That must have been how the first caves were begun, or so Ardhanari imagines, the stream and grove of elm trees behind him as he surveys the cliff face. The sun is close to the top of the cliff, and soon to descend beyond sight, beyond the Mingsha, the Singing Sands. Some four hundred years ago, after those monks emerged refreshed from the stream, did their tears finally materialize? They must have felt a chill of silence in this narrow corridor between the trees and the cliff face, the way he's feeling that shiver now. He wraps his arms in front of his naked chest.

Was Dunhuang the pilgrim monks' final stop before heading back eastward, or were they on a much lengthier trek, heading west to India? As they gazed up at this cliff face, which one had the brilliant idea? Which monk pictured his body enveloped within the dry coolness of a cave, listening to the sound of his own breathing, embraced by the austere serenity? His body craved that shelter, an antidote to the harsh openness of the desert. Had not the Buddha and his bodhisattvas protected them from the dangers of the desert? It seemed only sensible to create sanctuary here and give thanks.

The monk wielded a jagged piece of rock like a weapon, trying to make a dent in the side of the cliff. He even poked at the stubborn façade with his walking stick. The other two leaned their sore backs against large boulders nearby and watched him, chuckling in amazement at their friend's determination. Slivers of rock chipped away, but the task was impossible without a pickaxe and shovel. Although the hole he made was small, he had exhausted himself. Gone was the relief he experienced when he dipped his body into the stream. But he had made up his mind. He would return with digging implements.

Ardhanari's daydreaming is interrupted by muffled echoes of voices from the cave to his left. He picks up his cloth bundle and heads in that direction.

Inside the cave, lit by torches, a crew of five men work quietly, mixing chopped pieces of straw with the mud they dredged up from the stream below, then applying this mixture onto the walls. He recognizes his cousins Ram and Arun supervising the men. They are, of course, middle-aged now, like him, but with faces that still bear traces of their youth. Squatting down in one corner, studying a parchment laid out on the floor, Old Gecko is talking to another man, giving him instructions about the mural to be painted.

Ardhanari shouts out a greeting, and the men halt their activities temporarily to look at the new arrival. Old Gecko stands up and walks up to Ardhanari. "So you got my letter and have come! Thank you, Nephew. My, how you've aged." He places his hands on Ardhanari's arms and looks up at him.

How ridiculous, thinks Ardhanari, *when I'm fifty-six and he's seventy-eight.* Whatever Old Gecko's secrets are, he is surely tortured by them, Ardhanari decides as he studies the old man's face, as weathered as an olive's crinkled skin after it has been soaked for ages in vinegar and spices. Sour yet blazing hot with years of suppressed frustrations. The sparse goatee, now white, the hairs flimsier than those on the tiniest calligraphy brush. The right eyebrow lower than the left, hugging the curve of the eyelid. That hasn't changed.

"Uncle, I was surprised to receive your letter after all these years."

"Yes, of course. But we're really desperate here, you see. Your reputation travels all this distance to reach our ears, don't you know? We kept hearing that you make beautiful sculptures in Chang'an, my dear Nephew! Finally, I simply couldn't stand it anymore, and had to write you. It's probably my last commission from the Cui family. I'm too old for this." He nods in his sons' direction. "It'll soon be time for them to take over."

He orders his assistant, Alopen, to carry out some tasks. Then he pulls Ardhanari to look at the parchment.

"You see how we're going to take advantage of the already existing niche here in the west wall?" Old Gecko addresses Ardhanari in their local Khotani dialect. Ardhanari feels a strong rush of emotion listening to the sounds of their language. It's been so long since he spoke this dialect. He steals a few glances at his uncle. Is he really ill? If not, what could have compelled the man to write that letter? Old Gecko points to the spot on the sketch where there are seven circles drawn in, all to fit within the niche, and says, "Sakyamuni Buddha seated as the central figure on an octagonal throne, and the six bodhisattvas standing around him."

"Seven sculptures in three months? That's not possible!" protests Ardhanari, shaking his head vigorously. No one he has worked for in the capital has made such unreasonable demands. Panicking, the thought flashes through his mind, *My uncle's expectation is the worst thing when I'm already upset about my abilities.*

"You just concentrate and work hard. I'm sure you can do it. A sculptor like you, with such renown in the big city."

Ardhanari detects a suggestive undertone, as if Old Gecko is referring to another kind of reputation. Perhaps his uncle has heard rumours from people they know in common, those who travel as merchants or artisans back and forth between Khotan, Dunhuang, and parts east and south on the caravan trail, especially Chang'an. A reliable web of connections means that even thousands of li cannot ensure protection from the infamy and humiliation of gossip. *How much does my uncle know?* wonders Ardhanari.

He looks back at the niche. "I'll need some help with preparing the sculptures. I'll work on the armatures back there while the murals are being painted."

"Do what is needed. After this first layer of mud has dried thoroughly, which might be tomorrow or the day after, the crew will slap on a layer of plaster. In another few days, after the plaster has dried, these men from Dunhuang will leave us, and the rest of us can begin laying down the outlines of the mural on the walls and ceiling. You can take the time then to start your work."

He stares at his uncle. How can this be? Old Gecko shows no signs of any illness. He moves his body with ease, his voice clear and unwavering.

One Week after Xiaoman 小滿 Jieqi
Forming of Grain
Fourth Lunar Month
Last Quarter Moon

MOUNT HUA

Baoshi has prepared himself for the trek by putting on a clean hemp shirt and pants this morning. His straw sandals are already on his feet, and he has wrapped a short brown jacket tightly around him with a faded black sash. While Baoshi watches, Harelip retrieves his old leather satchel and shakes it out at the entrance of the shack. A pair of spiders drop to the ground and scurry away. At the table, Harelip gathers together a few essentials. A waterskin he had bought at the market in Chang'an during the time he was at Da Ci'en Monastery. Baoshi can fill it with water from a stream on his way down. Two flints for starting a fire. A knife. Food, he can pick from bushes or dig up from the earth. In the city, the boy can beg. He drags out a begging bowl hidden under the altar, the one he had to use on his journey to Mount Hua. He unwraps the bowl from its swathe of rags. He stares into its dusty interior, thinking about that time a drunk had filled it with millet wine. He runs a finger along the inside rim, clearing the dust to reveal the dark brown wood underneath. He starts to wipe the bowl, but the dust irritates his lungs and he's seized by a coughing fit. Baoshi runs up to pat Harelip firmly on the back. All of a sudden, a stinging pain travels up Harelip's throat.

"Master!" Baoshi's eyes widen with shock at the sight of blood colouring Harelip's mouth.

Harelip stumbles out of the shack. He repeats a chant silently, calling on the mercy of Buddha. Dizzy, he collapses to his knees and lowers his head to the ground. He takes a few deep breaths before pressing down hard on certain points on his chest. The pain retreats, his throat relaxes, and he regains his composure.

Baoshi squats down next to Harelip. "Master, I cannot go. You're not well enough for me to leave you here alone."

"No, my son, quite the contrary. You mustn't delay."

Harelip returns inside and resumes his task. He moves swiftly between the table and his cherished cabinet with its fifty small drawers. On the table he builds up two separate bunches of herbs, one for internal injuries and the other for dealing with poisoning from snakebites or toxic plants. He places each cluster of herbs into a hemp pouch. Finding two broad strands of silk, he writes on them with his tiny ink brush and secures the pouches with the tags. Next, he wraps an extra layer of hemp around each pouch. Finally, surveying the objects he has collected on the table, he feels satisfied and places the objects into the satchel.

"Ready?" Harelip asks Baoshi.

Baoshi nods reluctantly, knowing he'll never be entirely ready. Harelip hands the satchel to him, and they walk to the entrance where Baoshi picks up his walking stick and straw hat. Harelip pulls out the jade pendant from inside his robes. He lifts the necklace over his head and places it around Baoshi's neck.

"My gift to you for the pilgrimage. Never remove it from your person." He holds the pendant up to the light and caresses its surface with fondness. It has not left his body for all these years on Mount Hua. How strange to now gaze at the pendant from this different perspective. Its outline seems sharper, more defined. A yellowish-green owl, wings outstretched, with brown veins running through the whole piece, as long as his fleshy thumb.

"This too is a miracle of Heaven. Jade, congealed from a dragon's breath. For thousands of years, people in this land have revered and admired its subtle qualities. Lately, however, especially at Court and in many temples and monasteries, people are bedazzled by the glaring sheen of gold, and they've hardened their hearts against this other kind of beauty." He pauses to collect his thoughts. "You must wear this for two reasons. First, to always remember who you are and thereby to notice the miracles you'll encounter. Second, this jade pendant will help you find Ardhanari. It was his gift to me. When he sees it, he'll definitely recognize it, having carved it himself. Only then can he trust you enough to follow you back."

"But what if I can't find him? What should I do then?"

"You surely will find Ardhanari. Go to the central western sector of Chang'an. There's a market there, and in it, a tea shop run by an old Turkish singer. Ask him to take you to Ardhanari. You'll know what to do, my precious stone." He touches the leather string that now curves around Baoshi's neck, and lifts the jade up to take a final look. How long before he sees this pendant again? Tears roll down Baoshi's cheeks, while Harelip tucks the pendant back inside Baoshi's jacket and rests his hands on the boy's shoulders.

"Now look at me." Harelip gazes intently into Baoshi's face, and the boy returns the focus. "You'll meet all kinds of people. Liken this journey to your first exploration of the creatures that inhabit the forest areas on this mountain. Be empty of assumptions, but never fail to be cautious. Appearances don't define character. Be close to your Two-in-Oneness. Remember, words are merely sounds. They're nothing until one imparts meanings to them. You'll experience a wilderness of meanings out there in the city. Choose only those interpretations that unfetter your mind."

Baoshi nods, biting into his lower lip.

"Remember the parable of the water in the pond?" Harelip looks at Baoshi in a particular way, and Baoshi understands immediately what is being asked of him.

Baoshi clears his throat and takes a slow breath in before he begins. "Each person's essences might be compared to the waters of a pond and the body to the embankments along the sides of a pond. Good deeds are like the water's source. If these three things are present, the pond will be sturdy. But then ... but then ..."

"The heart," Harelip prompts.

"Oh, yes. If the heart does not focus on goodness, then that pond lacks embankments, and whoosh! Water runs out." Baoshi motions with his hands to emphasize his words. "If a person fails to accumulate sufficient good deeds, the pond is cut off at its source and the water will dry up. If one breaches the dike to water fields as if it were a river or stream, then, even though the embankments hold, the original flow will leak off and the pond will eventually empty. Then ..." He wrinkles his forehead and shakes his head. He can't remember the rest.

"Then the bed of the pond becomes scorched and cracked. That is when all kinds of sickness will emerge. If one is not cautious about these things, the pond will become an empty ditch."

At the completion of the parable, Harelip continues, "One small correction. When you said, near the beginning, that when all three things are present, the pond will be sturdy."

"Yes?"

"Not just 'present.' All three things have to be complete."

"Yes, Master."

"Reflect on this parable. On your journey, you'll have many opportunities to ponder its wisdoms. Remember everything I've taught you. Now it is up to you to apply what you've learned and to answer your own questions. May Buddha bless your pilgrimage. Be grateful for everything and everyone who comes your way."

Baoshi vows silently that he won't forget all that Harelip has taught him. Harelip turns around and enters the shack. Baoshi hears the cymbals that signal the second morning meditation, at the start of the Hour of the Snake, then Harelip's low voice chanting. He looks up toward the northern peak. He wishes he were going up there, instead of having to make his way down the mountain. He'll miss the view from the peak. With a heavy heart, he heads down the path along the eastern side of Mount Hua.

The rain leaks through one spot in the roof, its timid dripping rhythm filtering through to Harelip, drawing him out of his meditation. He hurries up from the cushion to grab a bowl and place it under the leak. Staring down at the accumulating pool of water in the bowl, he imagines Baoshi slipping on the rocks and hurting himself. He panics, feels an urge to run down the mountain in search of his child. But he calms himself down using a soft, whispering tone, the way he would speak to wounded deer or birds.

He returns to the cushion and ends his meditation period with three strikes of the cymbals. At the door, he stares blankly into the distance while noticing how distressingly quiet the shack is without that miracle of Heaven. Yet he had lived here alone for a long time before Baoshi came along. Surely it will be a matter of getting used to the silence again.

He looks around the shack, bereft and frightened, then sits down at the table to check his three pulses. Empty heat in the lungs. He puts together a slightly altered combination of herbs from his medicine cabinet. Too soon to tell, he tries to encourage himself.

Thirty-six years ago, when he had just turned thirty sui, he left Chang'an for Mount Hua because of a dream. The dream arrived a week before New Year's Day, when the Feng and Shan rituals were to be conducted on Mount Tai.

Sleeping in the large dormitory with the other monks, Harelip felt a chill descend on him as he lay on his bed thinking of the upcoming ritual. It would be the first time an Empress was going to ascend the mountain alongside her Emperor, acting in the role of First Assistant. Wu Zhao had been ruling in Gaozong's stead for five years by that time, since he fell ill and could hardly speak or move one side of his body. Harelip pondered this imminent event with a touch of agitation. After all, he thought, Feng and Shan rituals were so rarely conducted by previous Emperors. Rulers performed such rituals only if they were confident that their rule was sanctioned by Heaven, that they had achieved complete pacification of the empire.

He tossed about for quite some time. When he finally fell asleep, he dreamed that he was climbing Mount Tai behind Wu Zhao, but she turned around and stared at him with eyes full of rage. She lurched forward and pushed him with such an uncanny force that he was propelled through the air, hurtling over the precipice.

When he woke up, his limbs hopelessly weak, he was sure the dream was a warning meant to save his life. He was reluctant to leave the capital, but what choice did he have? Up until then, he was willing to comply with the wishes of his monastery superiors. Willing, yet devoid of true enthusiasm. The dream shocked him, not only for its fierce aggressiveness, but because it resonated with misgivings he hadn't been able to admit to until then. Hadn't his superiors chided him for his tolerance of Daoist principles? For not being pure enough? So why include him in their retinue?

One week later, just before they were supposed to set off for Mount Tai, he hid in the storage cellar below the kitchen, bearing with the stink of pickled turnips in earthen jars and salted radish roots hanging from the ceiling. He heard voices calling out for him and the thump of searching footsteps overhead. Angry voices above saying, "What's the matter with him? How dare he!"

He had chosen the storage cellar because all the other monks knew that he despised the smells trapped inside. No one thought of looking for him there. He came close to vomiting too many times, but he managed to suppress the urge with a great deal of effort. He imagined the scorn and puzzlement of the other monks. To decline to participate in the Mount Tai procession was akin to treason against Nü Huang.

He hid in that ghastly cellar until no more light entered the room from the window. Clothed in complete darkness, he tiptoed out of the cellar, tied on his boots, and fled from the monastery, but not before grabbing the Buddha figure from the apothecary and a begging bowl from the side storehouse. These he tucked inside his jacket before running away as quietly and quickly as he could.

Now, Harelip glances at the Buddha figure on the altar. *Ah, that's right.* He sighs with the memory, both he and this treasured Buddha are truly in need of repair. Together they abandoned that distinguished life in the city, and together they've aged and become decrepit. He chuckles at his own joke.

Every detail of the escape is still vivid in his mind. He was tempted to run over to Ardhanari's place and hide there, but he persuaded himself that it would be too much of a risk. How easy it would be for others to find him. He couldn't lose himself easily in a crowd, with his deformed mouth and monk's robes. It would have been too dangerous for Ardhanari, or anyone else, to hide him.

His old arguments swirl inside him. Why is it, he wonders, that his most formidable reasoning hasn't succeeded in dispelling doubts? A pang of regret grips his chest. Love and its promise are hard to leave behind. He closes his eyes for a moment, sees Ardhanari's dark body glistening with sweat as they lay together in bed. He has deceived himself, believing he's incapable of nostalgia. His soul yearns for that which is past, yearns for a possibility that was never fulfilled.

How far away Chang'an is. It had taken him five days to travel from the capital to the base of the mountain. Five days that marked an irrevocable departure from his previous life. He's never gotten over the pain of abandoning Ardhanari. He chose Mount Hua because it was the nearest sacred mountain, treacherous enough that not many would make the pilgrimage, especially at the end of winter. No one would ever suspect that he fled here. Harelip shakes his head. There are just too many feelings coursing through him this morning, but he mustn't get swept away.

There's a great deal that separates me from that life, he reflects. All these years of seclusion with much left unsaid and unfinished. The new dream has brought him both turmoil and hope that he may be able to see Ardhanari again and tell him what had happened. That surely would grant him some peace, and he would be able to leave this life with a diminished burden. He lowers his forehead and weeps.

MOGAO CAVES NEAR DUNHUANG

It's rather strange to be back, Ardhanari reflects as he peers into the earliest caves, the tiny cells that those first pilgrim monks created. As young boys, he and his cousins were small enough to slip into them. All his memories of childhood return, flooding him with intense emotion. Memories of his father working here with his uncle, while he, Ram, and Arun raced wildly past the rows of caves, playing games.

His family lived for three generations in Khotan, and it was only in his father's and uncle's generation that they converted from Hinduism to Buddhism. They never told him the reason for that sudden change. All he knows is that the change coincided with his father and Old Gecko starting to work in the Mogao Caves. Still, his mother and father named him after Ardhanarishvara, one of the principal manifestations of the Hindu god Shiva, Lord and Creator of the universe.

An apparent contradiction that never got explained.

His parents taught him and Meru to cradle their most precious secrets closest to their hearts. But there was too much restraint in his life, and he often felt his rebellious spirit rise up, especially after his parents died, both claimed by an inexplicable illness. How is his sister doing now? They were never close, and the last he heard, she lived with her husband in Khotan.

As he walks around, he recalls his youth spent wandering these caves, gripped by a sense of awe that often left him gasping, speechless. He liked standing inside a particularly colourful cave, spinning as fast as he could so that when he stopped, he would be drunk with the frenetic shifting of the visual universe. Images crashing and collapsing, until it was impossible to know where one image ended and another began.

With a parchment and a piece of charcoal tucked into his antariya, he climbs up the scaffolding to the second level of caves. The more recent figures of Buddha have voluptuous robes, draped with such confidence that it becomes easy to forget that both bodies and robes are made of clay or wood. The figures have been painted with reds, yellows, and greens. Their bodies vibrate quietly, with traces of their creators' lives. Alive, like moving water. The illusion of vitality is so powerful that he feels the figures could walk off their platforms and into the open air outside.

Within these figures lie secrets waiting to be discovered. Some have one hip raised higher than the other. He smiles, as a gentle pleasurable sensation spreads through him. That's right, these recent figures bear witness to the influence of Indian art from the Gandhara region. How interesting that the spread of Buddhism to Zhongguo was accompanied by such an emphasis on the body's insistent pulse.

Ardhanari touches the sensuous Buddha face, whose lips hold unspoken suggestions. He wants to taste the heat locked in those lips. Yet Buddha's blissful, half-lidded eyes refuse him.

He pulls away from the figure and sighs. There are too many memories here at the caves, not only of his parents but also of Harelip. Here, where he's surrounded by depictions of pilgrim monks and the deities worthy of their devotion. He remembers one of Harelip's jokes: *Buddha was not a Buddhist.* Uttering this statement with a wicked glint in his eyes.

A man's heart could grow bitter after years of not knowing why his lover abandoned him. An embittered heart is ugly. All the outer embellishments, however pleasing to the eye, would do nothing to alter that heart's poisoned state.

He makes a few sketches on the parchment before going outside. The sun is almost directly overhead. He squints from the light. He had better start work on the sculptures soon. He must convince his uncle to hire some assistants for him from Dunhuang. And he must definitely stop thinking about the past. What's the point of all this nostalgia when it only causes his heart to ache?

He walks by the nine-storey pagoda where the gigantic figure of Maitreya is housed. To think that the Female Emperor could ever dare to proclaim herself Maitreya, Buddha of the Future, the one who will deliver humankind from suffering. Are there people who believe such a preposterous claim? It was Bodhidharma, the Indian monk, who preached to a Liang Dynasty ruler that there is no Buddha save the Buddha in one's own nature, a message that didn't gain Bodhidharma much applause or sanction from the Imperial court, and so the monk departed for a quiet life elsewhere.

He's disinclined to visit the pagoda cave, even though it has become one of the most frequented since it was completed seven years ago. He doesn't wish to be overwhelmed by such a colossal Buddha figure. Inundated with grandeur, he's already suffering from an inability to digest it all. Instead, he is hungry for some small, quiet revelation.

Nü Huang's Study
The Inner Palace at Taijigong
North Central Chang'an

Palace Diary: My Thoughts on Immortality

*N*o one knows where the immortals reside. There have been countless stories and not enough proof. They say Laozi was taken up into the invisible, infinite realms by a pair of magical cranes. Over the centuries, sages are reputed to disappear mysteriously, leaving their clothes in a messy pile on the ground, presumably at the last place where they inhabited their mortal bodies. We are supposed to believe, based on such paltry evidence, that transcendence has occurred, that these mere men—and a handful of women—have been able to transform flesh and bones into the pure essence of breath, of cosmic qi, taking themselves into realms beyond mortal existence and suffering.

I am, of course, skeptical. Still, it behooves an Emperor to be open to all possibilities. I have an insatiable appetite for such myths. They offer a scent of some mystery around the corner, of a beauty whose fragrance lingers on, in an interminable trail of seduction.

I remain open to being convinced. After all, certain concoctions have sustained my youthfulness and vitality for years, especially the Eternal Spring potion. I wonder about the recent elixirs, said to be necessary now that I am older and require extra fortification. Apparently, one cannot merely be sustained by the ingestion of the Eternal Spring potion. "Your Majesty," those Luoyang alchemists insisted, "you must now take the Jin Dan elixir in addition to your monthly Eternal Spring potion." What? It took those alchemists in the Eastern Capital three miserable years to come up with their version of the Jin Dan elixir, the Golden Elixir of Life. A single dark pellet twice the size of my thumb. I had to eat it bit by bit with some tribute tea to dissolve it. Vile taste. I ingested that elixir two years ago. Not only did it fail to work, but I have been sicker ever since. Just what kind of immortality pellet is that? Worthless. I had those men demoted and sent away to different small towns across the country, so that they cannot indulge their alchemical connivings again.

Now I am willing to try this group of alchemists here in Chang'an who convince me that they take a more enlightened approach to making the Jin Dan elixir. My retinue of alchemists has been furiously working at it, making another pellet for me. Even as I speak, they are slaving in that dank Repository of Da Fa Temple in the western sector of the city. My poor little rats. But I do pay them handsomely. I have increased each man's salary to three bolts of silk and two full purses of silver. They are fed well, all their needs looked after. Nü Huang is generous.

I am kept informed of the alchemists' progress. They insist that the ancient formulae need to be interpreted differently. Apparently, that had been the error of the Luoyang alchemists. Not enough cinnabar—that red sulphuret of mercury—and perhaps a touch more of orpiment—yellow sulphuret of arsenic. That makes sense to me. When I gaze at cinnabar, does it not suggest, with its rich redness, a passionate vitality? Cinnabar, capable of the greatest transformations of all the minerals, since it changes, when heated to a high temperature, into mercury, that most elusive of substances. Yes, those marvellous globules that can glide along surfaces. How I love shiny things! This cinnabar, when ingested, must stimulate the body to acquire a magical liveliness. What else is going into this new version of the Jin Dan elixir? The everlasting sheen of gold, distilled into gold essence, and the eternal clouds of dragon's breath suspended in jade. There is a whole host of substances my alchemists are including in the elixir. They have informed me that cinnabar, arsenic, and gold are the three primary ingredients of their formula, and they are including these in even higher concentrations.

Movement, transformation, change—these are the characteristics of the universe. Where there is movement, there is life. And where there is life, there is transformation. Just thinking of these men sacrificing themselves on my behalf gives me a rush of pleasure and renewed vigour.

The Emperors in our illustrious history all employed alchemists and practised the Daoist bedroom arts for rejuvenation. The historiographers would record that Emperor so-and-so had twenty concubines. Fact. End of story. Previous Emperors were not criticized for such behaviours. But every time I take one or two lovers, the whole court is abuzz with gossip and scandal. Outrage seethes under the cloaks of the strict Confucianists; jealousy ferments under the finest silk garments of the ladies of the palace. I must conclude that the uproar exists because I am a woman.

Is it so shocking that women would yearn for power and immortality? That we might wish to pursue and conquer rather than be caught in a web spun by others?

Humour and delight are my prerogative now. Who cares what the officials and the Imperial household say about my indulgences? Let them gossip. They are all jealous. I have succeeded and survived while others have lost their lives. Jealousy is a dangerous emotion. It topples those who are in its grip.

If it emerges that this latest Jin Dan elixir does not work, and I follow in the path of previous Emperors, I will not despair. At least I will have recorded these insights in my Palace Diary, and hence obtained another kind of immortality. I hope to have all my stories recorded for posterity regardless of what the historiographers may later say. In my old age, I will not succumb to the foolishness of fear.

"Are you writing down exactly what I'm saying? Make sure now. I'll have your words checked, Shangguan Wan'er. Don't play any tricks on this shrewd old woman. Remember, I can have your head in an instant."

"Did you want me to write that last bit down, Your Majesty?" asks Wan'er.

"What?" asks Nü Huang, as she squints at the calligraphy.

Wan'er repeats verbatim Nü Huang's last few lines with an absolutely serious facial expression. Nü Huang smiles, amused. She likes it when Wan'er is focused and yet lighthearted.

"Oh no, leave that out, my dear. Of course not! An impulsive moment there. I was merely stating the obvious, and no one needs to hear that, do they? End the entry with the line, 'In my old age, I will not succumb to the foolishness of fear.' Right there." Nü Huang pokes her index finger at the place on the scroll where the calligraphy ends. She continues, smiling in the subtly restrained manner so familiar to Wan'er. "You know I was only saying those last few words for dramatic effect, don't you? I would never hurt you, my child."

A shiver runs down Wan'er's back as she rolls up the scroll and stirs the water vigorously in the cypress brush-pot with the calligraphy brush. The ink washes off, turning the water instantly black.

"We are finished for now, but I would like you to come back for another dictation this afternoon. But don't leave just yet. I want to talk to you about a special mission you must conduct on my behalf."

"What might that be, Your Majesty?"

"A few errands that I can entrust only to you. You must travel out of Taijigong within the next few days without anyone's knowledge of your purpose. Make whatever arrangements to take your leave from here. Do nothing to arouse suspicion."

Wan'er's curiosity is piqued by the pronounced anxiety in Nü Huang's voice, but she knows she must sit patiently and wait. Nü Huang lifts the wide-mouthed cup close to her nose and sniffs at the tea that Ah Pu prepared for her, imagining the fragrance of tree trunks awakened by a light rain, and nods in approval before drinking. Wan'er also drinks, imitating her sovereign's mannerisms. This has become an automatic habit. As Imperial Secretary, she must prepare official documents, tend to the collections of writings housed in the main Imperial library, and write poetry for court celebrations. Then there are the other compulsory acts of loyalty, seemingly small yet of great consequence, including these daily gestures of imitating her sovereign in order to pay tribute.

"The Jin Dan elixir I just spoke of. I have word from the Abbess of Da Fa Temple that it is ready for me. I do not want an ordinary messenger to retrieve the elixir from the Temple. That would be too risky. Traitors would be delighted to intercept the elixir and contaminate it, for instance. I have decided that you must make the journey to Da Fa Temple alone and bring the elixir safely back to me. Do you understand?"

"Yes, Your Majesty. I am honoured."

"There is something else I want you to do while at Da Fa Temple. You must not tell anyone. Swear to me."

"I swear myself to secrecy." Wan'er bows her head and places her right hand over her heart.

Nü Huang leans forward and gestures for Wan'er to come closer. She whispers into Wan'er's ear her second request, her breath hot and urgent.

Listening intently, Wan'er blushes. Straightening back up, she pauses to reflect on Nü Huang's request before she responds. "I understand, Your Majesty. I will ask the Abbess and hear what her advice may be regarding this concern of yours."

"Good. You may go now. Return this afternoon at the Hour of the Sheep. Don't be late this time, or I shall worry that you are involved in a dastardly plot against me." Nü Huang dismisses Wan'er with a swift wave of her hand.

Wan'er clenches her jaw at Nü Huang's comment. She forces a smile as she takes her leave. Walking down the covered arcades, heading east toward her apartment, she thinks about her assignment with a mix of pleasure and worry. To leave Taijigong on an unusual mission, and a secret one at that. She has carried out some errands for Nü Huang before, while they were in Luoyang, but this will be her first one since the move back to Chang'an.

As she turns the corner, a figure rushes into her, upsetting her armful of scrolls, which tumble to the ground. Her foot has been stomped on, and she yells out in pain.

"What? Who ..." As she falls back against the wall and regains her balance, she notices it is Changzong, the younger of the Zhang half-brothers. "Look what you've caused me to do!"

"What a temper! Tsk, tsk." He waves an accusatory finger at her.

"Impudent fool," Wan'er mutters under her breath, as she feels the anger flush through her neck. She checks herself, suddenly aware of the dangers of going too far. How quickly the words have slipped out. She clutches at her foot even though it is no longer hurting and pretends to be on the verge of tears.

"Have I hurt you? Why didn't you say so?" Changzong looks sympathetic. He helps recover the three large scrolls from the ground. "By the way, Lady Shangguan, since I've run into you, I could be the one to give you the good news."

"Good news?"

"Oh, yes. There will be an Immortal Crane Event around the time of the Autumn Equinox. For me! Because I resemble some Daoist

Immortal, according to His Excellency Minister Wu. This means that you will get to organize poetry contests and other such literary activities, where the best scholars will compose tribute poems for me. Wonderful idea, don't you think?"

She doesn't answer but nods her head in grudging acknowledgment before she resumes her walk, her scrolls gathered up once more in her arms. Why did Sansi suggest the idea of such an event? Changzong is such a silly boy, smiling and giggling without cease. Doesn't he have any moments of melancholy?

In her apartment, she throws the scrolls down on the long table. She can't be bothered to make the trip down to the Office of Historiography right now, or even to lock up the scrolls in her special camphor cabinet. *Let someone steal the scrolls. Why should I care?* she fumes to herself. *And why does the old woman go on and on as if her thoughts are the most critical ones in the whole universe?* Such a singular, all-consuming focus. And to utter such a threat to her, knowing full well that it would frighten her, then to deny its impact by saying, "I would never hurt you, my child." An absolute lie.

Wan'er's throat tightens up. She isn't sure which is worse, being threatened by Nü Huang, or hearing that she is to write tribute poems to Changzong. She strides back out immediately. She must go see her mother now.

MOUNT HUA

Baoshi has walked down this path many times with Harelip but never completely to the base of the mountain. Even though the path is familiar, he never fails to shudder at the sight of the steep descent. He remembers his hand being held too tightly by the guide as the three of them battled against the winds and the patches of ice, climbing up to Harelip's shack.

Baoshi keeps his eyes focused on the steps closest to his feet. The path of narrow stone stairs veers down almost vertically in some places. Sometimes he feels as if he is treading air, miraculously suspended in an ether of nothingness. The peaks loom around him, hard-edged granite cliffs. A mountain that's as treacherous to descend as it is to ascend yet called by such a pretty name, Flower Mountain. He's never understood it.

He turns off the path to follow a stream threading its way through the rocks and passes by a few makeshift shrines. After filling his waterskin, he resumes his trek. Farther down, he encounters two gigantic boulders with a narrow gap between. He manages to squeeze through, walking down a dimmed passage of about a hundred steeply descending steps. His legs begin to tremble with the effort, and he stumbles once, catching himself against the side of one of the boulders. He emerges from the passage breathing a big sigh of relief.

Nearly a third of the way down, Baoshi rests on a large rock. His body is drenched in sweat and he feels a little light-headed. Far below him, the view is partially obscured by wisps of mist. He takes a few sips from his waterskin and wipes his scalp and neck with the sleeve of his jacket. Checking the sky, he's surprised by the quick transformation. The clouds have acquired a red tinge, a sign of approaching turbulence.

He looks down at the Yellow River, glimpsed through the mist, and catches sight of the Wei River, its western tributary. Somewhere near the Sanmen Gorge is his family home. His father often stayed up until the early hours of the morning drinking with his fellow merchants. Baoshi's bedroom was at least eighty paces away from the reception hall, but he could hear the men's revelry echoing down to him along the corridors. After all these years, that's one of the strongest memories he has of his father, apart from that awful trek up the mountain.

Rumbling sounds overhead. Storm clouds thicken across the sky. It happens without warning, the lightning and thunder, the first drops of rain. Baoshi places his hat on his head and starts to search for the trail that takes him into the heart of a wooded area. He spots a thin white rag tied around a tree, then follows the trail until the fresh wet scents of tree bark and leaves greet him. He is soothed by the sound of rain filtering through the canopy of leaves. He admires a pine tree whose bark peels, exposing its cream-coloured trunk. A few magnificent spruce trees tower above him. The rain begins to pour down heavily. He follows the winding trail, his breathing becoming more rapid as he rushes toward the thatched pavilion, his sandals squelching in the mud. The pavilion is a humble one, cobbled together from the branches of elm trees. Its thatched roof has been overwhelmed by a generous growth of moss. A tree stump rests under it for the weary traveller.

Shivering slightly, he notices the pile of twigs in a shallow pit dug out next to the tree stump. Crouching down, he picks a twig up with its burnt tip and sniffs at it. A trace of smoke. And heat. Someone was here not too long before him. Where might the traveller have gone to when there are signs of an approaching storm? He casts quick glances around. No sign of anyone.

A chill creeps across the back of his neck. A voice from behind him whispers, "You have the soft lips of a woman."

Baoshi turns around to look, but there's no one he can see. Instead, sighs begin to echo around him. Harelip has told him about mountain spirits who beckon to the sadness in mortal creatures, always ready to lure them to the brink of insanity or oblivion. *Do not treat these spirits with anything but the utmost respect. Do not offer them any opening to reach your grief, or they will compel you.* The spirit has been swift to sense the welling up of sadness in him. Perhaps it also has intuited the trepidation with which he has begun this pilgrimage.

LADY ZHEN'S APARMENT
THE INNER PALACE AT TAIJIGONG
NORTH CENTRAL CHANG'AN

"Mother," whispers Wan'er entreatingly at the open entrance to her mother's apartment. No one replies. Wan'er calls out more loudly.

Lady Zhen's maidservant, Wisteria, emerges from behind the spirit screen in the modest receiving hall, her feet uncomfortable in her new slippers. On seeing Wan'er, she bows in greeting. "Lady Shangguan, your mother is resting."

Wisteria keeps her head lowered, awaiting further instructions. Wan'er pauses. There is an understanding implicit in their exchange. Wisteria has previously reported to Wan'er that her mother is not sleeping well at night and needs to nap more frequently in the day. Quite often, according to the maid, Lady Zhen talks during these daytime naps. The strangest things. When pressed, Wisteria had refused to elaborate.

"Inform my mother later that I came by." As she turns away, she changes her mind. "No, wait. I'll look in on her. I promise to be quiet." She removes her shoes and puts on a pair of brocade slippers before proceeding down the narrow corridor past the study, neglected and unused for years.

The corridor runs between rooms on the left and a tiny courtyard on the right. Wan'er peers through one of the hexagonal leak windows into the courtyard. A rose-purple azalea in a large porcelain pot is flanked by several dark brown yixing pots with miniature versions of juniper, cypress, and maple. Slanting rays of light pass through the gaps between the ceramic cloud patterns in the leak windows and fall on the coloured pebbles of the courtyard, imprinting cloud shadows onto the paving.

Entering her mother's bedroom, Wan'er tiptoes across the terracotta floor, walking around another screen to the other side, where her mother lies asleep. She sits down on the chair nearest the bed, watching her mother's torso rise and fall gently with each breath. Lady Zhen's eyes are tightly shut, her arms resting on top of the light quilt, the fingers of both hands spread out like fans.

Nothing happens for quite a long time. Wan'er is about to leave when she hears the first sounds. The voice is clearly her mother's—why does it sound so unlike her? The way each word is dragged out, as if it were coming from somewhere far away, distorted by the distance it has to travel. As if it had to force its way through her.

Is her mother ill? Catching some fever? She wants to place a hand on her mother's forehead, but that might startle her. Wan'er leans closer, trying to decipher what her mother is saying.

"The crescent moon, a dangerous hook, then the fullness of a moment passes quickly ... seize the chance to ask for a prophecy ..." These are the only phrases Wan'er can make out clearly. As her mother speaks, her fingers move together and apart across the pale pink quilt.

A prickly sensation starts at the base of Wan'er's neck, causing her to shiver.

"Revenge ... revenge ... this is all I know ..."

"Who are you?" asks Wan'er cautiously, clenching her fists.

"Don't you know? Too young to remember? Or perhaps you weren't born yet. What do I know? I know only revenge."

A rustling sound from behind makes Wan'er flinch and look back. Nothing. The eerie sensation passes. Her mother's breathing resumes its regular rhythm. Relieved, Wan'er walks away.

Lady Zhen rouses. "Wan'er? Are you leaving already?"

Wan'er returns to her mother's side. "I came in to sit with you while you were taking a nap. How did you sleep?" She tries to sound calm, but her heart is still beating fast.

"Daughter, I've not been sleeping well at all."

Her mother's voice has resumed its pliant, tender quality, a characteristic that evokes an acute pang of sadness in Wan'er. Through all the hardships they have faced, Lady Zhen's voice has remained gentle, never acquiring a hard or embittered quality. Although Wan'er hungers to hear her mother's soothing voice, she sometimes worries that its tone betrays weakness.

"You seem to be more troubled in your sleep these days. I will request that the Imperial physician pay you a visit soon."

Lady Zhen sits up and smiles warmly, touched that Wan'er shows concern for her.

"My dear, this is not something that the physician can help me with. It is more a matter for someone schooled in the mystic arts."

"Mother, you must be careful what you say. You know that we're not allowed to consult sorcerers."

"Of course I'm careful. I'm only saying this to you, am I not? No need to be afraid on my account. I'm an old woman now, and no one has any reason to do away with me."

"Do you know what these disturbances are about? Why have you recently been plagued by them?"

"There are some restless presences moving through the Inner Palace. They are stirred up because we have moved back from Luoyang."

"Tell me what you know. I heard you speaking while you were asleep. You said something about ..." Wan'er hesitates.

"Revenge," says Lady Zhen, her face shadowed by the weight of the pronouncement. "I don't know why they've chosen to visit me. They mean me no harm." She sighs and lifts a hand to her chest. "I am quite fatigued from their conversations."

"Do you have any idea who these presences are?"

Lady Zhen gazes into her daughter's eyes with a penetrating directness that startles Wan'er. "They're troubled by Nü Huang's return. You know who they are. The two who died tortuously in the southeastern section. I can't say their names aloud."

Wan'er clutches at the fabric of her gown, needing to feel the raw silk fabric rub against her fingers. She has never questioned her mother's intuitive gifts. Lady Zhen began to have unusual dreams when she was pregnant with Wan'er. She dreamt she would give birth to a girl who would grow up to have the power to measure out the world with giant scales. As Lady Zhen faced the two sovereigns Gaozong and Wu Zhao, cradling her precious Wan'er, she stretched out her arms as if to present the infant girl as proof. *I told them I had asked you when you were a month old, "Are you really the one who will measure out the affairs of the world?" To my surprise, you could answer me, "Yes."*

Shangguan Yi's treason had cost both him and his son, Shangguan Zhi, their lives. Yet Wu Zhao believed in the prophetic nature of Lady Zhen's dream, as well as the story about the infant Wan'er's reply. That was the reason she and her mother were spared, and why Nü Huang groomed Wan'er from a young age to be her personal secretary and scribe.

Wan'er brings her mind back to the present. "Do you think there's anything to be done about these presences?"

"What can be done? No one has succeeded so far in exorcising them."

"Indeed, Mother."

"Wan'er, I am uneasy about something else."

"What is it?"

"Do your best to be watchful. Stay out of the way of those meddlesome half-brothers. You must be careful. You're all I have left, and I don't want you to suffer the same fate as your father and grandfather.

Do you understand, my dear? My heart would break if that were to come to pass."

Wan'er strokes her mother's wrist lightly. "You must not dwell on such morbid thoughts. True, our lives have been painfully altered. But as you know too well, I have no choice but to obey Nü Huang's wishes. I am her slave and Imperial Secretary." Wan'er pauses and decides to steer the conversation away, lest her mother sink into a fretful state. "Wisteria is loyal. She didn't repeat anything of what you were saying in your sleep. Even to me. This must mean that she does the same with everyone else?"

"I'm sure of it. You mustn't worry about me. These presences will leave me alone soon."

Wan'er raises her eyebrows at this comment, intrigued but certainly not quite ready to hear more. Too much has occurred this morning.

"I must go now. Please let me know whenever there's anything you need." Wan'er touches her mother's cheek. Lady Zhen keeps Wan'er's hand gently against her face, enjoying the feel of her daughter's warmth. How strong and capable Wan'er has become. She is filled with affection and pride.

At the Foot of Mount Hua

Zhu imagines it must be a vision approaching. A boy, surely not much older than herself. The boy's head is shaved, and he's dressed in tattered clothing, carrying a satchel slung across his body and striding forward with the help of a gnarled walking stick.

She studies his face as he comes closer. Eyes wide apart yet deep-set, a nose that flares slightly at the nostrils, and a mouth that makes her think, strangely enough, of their neighbour's newborn. She addresses him in a quiet, confident voice. "You're the one who lives with Harelip, aren't you?" He answers with a grin. She takes an instant liking to him and grabs hold of his hand, leading him into the village.

Dogs bark as they approach. Women and children emerge from their caves and climb up the steps to the main path. Here and there, an elderly man or woman peers out the window of a cave or leans against the entrance, staring at him. Those who have made the trek up Mount Hua to see Harelip recognize him. The Stone Boy. They call him this because they learned his given name was Baoshi, and they appreciate that this precious stone dropped into the monk's lonely life is a blessing for Harelip, and for them as well.

Zhu's mother is the first to approach him. "Baoshi, I am Ke, the chief's wife. What brings you to our village? Is Harelip all right?"

Baoshi bows deeply to her. "Yes, Master is fine. He has sent me to Chang'an. A special task."

Her face relaxes at hearing this pronouncement. The other women giggle while casting shy glances at him. The Stone Boy has a lilting voice, no longer a child's thin timbre but possessing a freshness that enchants them. They stare, look away, then return to their gawking, while some of their children cling tightly to their mothers. The bolder ones rush up to him and pull at his clothes.

"Stay the night with us before you set off. When I heard the dogs, I thought it was my husband, Qian, and his team of men returning." Ke pauses to assess his condition. Dirtied sandals and muddied hems of pants. "You'll need a good washing up, won't you?"

"Most grateful. Thank you." He bows again.

She's pleased. Harelip has taught the boy well.

"Where are your husband and his men?"

"They've been away for three days now. They went up to join men from the other villages slightly north of us to work on repairing the damaged embankment there. The water level of the Yellow River has risen quickly in the past week because of the rains. We could lose the harvest and ..." She cannot finish but repeats instead, "Come to our home to eat and rest before you set off again."

The crowd of women and children follow close behind as Ke leads Baoshi down the steps to her cave. The villagers linger outside the entrance for quite a while, one by one reluctantly leaving after they've had their fill of staring at the Stone Boy. Zhu enters the cave after watching the commotion from their courtyard, her brother following soon after. Their grandmother sits, half-hidden in the darkest corner of the cave, her leathery hands plucking the ends off green beans in a basket on her lap. She drops the ends into a bowl on the earth floor. Grandma mutters a greeting as she waves a handful of green beans at Baoshi. A few rotted teeth are scattered like lost souls in the dark cavern of her mouth. Still, her eyes are mirthful and lively.

Drinking a cup of hot barley tea, Baoshi studies Zhu's calm expression as she sits across from him.

"What's your name?"

"Zhu." Her reply is quick and unhesitating.

"As in 'pearl'?"

"As in 'pig,'" interjects her brother, Shan, just before running outside.

"That's right. Pearl." She answers resolutely, without betraying any hurt feelings.

"I am a precious stone and you, a pearl. We are twins," he jokes, feeling his humour return to him with several more sips of tea.

Baoshi looks through the open doorway into the kitchen and watches Ke work, his mouth watering with anticipation. How loudly his guts are gurgling as he waits.

"Ready!" Ke exclaims.

Everyone huddles around the low table and slurps up the wheat noodles spiced with chili oil. They're picking at the mound of steaming-hot dumplings from the large bowl in the centre when the dogs begin their chorus of yapping, followed by the strained shouts of men and the thudding rumble of carts.

The donkeys have come to a full stop. Only eight men are walking. The women and children rush toward their men. All too quickly the villagers realize that a third cart is missing along with two donkeys. The cries of grief break out as three women push past the others to discover their husbands' corpses piled onto one of the two carts.

Baoshi stands at the edge of the crowd, time warped and stretched by each gasp of sorrow. His heart's fears pound loudly in his ears. He wants to flee, to avert his eyes, but Harelip's voice asserts itself sharply: *Be brave for their sakes.* Baoshi instinctively straightens his back at the sound of Harelip's voice. He moves slowly toward the crowd, his limbs heavy as iron.

Ke's trembling hands caress her husband Qian's haggard face and grasp his arms as he reaches out for her.

"Why has this calamity come upon us?" gasps one of the widows, her voice tightened by sorrow.

"What have we done to deserve this?" cries a second, who thumps her chest repeatedly in utter shock. "It is all wrong, the yin has overwhelmed the yang! This is inflicted on us because a woman is on the throne!"

Qian raises his voice above the cacophony. "There were many men lost from the other two villages." Baoshi examines the wound on the man's leg. A deep gash runs the length of his right calf. The makeshift tourniquet is already soaked with blood. "The embankment ... it was impossible ... we failed ..." Qian's voice cracks under the memory.

In the second cart lies a man whose eyes are open, but who can't speak or move. Baoshi climbs into the cart and bends forward, ear to the injured man's chest. The man's breathing is faint. He holds his wrist to track the three pulses.

"Quickly! We must bring him inside."

With the man safely placed on the kang, Baoshi brings out the hemp pouch of herbs for internal injuries and instructs the wife how to brew them. He places one hand gently on the man's chest and addresses him in a low voice. "Don't be afraid. I can help you."

How often had he heard Harelip reassure the sick ones that way! But he's witnessed Harelip deal with someone in extreme shock only once before. A slight tremor of fear rises up in Baoshi's throat. What if he isn't able to help him? Baoshi moves his hand in front of the man's face. A slight response. The man's gaze seems transfixed elsewhere. Baoshi keeps one hand on the man's forehead and slips his other hand under the back of his head, sending energy to drain some of his terror away. He passes his hands over the man's body, scanning his organs.

Baoshi sits in the dark, practising neidan, the secret rejuvenation techniques. He must recover some of his energy. Four days have passed since the men reached home. He had sensed some force in this injured man, apart from the physical wounds, some trace of a malevolent influence. He doesn't know exactly what this presence did, but it had come from the river and lodged itself in his legs. It will take weeks of medicinal brews before the man is completely well. Someone will have to get the herbs from Harelip.

He had to reset the man's leg and wrap a mud cast around the thigh. As he did that, he recalled with tenderness all the people he has been close to or had to help. Vague flashbacks of seeing his mother's naked body yet never his father's. Glimpses of Harelip as he washed and changed. Then there have been those who went to Harelip for healing. No one whom he has seen naked has a body that looks exactly like his.

He opens his eyes to look at the prone, sleeping figure. He knows what it's like to be gripped by a feverish delirium. The memory of that first foray into the forest now enters his mind, as if to comfort him, as if Harelip were next to him, whispering, *Surely you remember?*

Still weak from the effects of a fever, he had followed his new Master into the woods with a show of bravado. He was curious, wondering about the secrets of living on the mountain.

"First, the sun 日. Then, the moon 月," Harelip said as he scratched out the two characters side by side on the ground with a twig. "The sun is the hard brilliance that sustains all life. But we must of necessity also rely on the movements of the moon. Look at the characters. What do you notice?"

Baoshi recognized the basic characters, but he sensed that his Master wanted him to find something new, something he hadn't seen before.

He was stumped but stammered, "Th-the look. There's that opening in the moon, whereas it's closed below for the sun character."

Harelip smiled and continued. "Some secret skills I will show you are like the yang energies of the sun. Too much brilliance and one could be singed to death. Fighting energy surges forward, concentrated, tight with hardness. Other skills are more like the moon, internal, unseen, moving softly and mysteriously. These are the yin energies, healing skills that you would use to restore yourself and others. As you progress in your learning, you'll discover how these yin skills also can be used in defending yourself."

Yes, he remembers very well. Baoshi furrows his eyebrows as he recalls practising Knife Hands, the sides of his hands striking the bags of pebbles repeatedly until they were swollen and bruised. Then Harelip would apply a special ointment and cover his bruises tenderly with hemp bandages. He learned how to generate striking power from deep within his belly, whether it was a weapon he was wielding or his bare hands. But he also learned from his Master how to rejuvenate his inner body with neidan breathing techniques. He can feel the energy powerfully surging through him now, returning to him what he has expended in the past few days.

When dawn arrives, the roosters signalling the start of a new day, he allows himself a long-drawn-out sigh. He must go. His work is finished here.

Outside the cave, Qian and Ke wait for him.

"We have a request of you, Precious Stone," Qian begins, holding out a letter folded carefully. "The village needs your help."

"There is a Bronze Urn in Chang'an," adds Ke. "That's how peasants like us reach the Emperor. Please go there and put this letter in it. You've been so kind."

Qian adds, "Without a reprieve from Nü Huang, we'll have to deal with the ire of the local officials at not being able to pay the tribute grain at the end of the summer. And then we may have to resort to making further sacrifices."

At this remark, Qian and Ke look forlorn and worried. Baoshi accepts the letter with both his hands and bows. He slips the letter carefully inside his jacket and swallows deeply, recognizing the added burden to his pilgrimage.

Mogao Caves near Dunhuang

"I've noticed," begins Alopen, "that you're puzzled by your uncle's motivation for summoning you, aren't you?"

Ardhanari doesn't reply but quickly unfurls his sleeping mat next to Alopen's prone body and lies down, pulling the light quilt over his body. He resents that there isn't even a coal brazier for these cold nights in the desert, and he has to huddle close to Alopen for warmth.

Gentle snores escape from the others sleeping to Alopen's left, followed by the occasional snort and a flurry of wheezing sounds.

"All right, let me tell you what I know. It's true about your reputation preceding you ..." Alopen pauses, and Ardhanari's back tenses up, wondering what he's going to reveal next.

"One of the Cui family's sons saw your work in Chang'an, liked it, and found out that you're Old Gecko's nephew, so he pressured Old Gecko to get you back here to work on the sculptures. It's really as simple as that."

Ardhanari raises his eyebrows in surprise. "What a strange way to get me to return. I mean, he made it sound as if he was close to dying."

"Well, the boss sure is shrewd, isn't he? His letter worked, and that's what counts."

Ardhanari closes his eyes. He pretends to fall asleep, but his mind is acutely awake.

He thinks back to when he first met Harelip at Da Ci'en Monastery. He was repairing a damaged sculpture, singing while he worked, and this monk followed the sound of his voice to where he was. Some glimmer of recognition passed between them. A fire sped from Ardhanari's eyes to the centre of his belly, rapid and convincing. They exchanged names. The monk insisted that he be called by his deformity. He had proclaimed, "I am the sum of all my deformities, seen and unseen."

Then there was the time when Harelip went looking for him at the Turkish tea shop, back when Hamed had his business at the edge of the Western Market. Ardhanari smiles wistfully at the memory. It was all too wonderful. How long did their affair last? He can't quite recall. Maybe two years, or slightly less. Harelip never showed up for their last meeting. The next day, Ardhanari went to the monastery where they had first met, to ask questions. He was met with blank expressions. A monk answered him stiffly, "We don't know where he is." Then he cast disdainful glances at Ardhanari, eyeing him up and down.

Did Harelip grow fearful of their quickly developing intimacy? Why couldn't anyone who knew Harelip tell him where he'd gone?

If his parents were alive today, what would they think of his life in Chang'an? And about his friends, the jogappas? He imagines his parents' scorn: *Women? How could you call them women? Men who renounce their rights—surely they are the worst of the worst.* He retorts inside his head to his parents, *Believe it or not, they are women because this is how the jogappas see themselves. The best of the best.* He clamps down on his teeth and clenches his jaw.

Maybe he is completely mistaken. Maybe his parents wouldn't be too surprised. He shrugs with resignation and curls up on his side.

OUTSIDE CHANG'AN

Baoshi looks up at the night sky from his spot on a slope slightly away from the road. The moon is dark, while the stars are resplendent. He relaxes his body into the earth and moans with relief, grateful for the rest. He has just finished the last of the food the villagers gave him for the journey. He unties his straw sandals and massages his sore feet. He has been walking for four days now, allowing himself only a few hours of sleep each night before setting off again at the crack of dawn. This will be his fourth and hopefully last night before reaching Chang'an. So far, only one cart driver has stopped for him, asking if he wanted a ride. That was yesterday. But he had said no, thinking about Harelip's words, that he is a walking boy, setting out on a pilgrimage. He must honour his Master's words; although tonight, feeling the blisters on his feet, he wonders if he was foolish to decline the ride. *Words are only sounds, nothing until you give them meaning.* That's right, he remembers Harelip saying that. "Well, I prefer to walk," he mutters to himself as he rolls his shoulders back and presses his lips resolutely together.

He has a sip of water, then shakes his waterskin to check how much is left. Perhaps twenty mouthfuls. The night before, the owner of an inn was kind enough to let him fill his waterskin at the trough, but that was all he would do, stating firmly he had the place filled with guests. He had told him how much farther Chang'an was. Why did the innkeeper look so unhappy, with such a sour expression on his face?

People are rather strange sometimes, he thinks as he lets his eyes rest on the beauty of the night sky. He wonders what the city will be like. His thoughts return to the concerns of the villagers. Now he has an extra task to fulfil. He taps his finger absentmindedly on his jacket, just above his left breast. The letter he must deliver on behalf of the villagers to something called the Bronze Urn.

He thinks about the parable of the water in the pond. Water is precious, he muses, just like the twenty mouthfuls he has left in his waterskin. Then there's the water in his body. Water in the clouds. Water of the Yellow River, which became far too menacing to be contained by the embankments. What wisdom does the parable offer about the disaster that affected the villagers? Who was responsible for the disaster, Heaven or Nü Huang, who some villagers believe has incited Heaven's anger? Or was it the weakness of the embankments? But that raises further questions. Baoshi shakes his head. Not very simple.

He starts to sing a favourite tune of Harelip's.

> *A sad song in place of tears*
> *I gaze into the distance instead of returning*
> *Miss the old home*
> *Heavy and listless my heart*

Desiring family long gone
Wishing to cross water without a boat
Unspeakable thoughts in my heart
Tossing in my depths.

He sings the song many times, each time softer and softer, his eyes getting heavy with sleep until he dozes off.

IMPERIAL PARK
NORTH OF TAIJIGONG

"Where is Her Majesty sending you?" asks Sansi, puffing and wheezing as he dismounts from his horse. He was never much of a horseman, and it proves to be a challenge keeping up with Wan'er. Their predawn ride through the Imperial park has not been witnessed by others.

"I had to swear to secrecy." Wan'er stares down at Sansi from her position on the saddle. "You haven't answered my question before you asked one of me."

"Which was?" Sweat marks the boundary between Sansi's grey hair and the rim of his black silk fu tou. He bends forward slightly, aware of a momentary pain in his right side, then pulls out a bright blue handkerchief to wipe his face and neck.

"What in Heaven possessed you to make such a ridiculous suggestion?" She turns slightly away to gaze into the far distance. West of them is a large lake with a humpbacked stone bridge. She studies its curved outlines, imagining it to be a serpent rising out of the lake. She wishes she could will it to move toward Sansi and choke him with its powerful body.

"We must continue to humour her until the way to proceed is clear.

The Immortal Crane Event, with all the preceding preparations, will provide a very fine distraction while we make plans."

"But why say that he's the reincarnation of a Daoist Immortal?"

"You must admit that it was clever of me to say the very thing dear to Nü Huang's heart." He straightens up and grins proudly at her, tucking his handkerchief back into his belt.

"I'm not looking forward to this venture. What a humiliating position to be in, having to write tribute poems to that dim-wit and to insist that other notable talents of our court follow suit! It brings shame to our refined tradition of poetry and goes against what we strive for."

For Sansi, there is no such conflict or challenge to integrity. Such tasks are mere performances, superficial yet necessary. The Imperial Secretary has been writing and commissioning tribute poems and literary works for court occasions all these years, so why should this be any different? Just another duty to be performed. He swiftly turns his back to her and strolls east to the edge of the swamp. His eyes are focused on a growth of tall reeds. Partially camouflaged by the reeds, two cranes are foraging for food in the company of ducks. The cranes' white bodies, their sinewy black necks, and the touch of red on their crowns cause him to shiver with pleasure.

Why can't Wan'er have more of a sense of humour? He doesn't like it when she's angry. He imagines the scar on her forehead to be throbbing and pulsating with some kind of discontentment. A person once marked will always be marked. He's convinced that her grandfather's disgraceful treason continues its legacy in her. Shangguan Yi miscalculated—he shouldn't have trusted in Emperor Gaozong. The minister and scholar-poet lost his life because of it, and here is his granddaughter, barely able to rein in her anger.

By the time he turns around, Wan'er has dismounted. He speaks in a firm tone. "There's nothing to debate. The event is months away.

You can decide for yourself when the time comes whether to defy Nü Huang's wishes or to obey them."

"You talk to me as if I can choose, while we both know what the truth of my situation is. I'm appealing to you for some understanding of my innermost emotions, my deepest yearnings. How despicable it is to have to concoct beautiful language for one whom I intensely dislike, to have to grovel and drool at the hem of his conceited gown."

She walks up to Sansi, knowing in her bones that he has no sympathy for her dilemma. He continues to remain cool, a reptilian cool, limitless in his capacity to absorb the heat of her anger. He, the man of immense privilege, whose aunt rules on the throne, and who doesn't mind doing and saying whatever it takes to ensure his own success. Who is she in comparison? A slave elevated to favour in Nü Huang's eyes yet still tugged this way and that by her owner's every whim. Isn't she the one to whom the Holy and Maternal Emperor confides the most vile and most vulnerable moments?

"How long will you be away?"

Without answering, Wan'er remounts her chestnut horse and, squeezing Nomad's body firmly with her legs, gallops away.

MOGAO CAVES NEAR DUNHUANG

The crew of men who prepared the walls of the cave have returned to Dunhuang, happy that they've gained merit toward their next rebirth. By the time Ardhanari enters the cave, Ram and Arun are already perched on the top rungs of ladders, holding cloth bags filled with powdered charcoal. Old Gecko orders Ardhanari and Alopen to climb up the other two ladders, then he passes them a large, coarse parchment. While Ardhanari and Alopen hold up two corners of the stencil, Ram and Arun pound the cloth bags against it at the other end, releasing the charcoal and thereby creating the outlines of the design on the ceiling.

Old Gecko stands below with his arms crossed across his chest, watching them work. Once finished, the four men climb down, move their ladders and repeat the procedure on the next section of the ceiling. They're about to complete laying out the whole outline of the ceiling when they hear shouts of the arriving food vendors. Old Gecko gives a reluctant nod. The men scramble down the ladders and rush out, grateful for the lunch break.

Ardhanari takes a detour to the other side of the cliff to pee against the rock. His warm urine shoots out onto the even hotter sand. Somehow, the act of peeing causes him to sneeze violently.

He turns the corner and emerges into the open area. Old Gecko stands to one side, looking askance at his noisy crew as they eagerly chomp on their fried green onion pancakes and slurp noisily from bowls of cold wheat noodles seasoned with sesame oil and fish sauce. The overhanging rock casts a long, slender shadow at noon, enough for the men to rest under. This scene could be material for a mural. What is the term? Bian xiang 變像, transformation image. But far from being a scene of religious epiphany, his mural will depict ordinary men, their bodies shielded by shadow, doing nothing glamorous or heroic. The mural must capture in fine detail how thoroughly their faces and hair are sprinkled with dust, their hands caked with mud and paint, and their tunics and antariyas stained. They laugh, cough, and chew, free from any consideration of etiquette as they rest their sore bodies against the cliff face.

Old Gecko sips his tea slowly and with deliberate loudness, pausing between sips. That way he doesn't have to remain quiet while the men cackle like fiends. The old man swears by the special brew he drinks every day. He says that it keeps his mind clear, his body agile, and his eyes sharp as a hawk's. He prefers to eat in private after everyone else has finished eating. Ardhanari thinks his uncle is too aloof and fussy, but he doesn't dwell on this any longer when he spies two bowls of noodles and two pancakes on a flat piece of rock under the shade.

"You know," Old Gecko begins, "we'll have to finish our work in the cave before the weather gets too cold. It doesn't leave us much time."

The men stare coldly at Old Gecko but continue eating. No one replies, but there's an abrupt suspension of the lighthearted banter. Ardhanari squats down with his food and slurps the noodles with gusto.

"You resent me, don't you? You forget I'm merely a pawn of the Cui family, exactly like you. Our reputations and our wages depend on finishing the work on time."

The sullen silence persists. Who knows where this speech is going?

Old Gecko continues. "Don't think I'm a heartless old man. I remember what it was like to be young and restless."

The men laugh nervously, including Ardhanari. This comment strikes all the men as somewhat ridiculous. After all, Ram, Arun, and Ardhanari are all middle-aged, while Alopen is in his thirties.

"Listen, I'll go into Dunhuang tomorrow to make arrangements for extra help. That will make a difference. If we work very hard for the next few weeks, we can afford a nice excursion into town, visit the local tavern, and spend some time with the 'chickens' there. Everyone will be more refreshed and return to the work with renewed vigour. I'll cover the expenses."

The men brighten up, chuckling. Only Ardhanari remains subdued. He has finished the noodles and is beginning to nibble on a pancake. His uncle is truly a sly one. *He wants to push us to our limits while promising to reward us. Of course he hopes we'll work harder and complain less.* Ardhanari is happy to hear, though, that there will be a few extra men hired.

"What's the matter, dear Nephew?" asks Old Gecko in a sardonic tone, directing a look of concern at Ardhanari. "Worried about cheating on some woman in Chang'an?"

Approaching Chang'an

By the time the sun reaches a quarter of its sweep across the sky, Baoshi catches his first glimpse of the city in the far distance. He quickens his pace until the image of Chang'an grows closer and larger with each step.

High walls of pounded red earth and tall watchtowers. Streams of travellers in carriages and carts drawn by horses or donkeys. A growing barrage of animal noises and the voices of people. He reaches the main gate in the southern wall of the enclosed city. Peering through the gate, he sees three wide lanes, flanked by two narrow ones. The wide central lane is practically empty, but the other two are choked with traffic. The wheels of carts rattle loudly in the grooved ruts. Baoshi follows the travellers on foot, entering the city along one of the narrow lanes, marked by rows of locust trees that seem to stretch ahead interminably.

Baoshi turns his head this way and that, his attention flitting from one new sight to another, his eyes wide with curiosity. He can't help but stare—there's just so much he has never seen before. Turbaned men with olive skin and curly beards stride about in flowing, cloud-coloured robes that reach down to their ankles. A man with eyes as fresh and green as forest moss. Women with their eyelids painted dark blue and their mouths obscured behind translucent veils. Farm folk with their donkey carts laden with cabbages, turnips, eggplants, peppers. Bamboo cages of chickens alongside baskets of eggs, expertly stacked to the brim, held in place by netting.

In the adjoining lane for traffic, camels amble past, followed by a horse-drawn carriage. A man sits on its roof, playing a mandolin while flashing appreciative gazes down at the women. His light, playful tune inspires giggles and applause. Baoshi is intrigued by the camels, with their long legs and half-lidded eyes. He mimics their mouth movements, feeling rather soothed by the action, but is jolted out of his reverie when a noisy battalion of men passes by, their torsos draped with heavy metal plates that jangle loudly as they march stiffly ahead, their spears held upright against their right shoulders. *Why*, he muses, *these men are just the very opposite of the monkey troops that live among the trees and rocks of Mount Hua. The monkeys chatter incessantly and move their bodies instinctually, never in unison like this.*

The letter jostles against his left breast, reminding him. Where is this Bronze Urn that he's supposed to deposit the letter into? First things first. He must get to the market then ask people about the tea shop run by Ardhanari's friend. Harelip told him it was at the edge of the market, in the western sector. He'll follow the farmers, just as Qian had suggested, since they're all heading there. Those carrying market wares on their backs grunt from the exertion. On the side streets, people and carts travel on the same path, no longer separated by lanes.

Baoshi startles at the thunderous sounds of large drums. He looks around, puzzled. He turns to ask the man next to him. The Hour of the Horse, he's told. The man points to one of the towers in the far distance. *Amazing*, Baoshi thinks, *drums to tell the time.*

"Are you also going to the market? Am I heading in the right direction?" Baoshi asks the man.

"Of course! Where are you from anyway? You seem to know nothing of the city." The man stares, incredulous.

"Why, you are right. I am from Mount Hua, to the east."

The man keeps staring at him with increasing consternation, and then moves abruptly away. Baoshi is puzzled. Why the wariness? Is curiosity not a valued characteristic in the city? He decides to follow closely behind a woman. She's balancing two wooden buckets, one at each end of a carrying pole. He peers into the buckets. Masses of small turtles darken the insides.

The travellers pass through different wards, each fang delineated from the surrounding ones by high walls and entered through a gate. In the bigger wards that they walk through, there's no lack of temple buildings. One temple complex is so large that it spans half the ward. He thinks about Harelip and wonders which one of these temple grounds was the one he lived in. The residential wards are smaller and quieter, where tiny houses huddle on both sides of lanes. He catches sight of children skipping in alleys, while a few old men squat on the pavements, smoking long pipes.

How much farther? His feet are miserably sore, and there are only a few gulps of water left in his waterskin. Into his fifth day of walking, every step feels much more painfully difficult now that he has entered the city. He can't wait to sit down under a shady tree and find food to eat. His hand reaches into his satchel, groping until it finds the hollow smoothness of the begging bowl. He never got any advice from Harelip about the bowl, so he'll have to make something up. *Just how large is this city? Surely the market can't be too much farther.*

Baoshi recalls how Harelip taught him to find his way on the mountain. The sun's position in the sky. The stars at night. The other signs of nature, like the location of the Yellow and Wei rivers in relation to the mountain, and the unmistakable peaks of Mount Hua. But here in the city, it is altogether different. None of the familiar signs other than the sun, which is not very useful at this moment, since it is almost directly overhead. Completely unsettling. He'll have to rely on strangers for help and risk receiving more looks.

Reaching the walled enclosure of the next fang, he notices that the farm folk are getting more animated and talkative. At the gate entrance, he peers into the ward, past the people ahead of him. The market! With a myriad of sellers at stalls that sprawl across the whole ward.

Sweaty hands and bodies push against him without apology or brush past as they hurry ahead to their destinations. He drifts through the crowd, threading through the stalls, surveying the faces of people around him. Sellers call out loudly to gain the attention of the customers. He shakes his head, as if trying to clear his ears of noise. Some stalls display fresh vegetables, while others are stacked with fresh slabs of pork or cages of live chickens. One stall displays substantial pig carcasses, cut open and hung on hooks. Baoshi feels a touch of nausea pass through him. His eyes feast instead on rows of salted fish, jars of pickled mustard greens, and heaps of salted vegetables. The delicious gleam of fresh greens, the smooth purple lengths of eggplants piled up beautifully into pyramids. How tidy and pretty. Customers line up to buy eels from two men. When he chances upon stalls where cooked food is being sold, he stares at the variety of edibles with his mouth wide open. All the possibilities, and he without any money! He watches to see how much money people use to pay for the food. Sometimes ten copper coins, sometimes five or six. Are there other walking boys here with their begging bowls? He looks around. He spots a few people sitting on the ground with their bowls, wailing and crying for attention. But none of these men and women have shaved heads. He hadn't realized until now that begging bowls aren't solely for monks and walking boys.

At the northeastern corner, he immediately senses a different atmosphere. It's quieter, without food stalls and loud wrangling. There are fewer people milling about. Small tables occupy much of the section, with two or three people sitting at each table. Instead of raised voices, there's a great deal of whispering. Baoshi wonders if they are playing games or sharing secrets. Small wooden signs hang over the front of the tables announcing what the service is. An elderly man studies the face of a young woman sitting across from him. Baoshi discreetly draws close enough to glance down at his table, where there's a drawing of faces labelled with the meanings of various features. The young woman cocks her head, eyes locked on his mouth, as if committing to memory every prediction that the man utters. At the next table, a man with three horizontal stripes of white paint across his forehead is being aided by a lively parrot that selects the customer's fortune from a box of wooden sticks.

Money changes hands with each termination of a whispered conversation. What is being paid for? Thoughts and guesses. *Strange,* Baoshi concludes. Harelip receives food or other materials in exchange for his help. Sometimes he's repaid with repairs to the roof or chopped firewood but never money. Baoshi recalls his father's handling of money, the silence in their home often punctuated with the clanking of silver and gold coins being counted. Baoshi cringes as the image of that pouch of silver flashes through his mind, the one his father dropped onto Harelip's table.

He stands in his spot for quite a long time, caught up in memories of his childhood, wondering if he would even recognize his father if he saw him here. Would his father recognize him? He stamps his feet and returns to studying the faces of the customers seeking answers. Some stare at the fortune teller they're consulting, heads nodding enthusiastically as if they're merely confirming what they already knew. Others carry years of worry on their faces and continue to look tense despite the wisdom shared with them. Baoshi is tempted to approach the worried ones and offer to press some points on their bodies to grant them temporary relief. A middle-aged woman with a mole nestled against her right nostril shakes a container of yarrow sticks, her face completely absorbed by her question. She stands up so that she can commit her whole body to the movement, shaking until one stick slowly emerges, raised from the rest by an invisible force, eventually tipping out of the container.

A strong gust of wind sweeps through the area, disturbing the donkeys and horses tied up at the posts. Papers are rustled, some blown away. The woman with the mole who has just been given her strip of paper with the Yijing hexagram clutches it close to her chest, while the face reader at the other table stretches his arms protectively across his papers.

Sand flies into Baoshi's eyes. He squints, rubs his eyes, then sputters some sand from his mouth. He uses the last of his water to wash out his eyes. When he recovers, he spots an old man in one corner with a begging bowl at his feet. What a startling bushel of white hair sticking up on the man's head! Maybe he can sit next to him, for he's desperate to get money soon, his belly painfully growling with hunger. Baoshi shields his eyes from the sand and heads toward the beggar.

The wizened man, wasted as a dried twig, sits upright on a stool, dwarfed by the gigantic sign at his feet. Baoshi stares incredulously at the message, the Chinese characters written in red ink: "I believe that my body will rejuvenate."

How is this possible, that someone who has progressed to this stage of physical aging can still believe this? He has heard from Harelip that the pure Daoist practitioners devote their whole lives to this venture. But his Master has made only lighthearted references to immortality, never putting any emphasis on that quest. *I may know about the external formulae for immortality, my boy, but sitting with oneself is still the more potent pursuit.*

Baoshi sits down next to the old man and pulls out his begging bowl. "Please tell me, sir ..." he begins, "do many visitors come, and do they give you enough money?"

The old man chuckles with amusement. "You're asking me how business is in the religious life? What a joke."

"What do you mean? What religion?"

"I believe in the resurrection of the body. The prophet Jesus came back to life and walked out of the tomb."

"When did this happen?"

"About seven hundred years ago, in the Far West."

"Oh? He must have done a lot of internal alchemy exercises."

The old man spits forcefully at the ground, landing a solid green gob in front of Baoshi's crossed legs.

"Aren't you an impudent one! Why have you planted yourself next to me, by the way?"

"Sir, I'm new to this city, and my Master gave me his begging bowl to use so that I can have money to buy food. I really have no idea how it's done, so I thought I would watch how you do it."

"Ho ho ho," chortles the old man. "Such a naive one! You must be told, then. Now listen," he begins, placing a cool hand on Baoshi's thigh, "you either rely on the ones who share common beliefs with you, or you have to perform something that truly impresses the onlookers. And, believe me, it takes quite an effort to catch people's attention. Those who merely sit and beg, offering nothing in exchange, don't fare as well. See my big sign here? It's an invitation to people who hunger for such a rejuvenation. They're the most vulnerable and will give me money because, in giving, they hope to save themselves. If I believe, then they can believe too, you see. I tell them what I think, without a shadow of a doubt, and then they go away quite satisfied."

Baoshi furrows his forehead and purses his lips. He supposes he could talk to people about what he has learned from Harelip, but he isn't keen on this idea. It's his Master who teaches, not him. He rubs the tight knot in his belly as he looks around for ideas. A man in a flowing crimson robe with a tall conical brown hat perfectly balanced on his head towers above everyone around him. His companions begin to chant to the beat of a drum. The dancer spins his body to the rhythms, arms outstretched, left hand raised higher than the right, palms facing up. The man's robe swirls in a blur of speed, yet he has a deep, inward gaze. Baoshi is impressed. A crowd of people gathers.

When the man stops spinning, the crowd applauds, but only a few onlookers drop coins at his feet. Baoshi's face lights up. He jumps to his feet, takes off his jacket, and begins to execute a sequence of movements, slicing the air with his graceful, swooping arms, lifting his legs powerfully in single, then double, kicks, sometimes pausing in one-legged balances, or squatting down on one leg while the other is extended, held almost horizontal to the ground. As he moves, he imagines himself becoming the animal he's mimicking. His sandals kick and stomp up a flurry of sand. A crowd forms quickly. Under the hot afternoon sun, he sweats profusely as he performs these moves.

When he's finished, the audience claps and cheers, some even urging him with "Another round!" A few copper coins later, he performs another set of movements. Two girls, less than half his height, try to imitate what he's doing, but they stumble over each other, collapsing to the ground in giggles. At the end of the second demonstration, a few more coins are dropped into his bowl. He bows gratefully to his onlookers.

As the crowd disperses, Baoshi notices a man staring at him. The stranger rests his hands against his hips, feet slightly apart. The man's face is very pleasant to look at. Beautiful, expressive eyes and skin that's a little darker than his. He can feel the smoothness of the stranger's cheeks with his glance. His heart already pounding faster from the physical exertion, he catches his breath and gulps, feeling embarrassed by the man's stare. The stranger is dressed in a deep blue silk hu fu tunic with an inner green skirt that grazes the tips of his leather boots. His gown is girded by a thin leather belt from which hang several objects—a sheathed knife, a leather purse, and two decorative strips of leather inlaid with jade and rubies. On his head, he wears a stylish black linen cap, with crimson brocade flaps that cover his ears. The cap sits quite low on the man's head, almost covering his long, shapely eyebrows.

Baoshi forgets his hunger. The stranger comes forward and drops a silver coin into the begging bowl. Baoshi bows deeply at the waist and proclaims in the most respectful tone he can muster, "I am most grateful, sir."

"Well done, young man." He laughs.

Baoshi stammers, blushing from the attention, "Th-thank you."

"Why are you begging?" asks the stranger.

"I've come into the city without money. I am a walking boy."

"Oh? What does that mean?"

"I've been sent on a pilgrimage to look for someone."

"Does that mean that you walked all the way here? Where from?"

"I've walked to the city from Mount Hua, sir."

The stranger looks amused by Baoshi's answer.

"Have you been to Chang'an before?"

"No, never before."

"How brave. I envy you that freedom, dear walking boy."

To which Baoshi responds with a look of puzzlement. Freedom? This impressive stranger envies him? How odd.

The stranger continues, "Do you think it is at all possible, this idea of rejuvenation?" He tilts his head at the sign while the old man talks with a few curious onlookers.

"I don't know. Most of us don't have the ability or the luck. Maybe there's more than one kind of rejuvenation." Baoshi pauses to scratch behind his ear, distracted by a sudden itch. "Not necessarily by physical means."

"An open-minded young man. How rare." The stranger seems wistful, his gaze drifting off before returning to focus on Baoshi. "I must go now," the stranger says abruptly. "Good luck on your search." He pats Baoshi on the back and strides away toward his chestnut horse, his ponytail flung side to side by his swift movements. The stranger rides away without looking back.

Da Fa Temple
West Central Chang'an

In the spacious open courtyard, sixty soldiers practise drills in their full battle armour. The clanking sounds of their heavy metal breastplates rattle the air as Wan'er dismounts from her horse, Nomad, at the south entrance. The guards retract their crossed spears as Wan'er produces her Imperial scroll with the seal of the Emperor. Her riding boots make dull tapping sounds against the pavement stones. After placing Nomad in the stable, she ascends the steps to the second gate with a saddlebag draped over one shoulder.

Under the free-standing gate, three bays wide, two clay guardians loom on either side of her. Across the top of the gate is an elegantly carved epithet, its characters painted in gold: *The Great Way Is the Ultimate Weapon*. She admires the ruddy earth tones of the sculptures' muscular bodies and the fierce insistence of their gaze. To Wan'er, they are far more menacing than the men at the outside entrance. The guardian to her left has its mouth wide open in a clear warning scowl, but the other one implies another kind of threat with its mouth closed. Two guardians of the spirit realms. One to oversee the battles of life and the other to watch over the cessation of the breath. How appropriate that these guardians should stand at the entrance to where secret potions and elixir pills are being concocted.

Looking past the pillars into the courtyard, she watches the soldiers perform their drills. They show no signs of noticing her arrival. Their leader, attired in his full regalia, shouts out each drill with tremendous verve, his chest bellowing in and out with each command. He too seems oblivious to her arrival. These soldiers must be preparing to fend off border raids from the Northern Turks led by the Qaphagan. Will the Turkish leader not quell his desire to seize territories? Besides his greed for more land, he's upset that Nü Huang didn't fulfil her promise to grant him Princess Taiping's hand in marriage years ago. Wan'er has written out Nü Huang's letters—bullying and haughty in tone—which were met by his replies, full of annoyance at the paltry concessions.

It's easy to tell which soldiers haven't engaged in any battles yet. Their faces are fresh, youthful, unmarked by the horrors of war. They move their bodies awkwardly, barely accustomed to their new armour. She recalls the walking boy she met in the market. His face, she decides, is the most open she has ever seen, short of the expressions of infants. Open in that it radiated unmitigated curiosity. Possessing a quality that even these youths in armour cannot approach. Why is that? Despite the naïveté, there was most certainly evidence of wisdom. She surprised herself when she confessed to him her envy. A walking boy can go everywhere with so few possessions or obligations to enslave him, whereas she, with so much prestige and privilege, and with so fine a steed as Nomad, can travel only when Nü Huang decrees it acceptable.

Nuns from the worship hall beyond the courtyard have noticed her. She has to wait only a few miao before the bell from the eastern belfry tower rings out, and a nun, the keeper of the temple, emerges from the hall and heads toward her.

The keeper's face registers surprise when she reads Wan'er's scroll.

"Your Eminence," the nun speaks reverentially as she bows her head, "the Abbess is conducting a ritual east of the Golden Moon Gate for the monks and visiting worshippers. I'll show you to her study. It won't be long." The nun is polite and respectful, with a hint of caution and girlish nervousness. When has anyone of such high standing visited them from the Palace City, much less a woman dressed in a stunning riding outfit? It takes all the restraint she can muster to stifle her gasps of admiration.

Wan'er follows the keeper, who's more than a whole head shorter than her. While the nun plods ahead in wooden clogs, pausing to steal some furtive glances, Wan'er's eyes are drawn to the curves and details of the bluish-grey roofs of the temple. The mythical creatures perch on the corners and look out to their surroundings, ever watchful, ever resilient. The groupings of these creatures vary from roof to roof and corner to corner, as if to challenge the lazy, presumptuous eye. One can never be complacent, it seems to her, when every corner is rife with unpredictability.

They leave the shouts of the soldiers well behind. Wan'er catches a heady smell of aloeswood incense as they pass by the dim worship hall. The hypnotic voices of chanting nuns and the ringing echoes of a brass bowl being struck at regular intervals with a wooden stick resound in Wan'er's ears as she and the keeper continue along the corridor adjacent to the hall.

Behind the hall are the more private sections: the large dormitory, the library, the individual rooms for guests, the dining hall, as well as the Abbess's study. A few nuns walk by on the other side of the quadrangle and smile shyly as they bow to acknowledge Wan'er's presence. The keeper leaves immediately after opening the doors to the study. Wan'er drops her saddlebag onto a rosewood divan in the corner of the room. She takes off her linen cap and flings it on top of the saddlebag. The divan looks inviting, but she resists, knowing that it would be improper to stretch out on it. She settles into a large chair instead.

Glancing around the study, she sees that it is long and narrow, more like a corridor than a room, the walls crowded with calligraphic pieces and paintings. A large bear pelt with head intact hangs behind the sizable writing desk. In addition to the pelt's impressive size, its head has been fitted with an extended piece, a veil of sorts. On the head itself is a pair of eyes, and on the veil, another pair of eyes. She's shocked that something dead could have such a formidable impact. Wan'er distracts herself by looking at the works of calligraphy. A piece of seal script and two others in cursive style. Several odd clay figurines on a side table. She finally plucks up the courage to approach the bear pelt. That's when she discovers that both pairs of eyes are pure gold. It takes a while before she realizes there's a faint chirping sound in the room. She looks at the objects on the desk and spots the tiny gourd vessel. It has an intricate ivory lid, carved so that gaps in the design, between the delicate branches, allow for the passage of air. A cricket! So the Abbess has a pet. She caresses the curved sides of the gourd container. Smooth as satin. *Like a woman's body*, she thinks. Her index finger travels now to the ivory lid, feeling its textures. The cricket's call grows louder.

The sound of footsteps swiftly approaching startles her. Suddenly self-conscious, she rushes over to the divan and slips her linen cap back on, pulling it low enough to cover her scar. The Abbess appears wearing a ceremonial yellow robe with a bright orange and blue brocade trim that borders the hem of the gown. A large silver yin-yang pendant hangs between her breasts. She has been briefed about the visitor. By the assistant's flustered face and excited tone of voice, the Abbess could tell that the Imperial Secretary made quite the impression.

"Welcome to Da Fa Temple, Lady Shangguan. We are honoured by your presence. How may we be of assistance to you?" The Abbess bows to Wan'er, while noticing that the visitor's elegant, slender fingers twist anxiously at the fabric of her hu fu outfit.

Wan'er produces her Imperial scroll from the saddlebag. As the Abbess reads the scroll, Wan'er finds herself wondering how old the woman is. Certainly much younger than Nü Huang. Perhaps closer to her own mother's age. She looks for clues. The concentration of wrinkles around the outside edges of her eyes. The lines around her neck. A few age spots on her ears and on the back of her hands and wrists. But her voice is strong, showing none of the signs of an elderly woman. Her braided hair is thick and lush and has only a few strands of white. Wan'er stares at the silver pendant. An unusual representation of the yin-yang symbol, but what exactly distinguishes it from the countless others she has seen? It seems to her that an answer lies just beneath the surface, but she can't quite summon it at this moment.

"I've come on behalf of our Holy and Divine Sovereign. She has asked me to obtain the finished Jin Dan elixir from you, as well as consult you on a pressing matter." She's repeating what's stated in the scroll. Wan'er pauses, considering how best to continue. "The matter is quite a sensitive one. That's why it's not revealed in the scroll. I've been entrusted with the duty of describing Nü Huang's dilemma to you in person, with the intent of seeking your advice on Her Majesty's behalf. Nü Huang requests your utmost discretion. She obviously values your opinion."

The Abbess rolls the scroll back up and returns it to Wan'er. "Indeed, I am honoured that Nü Huang seeks my opinion. I had been informed that she would send a special messenger from Taijigong, but I didn't anticipate she would send such a distinguished member of her court here. We have heard of your talents and your reputation as a poet in Her Majesty's court, Lady Shangguan."

"I too have heard a great deal about your impressive skills, Abbess. Let us dispense with the formalities. I live my days at Taijigong having to follow protocol at every turn. It would be a relief not to adhere to them while I'm here. Please call me Wan'er." She smiles shyly at the Abbess. "May we discuss the second matter later this afternoon, after I've had a chance to rest?"

"At your convenience."

"Good. I shall request your hospitality for two days while I fulfil these duties." While speaking, Wan'er stares into the Abbess's eyes. She notices, with some puzzlement, that they're not the same colour. Not exactly. One seems bluish-brown while the other is almost green. How odd.

"Stay for as long as you wish, Wan'er. You're most welcome here."

They're silent for a few moments, listening to the soft rise and fall of their own breath, until that silence is broken by the cricket's calls once again.

"Your pet cricket knows when you have a visitor, doesn't it?"

"My cricket and I are one," the Abbess quips. "Please call me Ling," she whispers.

Wan'er blushes at the intimate tone. "Certainly," she replies quickly.

"I'll show you to your room. Perhaps you would enjoy a bath?"

Ling leads the way out of her study and heads toward the private guest chambers. Unlike the keeper of the temple, the Abbess doesn't look back, yet Wan'er feels the heat of that strange pair of eyes burning through her.

WESTERN MARKET
WEST CENTRAL CHANG'AN

After performing a third set of fighting movements, Baoshi bows to the applauding crowd as more coins are dropped into his begging bowl. Panting, he sits back down and asks the old man, "Do you know where the tea shop is?"

"My boy, you're really a country bumpkin! There are dozens of tea shops scattered across the market."

"This one is run by an old Turkish man who sings."

The man raises his scraggly eyebrows in a show of skepticism while his shock of white hair is ruffled slightly by the breeze. "Oh, is that so? Ask the bun seller over there."

Baoshi throws his money and bowl into his satchel and walks toward the bun seller. His mouth waters as he catches a whiff of the fragrant aromas. The customers cover their noses as they turn away after paying, disgust showing on their faces. After they're a few paces away from the cart, they smile with relief and bite heartily into their buns.

Baoshi is intrigued. He takes his place at the end of the line. He understands when he draws near. Foul odours escape from the bun seller's mouth, flaming with enough poisonous fire to singe the hairs of even the most insensitive of nostrils.

"Want one?"

"Oh, yes! But I only have these ... How many do you need?" Baoshi pulls out his coins to show the man, willing himself not to flinch away. The man snatches three copper coins out of Baoshi's hand.

"I'm new to this city and I'm looking for a tea shop run by an old Turkish man. He sings. Do you know the one?"

The bun seller squints his eyes and leans toward Baoshi, scrutinizing him.

"Why do you want to know? Not many Chinese people want to go there. Besides, that old man died a while ago. He was really old, you know."

"I am looking for someone called Ardhanari."

"Shhh, shhh!" His utterance only increases the intensity of odour issuing from his mouth.

Baoshi tries again, tears welling up in his eyes. "Please, would you explain what it is I'm doing wrong?"

The bun seller looks nervously at the growing line of customers behind Baoshi. "There now, don't cry." He quickly hands Baoshi a bun wrapped with a small lotus leaf, pulls the boy around to his side of the cart and whispers into his ear, "I'll show you where the tea shop is after I've finished selling my buns. They moved to a new location, new owner, next ward. In the meantime, have a drink of water from the pump over there."

Baoshi tears open the bun. His mouth can't gobble fast enough. The subtle combination of fragrances from the seasoned cabbage, bamboo shoots, mushrooms, scallions, and minced pork rise up to his nose as he chomps down with gratitude. It doesn't matter that the escaping steam burns the inside of his mouth slightly. When he reaches the pump, he bends forward and opens his mouth wide under the spout as he cranks the handle.

He releases two sizable burps then plops down on the ground. Rubbing his belly with satisfaction, he thinks about the handsome stranger. If only he'd lingered, he might have overcome his shyness and asked more questions. His eyes were captivating.

Baoshi's daydream is interrupted by the voice of the bun seller calling out, "Come along, it's time to go."

The bun seller has tucked the empty bamboo steamers away. He lifts his cart by its long handles and pushes it in front of him on its one large wheel. "The tea shop is not very far. You said you're looking for a friend?"

"My Master's friend. The former owner of the tea shop would have been able to help, but now that he's dead, I just don't know who can help me."

"Things change quickly in the city. When the Turk croaked, what followed was such a scandal, even I know about it. You see ..."

"Yes?" Baoshi nods eagerly in anticipation.

The bun seller makes another hissing sound through his lips, expelling more foul odour. He doesn't finish what he was about to say. They go down some side streets, leaving the market behind.

"Why were you so nervous back there in the market, sir? When I asked about the tea shop?"

The bun seller looks furtively around. The walls of the next fang are about fifty paces ahead. He speaks up again when no one is within earshot.

"I don't usually come through here. I'm making an exception today because I see you're an honourable yet hopelessly ignorant lad from the countryside and I've taken pity on you." He pauses, rolls his eyes up as if to contemplate thoughts in certain far reaches of his mind, before he continues. "All kinds of strange people go to that tea shop." He wrinkles up his nose to show his total disapproval.

As they pass through the gate and into the Foreign Quarter, the bun seller glances at people around them with growing nervousness. "I try not to go near them, the Hindus. Your friend Ardhanari is a Hindu, right? With such a name, he must be." Baoshi shrugs his shoulders. Taking a deep breath, the bun seller resumes without waiting for an answer. "I suppose they don't mind me as much as the Muslims do when they see me with my pork buns in the market! It's good there are walls separating the different wards. I like being safe in our fang each night when the curfew begins and no one is allowed on the streets.

The Foreign Quarter isn't that big anyway. It's a residential area with Hindus, Muslims, a few Nestorians, some Persians in exile ... A motley bunch, if you get my meaning."

The bun seller stops, dropping the handles of his cart. He tilts his chin up and points at his throat. "Do you see this? See?"

Baoshi stares at the bun seller's neck. A long scar runs from ear to ear, just under his chin.

"Oh my ..."

"See what I mean? I was robbed when I passed by one evening on my way home, and my throat was slashed by one of their ruffians."

"Sir, do you mean to say that you're now afraid of all the people who live here, ever since then? That's an old scar!"

"That's exactly right, my boy. Don't tell me that doesn't make sense to you!"

Baoshi doesn't know what to say. The man's firm tone of voice suggests that he has made up his mind. Baoshi is suddenly aware of some odd sensations in his body. His throat is itchy and uncomfortable while he struggles to come up with the very words that Harelip had used. Something about questions. More questions than answers. What, though? He frowns, perturbed by his lapse in memory. Then he stares wide-eyed at the bun seller and blurts out, "That is ... awful, sir! To allow such attitudes to fester in you all these years. It's not good for your health."

The bun seller's face puffs up in a crimson flush as he retorts, "Insult! What ingratitude! I help you out, and what are you but this pathetic bamboo shoot hurling complaints at me? Look over there!" He points ahead, his large hand waving wildly in front of Baoshi's face. "I told you it wasn't far away. The tea shop is at the end of that alley. Just follow it until you come to a fountain, and it's on the other side of it. Off you go!"

The bun seller turns his cart around, disappearing quickly into the crowd. Baoshi stands there, looking across the street at the alley on the other side. The bun seller's reactions have unsettled him. Barely a day in the city, and he has been close to tears several times already. He hasn't felt this shaky since his father dragged him up Mount Hua. His body starts to tremble, as if overtaken by a force beyond his control.

A boy with big dreamy eyes grabs Baoshi by the leg, holding out an open palm. "Pretty ... pretty ..." the boy says and points to the jade pendant, which has slipped out of concealment. The boy continues to grin, his palms raised up to Baoshi. Next he makes a circle with thumb and index finger of one hand, while pushing the index finger of the other hand through that hole. Again and again, all the while looking at Baoshi quizzically. *What is the boy trying to say?*

"Do you know Ardhanari?" Baoshi asks.

The boy shakes his head vigorously and runs across the street into the alley. Baoshi follows after him, but the boy soon dashes down a side lane and disappears from sight. Walking down the cobblestone alley, Baoshi admires the colourful fabrics on the women who bustle by. Some of them have gold studs gleaming in the sides of their noses or dots of red paint between their eyes. A man with curly orange hair and bright green eyes balances several digging tools across his shoulders. A woman with honeyed locks of hair rushes past him and ducks into a store selling dried fruits, spices, and tobacco. He stands close to the store window and sniffs, enjoying the wonderful aromas. Walking through this alley reminds him of the first day he spent in the mountain forest with Harelip, where he saw all kinds of animals and trees and marvelled at the miraculous variety. Recalling this, he feels much better.

The alley curves and twists like the body of a snake. Murmuring voices filter through half-open doors and windows, interspersed with the occasional clattering of pots or tools. The plaintive bleating of a goat. The scent of meat cooking. Who knows, maybe even a relative of that goat. Baoshi suddenly feels remorse for enjoying the pork bun as much as he did.

At an open area with a fountain at its centre, he hears voices singing in unison to the accompaniment of drums, bells, and a flute. The music comes from the shop on the other side of the fountain. Its entrance is flanked by a set of dilapidated doors. The doors were once a vibrant terracotta colour, but most of that paint has peeled away to reveal the faded layer of green underneath. A shingle hangs above the entrance, decorated with a line drawing of a woman carrying a copper pot on her head. Baoshi grins. This must be the tea shop he's looking for.

He crosses over to the entrance and peers in. Light filters into the tea shop through shuttered windows, creating a dim, shadowy world. A haze of smoke permeates the air. At the small round tables, groups of men sit drinking tea and smoking pipes, quietly listening to the music. Their eyes and bodies are turned toward a stage in the far left corner of the room.

Five women sit cross-legged on the modest stage, a wooden bowl and a shiny copper pot in front of them. The women are wearing vermillion muslin antariyas around their hips and saffron crossbands over their breasts. Around their necks are slung long necklaces of red and white beads. They wear their hair in buns knotted on the left side of their heads, with tiny white flowers nestled in their hair. The tallest woman in the centre is playing a flute. The one sitting at the very back beats energetically on a double-sided conical drum balanced across her knees, while another vigorously shakes a stick with many bells along its length. The remaining two are singing, their voices reverberating in rich, low tones.

Baoshi finds an empty chair just inside the entrance. The two singers' voices rise and fall with the drum's modulating volume. The mysterious melody soothes him. He closes his eyes. He sees a stream of water dancing over rocks in the heart of Mount Hua. His body begins to sway back and forth, caught up in the pulse of their combined voices.

The song gives way to a chant of only a few sounds repeated countless times. The customers begin to clap along. Baoshi opens his eyes to discover that one of the singers has risen from her seated position and is dancing in a slow, sensuous manner, stretching her arms and hands out over her head, then horizontally at her sides, sometimes even making sweeping arc-like movements, the bells around her ankles tinkling as she moves. Her face radiates a mix of entreaty and delirious, barely contained joy. Her eyes are made even more dramatic and appealing by the thick black liner accentuating them. Baoshi stares at the dancer, fascinated. When she lifts the copper pot onto her head and dances around with it, the customers applaud with fervour. Never has he seen such display of emotion in public. *Who are these people?*

There's a long pause after the performance. Then the tallest one speaks up in a different language. Her voice shocks Baoshi with its coarse, rumbling timbre. The other singers erupt into throaty cackles, an intermingling of high and deep voices. They emerge from the shadows. Customers approach the stage and throw coins into the bowl before leaving the tea shop. Baoshi gasps when he notices the lumps on their throats moving up and down. Men! Dressed so convincingly like women. His father never moved like that. Nor does Harelip. How surprising. Why, he surmises, despite those lumps on their throats, aren't they women in other ways, much like those he has just glimpsed in the streets of the Foreign Quarter? He squints at them with great interest.

The tall one approaches Baoshi. "Young man, we jogappas don't get too many handsome admirers, especially from the local Chinese. What brings you to the Foreign Quarter and particularly to the tea shop?" This performer speaks Chinese with soft purring sounds rounding off some of the words.

"He's mine, he's mine, you can't keep taking the best ones!" shrieks the dancer, jumping down from the stage and hurrying toward them.

"Calm down, you stupid teat! Who's stealing anyone?"

The dancer huffs with disapproval at the insult and folds her arms together in front of her chest. Standing next to the tall flute player with pronounced cheekbones, this one, with her curvaceous body, looks rather dwarfed. The tall one signals to the drum player to bring some tea, then turns her attention back to Baoshi.

"Tell us your name—and why you are brave enough to sit and worship at the feet of we jogappas. Perhaps you've heard of our fame?" More giggles from the others. The tea arrives, and all the jogappas seat themselves around Baoshi at the table.

"I am called Baoshi. I'm searching for a man called Ardhanari."

More giggles from the jogappas. Baoshi thinks they are probably laughing at the way he says his name in Chinese, "何處覓良人," which means "Where is the good man?" Isn't that the way Harelip said it? It was an easy name to remember because of that.

"No wonder you're not afraid of us. You've come to the right place, little sweet," chimes the sensuous dancer.

The singers introduce themselves. Sita, the tall one, and Lakshmi, the voluptuous dancer, can speak Chinese best. The other three—Indra, the drum player; Gita, with the bells; and Devi, the other singer—can say a few words here and there. Baoshi studies them carefully. Indra is the one with the most laughing wrinkles around her eyes, Gita has the pouting lower lip, and Devi speaks the least but shakes her legs vigorously while seated at the table.

Baoshi claps his hands several times in delight. "Ha, what a relief! I was worried about how I was ever going to find Ardhanari when I set off on my pilgrimage."

"Pilgrimage? Don't tell us! No wonder the shaved head," Sita says.

"You don't even have a single hair on your chin yet. How could you give up on this life so young?" asks Lakshmi. She turns to the others to explain what he said. Cries of disappointment all around.

Baoshi is amused. He hasn't given up on this life yet. What an odd remark.

"Young man, you look puzzled. Unsure if we're men or women, aren't you?" Gita blurts out in Chinese.

"I saw the bumps on your throats, but according to your dress, I'm guessing you're women. My Master said, 'Words are only sounds, and we choose the meanings we impart to them.'"

"Well said." Sita translates to the others, who laugh and smile approvingly.

"What was it you were singing earlier?"

"It was a song of dedication to our goddess Yellamma. That's whom we jogappas serve. The words? Let me think ..."

Before Sita can continue, Laskhmi speaks up, "Let me do it. I can—really, I can." She clears her throat and, in a clear, bell-like tone, begins:

> Oh, my heart,
> Yellamma
> Divine goddess
> To you, I offer devotion and love

Surrender to blessed passion beyond compare.

A ripple of excitement travels up Baoshi's spine. What emotion behind those words! Feeling the eyes of all the jogappas on him, he speaks again. "Please, can you take me to Ardhanari? My Master, Harelip, asked me to look for him." He clasps his hands together in front of his face and pleads earnestly, head bowed in supplication.

"Harelip ... Wasn't he a friend of Adhanari's?" Sita raises an eyebrow.

"So you know my Master!" Baoshi exclaims with delight.

"No, I was too young to remember him. I would have been just a child. All I know is that Ardhanari was fond of Harelip. Very disturbing for him when Harelip disappeared."

Gita pours fragrant milky tea from a pitcher into slender glasses that have delicate swirls of red and gold designs painted on the outside. Her pout relaxes into a smile. The conversation is punctuated with loud sips of tea.

"My Master had to leave the city a long time ago. He had no choice. He was worried about his safety. Where is Ardhanari? Won't you tell him that Harelip sent me? It's urgent. I need to take him back with me to Mount Hua."

"What?" the jogappas all exclaim together.

"My Master. He needs to see Ardhanari very soon. Please." Baoshi's voice quivers with fear.

Sita replies in a solemn tone. "Ardhanari's not here. He's gone far away."

"But where?"

"Near Dunhuang. Where the Mogao Caves are."

"No!" Baoshi buries his face in his hands. His eyes and forehead burn with the surge of upset. What is he to do now? He can't return to Harelip without Ardhanari.

"My Master had a dream, and he said I had to find Ardhanari and bring him back to see him before ... before ..." he breaks off, unable to finish.

Lakshmi, fluttering her eyelashes at Baoshi across the table, pipes up. "You mustn't get so upset. It's not good for that pretty face of yours. Let us pamper you. Hungry? You must be, after such a long journey!"

"Long? He hasn't even told us where he's come from, and you're already making assumptions!" remarks Indra, her laughing eyes wrinkling up even more in amusement.

"Yes, he has. He told us he's from Mount Hua," counters Lakshmi.

"How did you get here?" asks Sita.

"I walked."

The jogappas, wide-eyed and impressed, nudge one another.

"I heard that the old Turkish man who used to run this tea shop is dead," says Baoshi.

"He died ten years ago. Not long after he moved his tea shop here. He was very old, had no family in the city, so just before he died, he entrusted me with this business," Sita responds.

"I don't know what to do. How long before Ardhanari comes back?"

"At the end of summer."

"I can't stay here in the city and wait for such a long time! I also have to go to the Bronze Urn to deliver a letter to Nü Huang on behalf of a village. I have some money, but surely it can't be enough. Look here." Baoshi collects all the coins from his satchel, cupped in both palms, and shows them to the jogappas.

A long conversation ensues among the jogappas, full of speedy exchanges punctuated by a few long pauses before Sita addresses Baoshi again. "I speak for everyone here. We'd be honoured if you stayed with us upstairs in our rooms above the tea shop. You don't need any money. We'll feed you. We know about the Bronze Urn, and we can easily find out when it's next open. Can you fix things like broken furniture and squeaky doors? Would you be willing to help out with the customers?"

Baoshi nods emphatically. He falls to the ground and bows to them several times.

Sita exclaims, "Please, please! We're not used to such adulation!"

Baoshi gets up and sits back in the chair. "I'm so grateful. How can I ever repay you?"

"In whatever ways your heart desires, dearie," Lakshmi offers.

Da Fa Temple
West Central Chang'an

The Abbess murmurs as if intimately addressing her brush soaked with ink. "When there are secrets, mysteries definitely abound. Whereas mysteries are not necessarily tinged with secrets."

Wan'er stares at the tip of the large horsehair brush as the ink drips into the porcelain bowl. *Blood*, the thought crosses her mind, and she shivers as if tainted with it.

"Mysteries are as varied as the stars in the heavens, but how many of these mysteries are we able to grasp with our limited minds? If we can't understand as a result of our flawed thinking, why should we impulsively conclude that such things are meant to be unknowable or to remain a secret?" The Abbess releases herself into the movement of writing, the brush striking the paper on the low table.

The image materializes on the paper, the single character hua, 炛, done in the same calligraphic style as the scar on Wan'er's forehead. Wan'er is discomforted to see the character fully formed on paper. Two identical symbols side by side, with their curved, forked shapes, reminding her of the vulnerability of two humans lying together, their long bodies and arms outstretched. But they're turned away from each other, one's head at the other's feet, as if they cannot possibly apprehend the other's perspective. Isn't that an untenable co-existence?

"I hope you don't take offence at my forwardness. I've made this as a welcome gift to you, as this is the first time you have come to grace us at Da Fa Temple with your presence." Ling, with gaze lowered, speaks in a thoughtful, whispering voice. "Today, you return to my study without the cap concealing the scar. It's impossible to ignore the disquieting challenge of that mark." Akin to the decisiveness of her brushstrokes, Ling's words fly out of her mouth with confidence.

"Why? Because it's so ugly?" Wan'er finds her tongue loosened too. She backs away from the table where the calligraphy piece rests, as if trying to escape her own fate.

"Ugly? Do you think so? That isn't what I meant. Your mark is disquieting because it bears witness to the enormity of what happened, even before its existence. Your mark is a sign of the burden of others. You may have been taken in as a slave of the court, but what does that say about those who demand your unswerving allegiance? As for your opinion about the scar's ugliness, I am saddened by your distress. A mark, indeed, is not just a mark on the skin."

Wan'er's ears flush from a stinging shame. The Abbess has glimpsed the raw turmoil hidden beneath her scar. How dare she be so bold! Wan'er clasps her hands tightly behind her back and grits her teeth for a few moments. Isn't the Abbess concerned that she could report her behaviour to Nü Huang? How did Ling acquire such confidence? Wan'er slowly relaxes her grip as she admits to herself that she finds Ling's boldness rather compelling. The way this nun behaves bears no resemblance to how Nü Huang exercises authority.

"You must be alarmed at my directness."

Wan'er blushes again, feeling even more awkward. "I don't know what to say, Abbess. I'm being rude. I'll ponder what you've said. Thank you for the gift."

"As I said earlier, call me Ling. This is," she gestures to her calligraphy, "a modest gesture. Let us drink some tea and sample these sweets while we discuss the secret matter."

Before Wan'er begins, her hands pinch at the emerald-green gown she has changed into and start to crinkle the fabric between her fingers. She must put aside all her feelings about the calligraphy piece and her own scar. She must turn her mind instead to carrying out her duties.

"How shall I describe it to you? Perhaps to preface it by acknowledging that Nü Huang considers you an exceptionally gifted woman as Abbess of Da Fa Temple. You've earned recognition as a spiritual leader who's willing to take risks. Nü Huang is pleased that you've allowed the alchemists to pursue their work on your temple grounds. Aside from your generous patronage of the alchemists, for which Nü Huang owes you gratitude and a substantial reward, your assistance is sought for a recent challenge faced by our sovereign." Wan'er pauses to take a small bite of a rice ball, its core a smooth, sweet red bean paste. Delicious. She sips more of the tea, noticing how it tastes different from the tea served at the Inner Palace.

"Her Majesty has been troubled by bad dreams. She has suggested to me that there still may be strange presences who are quite unwilling to depart from Taijigong and who are so tenacious that they affect her health."

"There is a special name for these creatures."

"Oh?"

"Zhesi jisheng 磔死寄生—those who suffer death by decapitation and who cling like parasites to the living."

Wan'er shudders at the description. "How did you know?"

"Know what? That it was by decapitation?" Ling smiles unperturbed, finishing off her rice ball and pouring more tea into their cups. "I must admit that it wasn't difficult to guess whose demon souls these might be. Being aware of Wu Zhao's rise to power certainly means that I could make an educated guess as to who or what is troubling our Emperor. Besides, I have some records here at Da Fa Temple from my predecessor, who tried to help Her Majesty."

"Her Majesty has been astute in choosing you."

"What does she wish me to do for her?"

"This is why the request must remain secret. She requests that you act as a fangxiang shi 方相氏, an exorcist. She wants you to conduct a private ritual on her behalf soon."

"I see." Ling suddenly looks sad. She rises from her seat and walks over to the window behind her writing desk, staring out for what seems like a long time.

Wan'er stares at Ling's back. She has changed out of the ceremonial robe into a plain brown one, but the aura of mystery lingers despite the lack of embellishment, its force radiating out to Wan'er.

When Ling turns around, the sad look is no longer there. Instead, her eyes seem to be gleaming with a renewed fire. "Wan'er, do you understand why these zhesi jisheng are so tenacious?"

"I suppose it's because of the extreme degree of suffering they were subjected to, just before they died."

"Indeed. If enlightenment is achieved at the time of a person's death, the spirit shen 神 separates from the body shen 身, and the supernatural part of the spirit, ling, will be able to leave the cycle of reincarnation and live forever. Conversely, what if a person has not only failed to attain enlightenment, but as a result of suffering tremendously at the hands of others, her spirit has also separated violently from her body?"

Wan'er shudders as she listens to Ling, and the image of a tortured woman dying very slowly in extreme pain lingers in her mind. "Are you saying that the conditions under which one's spirit separates from the body determine whether a zhesi jisheng develops?"

"Determine? Not entirely. There are many who die violent deaths, yet only a very small proportion of these transform into demon souls, so there must be some other force operating that distinguishes zhesi jisheng from the others. With those two women in the Inner Palace, we can safely infer that the immense anguish of that separation of their spirits from their bodies was a necessary condition for them becoming demon souls. But what has kept them here, clinging tenaciously to Nü Huang, is their bitter need for revenge."

"The sheer force of bitterness," whispers Wan'er, upset by the resonances in her life.

Ling sits down behind the writing desk, across from Wan'er. "That is indeed the unfortunate aspect of calling them demon souls, since that term suggests only their ugly, troublesome facets—the focus on the afflictions they cause to the living. Yet there is a hidden aspect to them, the fact of their own misery, which lies at the heart of their perpetuating others' suffering."

Wan'er wonders if that's why Ling looked sad only moments ago. She speaks so intimately of demon souls, as if she has some means of understanding them.

"The Double Fifth is three days hence. I presume there are observances of rituals on that day at Taijigong?" asks Ling.

"Yes, we hang peachwood seals and aromatic herbs on all doorways to ward off the evil that threatens us on that day."

"Exactly. I suspect the Double Fifth will signal a shift of energies in Taijigong. As to what happens, we'll have to be watchful. Tell Nü Huang that I'm willing to conduct a ritual at the end of the old year, according to the ancient customs of exorcism. But if any further visitations occur before that time, I would like permission to enter Taijigong to deal with the demon souls. Please convey this message to Her Majesty."

"I will relay your opinion, Ling. I can assure you that Her Majesty will appreciate such a prudent strategy."

"You see, my dear Lady, if these creatures had such tenacity to distress Wu Zhao forty years ago, and still continue to trouble her the moment she returns here, it is an indication of the demon souls' great power to penetrate into the sovereign's mind and body. For such creatures, we must scrutinize their habits and natures, so that the exorcism is effective. An ill-prepared exorcism attempt will only end in failure, and possibly fuel the power of the demon souls."

"Well said."

Ling unlocks the cabinet and produces an amulet carved from jade, a pale white bracelet in the shape of a dragon's head and body, with a gold clasp. She wraps it in a piece of purple silk. "Give this to Nü Huang. Tell her to wear it at night or keep it near her while she sleeps."

Wan'er slips the amulet into a pocket hidden inside her sleeve.

"Shall we now proceed to the Repository for your visit? I believe they have the elixir ready for you."

The Inner Palace at Taijigong
North Central Chang'an

Nü Huang's Private Scroll: A Spell to Transform

I am sure Wan'er is wondering, what with our work on the Palace Diary, how much I will say, if anything, about her grandfather and father, and the circumstances of her own life. How can I possibly reveal such details in front of her? She is, after all, a slave, someone who owes me her life and her mother's life. I will not subject us to an awkward reminder of how we became inextricably linked. Was it true, what Lady Zhen told

Gaozong and me, about her dream while pregnant, of Wan'er weighing out the affairs of the world? It is surely a powerful sign of Wan'er's destiny.

A person's spirit is so clearly perceptible even in childhood. I noticed the force of Wan'er's independent and wilful self emerge very early, so that by the time she was five sui, it was unmistakable. A child who did not know the meaning of fear. Had she ever felt frightened? She must have. Yet she would act as if nothing could prevent her from following her every impulse. At five, she was a wild, unrestrained creature, babbling endlessly about her every discovery, investigating every nook and cranny of the palace, refusing to submit her will, even to her mother or me. What rageful tantrums she had! I had to find a way to tame her. If I failed to instill fear in her, it would be a threat to my authority over her as mentor and sovereign. However, if I succeeded in my endeavour, I would have at my service an engaging mind and a marvellous talent obedient to my will.

I decided I would have her branded. I fretted for months as to the kind of symbol I wanted to use. The symbol had to be chosen carefully because it would have tremendous power once it was burned into her skin. If I chose the wrong one, it could work against me. One day, while looking at copies of the ancient symbols, I came to the section describing characters that employed pairings of the radical ren 人. Two ren—two people in various juxtapositions. There was the character that had two ren, one behind the other, both facing west. The character meant "to follow." I ruled it out quickly because employing such a symbol might result in too drastic a diminishing of her creative energy. What use would I have for another compliant slave? I have thousands of those. They are handy, but what a waste it would be of Wan'er's spirit! Then there was the character with two ren facing east. Definitely not. This symbol signifies the comparisons people are constantly making with each other. It bears the energy of competitiveness and could potentially spur aggression and malice. The third character depicted two ren with their backs to each other, which nowadays represents the direction north, but originally, it meant "behind." In the cold winter months, we clever humans know to turn our backs to the bone-chilling winds coming down on us from the north, and that was how this character eventually came to refer to "north." This was not anything particularly pertinent to my intentions.

Only one character that paired the two ren spoke compellingly to me as I contemplated it. In ancient symbology, the ren were side by side, with the second ren on the right upturned and facing the other direction. In other words, two people who possessed two views of the matter at hand. Now surely that is a great advantage, to have two views of reality, I thought to myself. That is what I cherish as I listen to the counsel of my intelligent zaixiang, who are forever arguing from all possible positions. This character for hua evolved over time to be written as 化, and indicates a turn, a change, or transformation. It is the character within the term for alchemy, and it could also mean—to reform or civilize someone by personal examples of moral uprightness, as in ganhua 感化. When I read through the list of possible connotations of this character, I realized this was the very thing I was looking for. My greatest hope in choosing this symbol was to create a spell that would transform Wan'er from an unruly, disobedient girl into a more restrained yet creative person. Transformation, magic, civilizing influence—what a wonderful combination of meanings!

I ordered the blacksmith from the Imperial stables to fashion a brand small enough to mark the girl's forehead. He made a brand in the style of the Shang Dynasty, very similar to the shape of the word used on oracle bones. I reproduce it here, with the best effort I can muster at this moment: 化. At the day and time appointed by the Daoist diviner, the ceremony was conducted, with myself and Lady Zhen present, along with several ladies-in-waiting, the Imperial physician, and, of course, the expert blacksmith.

Fire possesses strength to cleanse and to exorcise even the most malevolent of influences. I cannot blame Wan'er for what she inherited from her ancestors. It was as if Shangguan Yi still strove to depose me through the rebellious nature of his granddaughter. She was labouring under the heavy inheritance of her ancestor's resentment. That was why the effect of the branding on Wan'er was so dramatic. It was to be expected. Lady Zhen did not have the same understanding I did. She was distraught, matching the child's screams with her own weeping. Could she not understand that the branding was necessary for her daughter's future welfare?

The ritual did effect a remarkable transformation. Wan'er was instantly subdued. Of course, the pain gradually decreased for weeks thereafter, and that was why she had to receive the constant attention of the Imperial physician.

From that day on, Wan'er no longer showed the same wild disregard for others. Her eyes flamed still but with a kind of cautious restraint that vindicates me for the wisdom of my decision. If her ferocity had gone unchecked, who knows what would have ensued?

Now, in my old age, I admit to a lingering touch of sadness. That spontaneous tendency of hers to be affectionate and playful was never to be experienced by me again after that incident.

An Emperor must bear a tremendous burden of responsibility. Wan'er has no idea that I branded her for her own good. I took her in as if she were my daughter, teaching her skills I learned from my own father. How many women of her time would be able to obtain such knowledge? She and I are rare creatures, fired with ambition that beckons us far beyond what had been prescribed for us.

Some day soon, she will inherit this scroll and any others that I have been able to write with my own hand. I would prefer she read these scrolls after I have left this world. I do not wish to have a direct conversation about any contentious events. It is comforting to rest in this thought: when I am dead, she will finally come to know what lies deepest within my heart.

DA FA TEMPLE
WEST CENTRAL CHANG'AN

Behind the worship hall, in what was the former Sutra Repository, the alchemists hear the bell summon the nuns to the last period of meditation before the evening meal. They know that farther east of them, beyond the Golden Moon Gate, the monks are also filing toward their recitation hall.

Suspended in the liminal world of perpetual dimness, the alchemists sometimes doubt the solidity of their own existence. However, today's announcement from the Abbess grants them a potent reminder of their relevance. They've been sent word that the Imperial Secretary has arrived at the temple and will soon visit the Repository.

The Repository was a storehouse for a vast number of copied sutras, portions of the Tripitaka teachings of the Buddha, and the writings of the monks who had run this Buddhist temple for more than two hundred years before it was given over to a Daoist sect by the Emperor Taizong. The Repository, five bays by three, with a second storey accessed by a ladder, now houses a group of twelve dedicated souls with their various materials and implements and one gigantic distillation vat. The men spend an inordinate amount of time sitting at their respective places at a long work table on the ground level of the Repository, peering at alchemical texts, straining their eyes, while behind them, the vat bubbles with the combined essences of all the young monks residing in the adjoining monastery.

Essences daily expended are collected by the alchemists' helpers, brought to the Repository, and dumped into the heated vat. The alchemists then watch over the vat until the boiling purifies the liquid down to a fine distillate powder, which accumulates on the underside of the vat's enormous lid. Following the standard formula, the men mix the powder with powerful herbs suspended in alcohol to yield the basic version of the Eternal Spring potion, meant to incite the yang powers of the frail Nü Huang.

This preparation is a standard procedure carried out so many times without much variation or surprise that it usually bores the alchemists—unless there's the rare luck of obtaining a gourd of fresh tiger's blood, which means they have to rush to purify the blood before adding it to the potion, followed by the thrill of immediately dispatching the potion via a messenger to Her Majesty.

For the past eight months, however, while making up regular batches of the Eternal Spring potion, the alchemists have been more preoccupied with the challenge of concocting the Jin Dan elixir. Ever since Her Majesty's return to Chang'an, blessing them with her commission, they've been frantically working to refine the formula. The men understand the immense shame and disgrace the alchemists in Luoyang have brought upon themselves, the ones who offered their sovereign the best of their endeavours, only to learn that her condition has worsened since she ingested that elixir.

Nü Huang is impatient. She has been sending them constant missives to hurry up. They dare not confess that they would feel a great deal more confident if they could be given another two years to experiment. This latest version of the Jin Dan elixir has been carefully wrapped in two layers of yellow silk and placed in an ornate gold-plated box. When the alchemists heard about the arrival of Shangguan Wan'er, they rushed around the Repository opening the windows and doors to ventilate the place, fearing that she would become nauseated by the stench or faint from the heat.

They sit at their table, fidgeting. The alchemical texts are laden with riddles and poetic allusions. The original creators of the elixir formula used language as a tool of concealment to guard the secret of their precious discovery. Ingredients as well as methods of extraction are couched in metaphors and obscure references. Alchemists in successive generations have puzzled over these riddles. What constitutes the correct proportions for each of a host of thirty-two ingredients that have mysterious code names like Dark Sweet Root of Rain or Fingers of Filigreed Bitterness?

The men often reassure one another that they must be on the right path, since their fundamental approach is to discover signs of Heaven as manifested on Earth. The codes and references must stand for those substances with the most resilience against the erosion of time and weather. To infuse the body with the correct combination and proportion of these magically ageless substances would allow the body to acquire the substances' indestructibility, thereby halting the process of degeneration and, in the ideal scenario, reverse the process of aging. They've deduced that previous interpretations of the elixir failed precisely because there had been insufficient amounts of arsenic, cinnabar, and gold. They're delighted at having reached this most precious of insights.

As the alchemists brood silently over these matters, they hear the voices of the Abbess and another woman as they approach the Repository. The men rise from their stools and fidget even more. When their visitors enter, the men bow and keep their gazes lowered to the ground. Most of them, though, catch sight of the Imperial Secretary's expression of disgust at the smell. She coughs loudly and strides across the room to the far corner, stopping to study a scroll done in their master's calligraphic hand:

Make the Void your cauldron
Nature, your furnace
Stillness, your primary ingredient
For your reagent, use quietude
For mercury, take your vital essence
For lead, your vital energy
For water, use restraint
For fire, meditation.

The Abbess offers an explanation. "The Union of the Triple Equation. Essence, energy, and spirit unite to form the Jin Dan elixir during deep meditation. It is a quote concerning the internal alchemy of meditation."

"I see," utters Wan'er, yet she has stopped paying attention to the poem, distracted by the few objects that embellish this stark yet spacious ground level of the Repository. Her eyes take in the gigantic vat, then roam the length of the work table, where the precious minerals, herbs, and potions are stored in rows of clay jars, wooden bowls, and bottles. Her gaze lands finally on the hand-held weighing scale. How many countless times has that scale been raised by the alchemist who must carefully decide where to position the looped weight along its thin ivory length? Everything proceeds from that decision—precisely how much substance is to be placed on the copper pan to balance out the weight.

The head of the alchemists summons up his courage and addresses Wan'er. "Lady Shangguan, here is the Jin Dan elixir. We are deeply honoured by your visit." He presents the shiny box to Wan'er.

"Yes, thank you. Nü Huang will send you the payment as soon as I return to Taijigong."

After the Abbess and the Imperial Secretary leave, the alchemists slouch back down at their table and cast worried glances at one another. Lady Shangguan reading the poem has stirred up their anxieties. Their master, who died at 112 sui, had told them there was basically no difference between what was wrought by external means and what was attained within the body by the work of the mind. Their master would shrug when asked, "Isn't meditation ultimately the fire required for the success of the elixir?" He never answered that question.

The Foreign Quarter
West Central Chang'an

Baoshi lies down on the mat on the creaky wooden floor, with a light quilt over him. He finds it hard to sleep, his mind racing with the conversations he had with the jogappas earlier. He rubs his round, hard belly. It is rumbling not with hunger but from the spiciness of the food. He was relieved, though, that there had been no meat in the meal. His stomach had felt a little unsettled after eating the delicious bun earlier at the market, and he's not sure whether it was because he hadn't eaten meat for eight years or whether it was the sight of the pig carcasses at the market that returned to haunt him. He moves his tongue around in his mouth, feeling its rawness.

One thing he found hard to understand was that the jogappas, with the exception of Sita, had left their homelands of their own accord. He knows that many people travel from place to place, just like those hundreds he was in the midst of earlier in the day. It troubles him to think that people choose to bid farewell to what was loved and familiar, sever such ties in order to launch themselves on a long journey to an unknown place. He didn't get to make that kind of choice when his father took him away. But this pilgrimage he is undertaking for his Master is completely different from that first separation.

He may not have left Harelip of his own initiative, but he set off on this pilgrimage wanting to contribute to his Master's happiness by finding Ardhanari.

Motivation is everything. And a dream is its beginning. His Master's dream is a mystery that must be listened to and fulfilled. It would have been cruel to remain on Mount Hua after such a revelation. Of course he has been engulfed by moments of sadness, but how trivial a price to pay to make his Master happy!

Baoshi shifts restlessly on the mat. He notices that time seems to pass much more slowly when he's impatient. He touches his forehead. It feels slightly cool, although his body is too warm. He kicks off the quilt and sighs, recalling the stories that the jogappas plied him with throughout their evening meal.

Sita's parents left their town in India, fuelled by a dream of living in the largest city on the face of the earth. Sita was born here and has lived in the Foreign Quarter her whole life. The other four jogappas, motivated by unhappiness and discontent, fled their former lives—lives that had necessitated that they act like men or face being reviled and threatened by family members or people in their villages.

It seems to Baoshi that many people have come here because they were lured by tales about the grandeur of Chang'an—Zhongguo, the central kingdom, and Chang'an, the heart of that centre.

He's too excited to fall asleep. He gets up, walks to the window, and contemplates the crescent moon. The surroundings are hushed at this early hour, just past midnight. He stares into this landscape of darkness, crowded full of shadows and unknown meanings, and thinks of the people in the village at the foot of Mount Hua. Their faces flit through his mind. He wonders how they are doing. The jogappas told him, much to his disappointment, that the Bronze Urn is not open to the public all the time. He will have to wait until two weeks after the Summer Solstice. That's about four weeks away—an eternity. On Mount Hua, that would amount to so many hours of meditation, countless more hours of gathering wood, finding edible plants and nuts, studying healing techniques, and practising his fighting drills. "Everything seems to take longer here," he mutters under his breath.

When his eyes are sufficiently lulled by the outside darkness, he stumbles back to his mat and covers himself with the quilt again, finally surrendering to sleep. Disjointed images appear. Faces of the villagers interspersed with faces of his parents. Harelip rising up from his meditation cushion yet falling over as he attempts to bow to the Buddha statue on the altar. His own body moves fast, much faster than he would like, down the steps of the mountain. Suddenly, in contrast, he cannot move, his walking stick dropping away from him into an abyss. His father strides toward him, a smirk on his face. When he reaches Baoshi, he tears off his clothes. The villagers have gathered below to witness his nakedness, the glaring contradictions in his body exposed.

He struggles against his father's hold, distressed at his immobility. With a shout, he breaks through. He sits upright, taking in big gasps of air. For a few moments he can't recall where he is.

"Are you all right?" Voices from the other room drift in.

"You had a bad dream." Sita appears and stoops down to touch his shoulder. He flinches away, overwhelmed by fear.

She whispers softly to him, "You're safe here, everything is fine. Remember me?"

He can't see her, but her voice soothes him. "Water, please. My heart is beating fast," he pleads.

"I'll fetch some from downstairs. Do you want someone to keep you company?"

"Yes." Fragments of the dream still float through his mind.

Sita leaves, and after a few whispers in the next room, Lakshmi appears and stumbles clumsily toward him. He knows it's her when she speaks up, "Poor boy, don't worry, we're all here." She finds his arm and squeezes it gently a few times. She sits down, wraps her arms around him, and rocks him gently, humming quietly. He allows himself to surrender to Lakshmi's embrace, yet his heart maintains its quickened pace, as if it has resolved to escape elsewhere.

When Sita returns with water, he gulps it down quickly. "I'll be fine, really. Fine. Just a bad dream."

"Your body is shaking!" exclaims Lakshmi. "Feel how he shivers!" she says to Sita.

Their hands touch his shoulder, his head, accompanied by a flurry of words and movements. "You're soaked! Let us find you some other clothes to wear." A cloth is applied to his scalp and neck to wipe off the sweat, then they try to pull his undershirt off.

"No, no! Please don't." He blocks their attempts with his hands and pushes them away.

A prolonged silence ensues before Sita says, "Let me get you some clothes."

A candle is lit to reveal their concerned looks. "What did you dream that caused you such upset, my dear?" asks Lakshmi.

Baoshi shakes his head. He has never described his nightmares to anyone, not even to Harelip. They're too frightening to speak aloud. They wouldn't make sense to anyone else. Lakshmi continues to stroke his arm. He listens to the other jogappas talk among themselves in the next room. He can tell that they're concerned.

Sita returns with a tunic and an antariya. "We'll leave you to change into these dry clothes. Why don't we keep the candle burning? Will that help you sleep?"

He nods again. "I'm sorry to trouble you this way. You're all so very kind. I'm grateful." His heart is finally settling down to an easier, relaxed rhythm.

"Call out if you need us," reassures Sita as she and Lakshmi leave.

Baoshi lies back down on the mat. He has narrowly escaped discovery. He stares at the candle flame. It was a frightening nightmare, but it was far more terrifying when the jogappas tried to take his clothes off. What would they have done if they had discovered his uneven breasts? Or his lower body with its male and female parts? Their shock would be too much for him to bear. The thought causes him to feel close to tears, but he pulls back from that panic, reminding himself that he was in fact not discovered.

He keeps very still, waiting until there are no longer any sounds of movement coming from the next room before he changes his clothes. He pulls the tunic on over his torso and clumsily wraps the antariya around his hips, tucking the cloth in to one side. He pulls the cotton quilt over himself, sits up, and keeps his eyes trained on the candle flame, not quite ready to fall asleep again.

The silence is occasionally punctuated by murmurs from the next room. He listens intently while staring at the flame, flickering from moment to moment, never staying the same. Finally, he blows out the candle. Sitting in the dark, he thinks of Sita and Lakshmi fussing over him earlier. The only person who has touched him in the past eight years has been his Master. A firm hand on the shoulder to summon him out of his daydreaming or a gentle adjustment of his posture while he practised his fighting forms. Harelip's touch always felt comfortable and never aroused any odd sensations. Sita and Lakshmi's hands don't touch him in the same way. He found their touch puzzling, although he can't find the words to describe the sensation.

He lies back down. Images of himself and Harelip naked as they bathed in a waterfall on Mount Hua. Feelings of tenderness as his mother and their maid dressed him. Now this other kind of touch from Sita and Lakshmi, carrying a different quality. Images of the stranger in the market enter his mind. He has never seen anyone so beautiful before, a face that caused him to forget all else around him. Hadn't the bustle of the market faded away as he stood there talking to the stranger? Baoshi sighs longingly.

A pleasant surge of energy arrives between his thighs, causing them to tremble and his jade member to come alive. He moans at this familiar occurrence. When this first started happening while sleeping on the kang with Harelip, he used to sneak outside and crouch in the dark, confused. If it was too cold outside, he first would wrap himself up in his padded long coat, shivering and a little scared of the power that throbbed between his legs. Now as he wraps his hands around his member, he recalls those first times, full of nervousness and desperation, and the urge to release himself from that tension. Surrounded by the ancient pine trees on Mount Hua, he would lie against the shack and look up at the stars, breathe in the exhilaration as he took his body far upward into that open sky. He has to conjure up that feeling now, imagine the stars in their marvellous mystery. His hands turn cold while his mind is overtaken once again with flashes of his dreams. His member softens in defeat. Tears emerge, along with the memory of that shameful moment his father exposed him to Harelip in the shack. As he lies in the dark, crying quietly, his thoughts turn once again to the stranger. How warm he had been, talking to him with such kindness! His hardness returns while the woman in him becomes moist with desire. He strokes his breast, thinking about Harelip's response when he noticed his growing left breast four years ago. His Master had instantly launched into stories about miraculous beings, from *The Classic of*

Mountains and Seas—stories about deities who had both male and female in them. Baoshi smiles, thinking about the existence of a myriad of possibilities, an infinite universe of creatures. Surely the jogappas, of all people in the city, can accept the unusualness of his body. Why should he linger in his fear of being discovered, especially by them? He inserts a finger into himself and, with the other hand, strokes and squeezes his member until he is taken beyond his sadness.

DA FA TEMPLE
WEST CENTRAL CHANG'AN

Ling reclines on the divan in her study, visited by images from her early days at Da Fa Temple. Back when she was a frightened girl, grieving the loss of her parents. How her heart had ached with rage and sorrow. She had been utterly confused and vulnerable—the world she had known, completely lost to her.

The conversation with Wan'er about demon souls in the Inner Palace had aroused sadness in her as memories surfaced of Qilan's sacrifice to stop Gui.

The candle flame flickers slightly from the light breeze entering the study through the latticed windows. Ling shuts her eyes and makes a deliberate effort to breathe deeply and slowly. She listens to the silence enveloping her, a silence that isn't purely silence, because the air around her contains sounds barely perceptible to most. Her hearing registers the soft rustle of bamboo leaves outside in the courtyard, the occasional steps of a passerby beyond the wall, and more intimately, the quiet rasping sounds made by her pet cricket as he rests.

She still feels the ache of sorrow whenever memories of Qilan return. Back then, as a girl and young woman, she couldn't fully grasp the depth of her feelings. The raw vulnerability of being orphaned still lived close to the surface of her consciousness, ready to sting when awakened. She had grown dependent on Qilan and felt strong admiration and gratitude for her mentor. *There has never been anyone else like her. And there never will be.* No wonder these feelings of heartache still arise whenever something happens to trigger her memories. It has taken Ling many years to admit to herself that she had fallen in love with Qilan. She didn't have the capacity or the language when Qilan was still alive.

Qilan's sacrifice and death catapulted Ling into a rapid and difficult transformation, one that has required her to be essentially self-reliant, even as she was learning from the elders and guiding the younger nuns. Qilan and Abbess Si were right—she was meant to become Abbess. She has grown to accept this legacy with gratitude. But she can't deny that she has felt a deep, enduring loneliness. No one to confide in about these feelings. A long, long time ago, if only she could have known then … she might have dared say something to Old Chen when he was still alive.

Tears flow fiercely, and her face flushes with the heat of grief. She might be the Abbess of the temple, but it's clear that sorrow never truly disappears, residing in the depths of her soul until it emerges, raw and present.

Is Qilan really gone? Although Qilan's physical form disappeared thirty-eight years ago, Ling continues to sense her presence, as if that beautiful and fiery fox spirit arrives unbidden, whispering a magic spell in her ear, sometimes caressing her cheek or creating a warmth that spreads comfort across her chest.

The encounter with Wan'er has awakened pangs of yearning. Is she mistaken in sensing that Wan'er too feels drawn, despite the moments of diffidence and aloofness? She wants to touch Wan'er deeply, beyond the superficial scar and the polite conversations. The Imperial Secretary is supposed to return to Taijigong tomorrow. Ling isn't sure how to proceed. But she must do something.

In the depths of her struggle, she hears the slow rousing of her cricket and the intensifying sound that signals his mating dance, that rubbing together of his front wings. *Sometimes it's sound that communicates feeling*, she thinks. And with that, she discovers what she will do next.

The box containing the Jin Dan elixir sits in Wan'er's saddlebag next to the amulet, both carefully packed away. Tomorrow, she'll have to return to Taijigong. She sighs at the thought. Duty is unavoidable. She feels too agitated to fall asleep.

After the visit to the Repository, she quickly returned to the guest room for a rest before proceeding to the evening meal. In the dining hall, she keenly observed the nuns, who matched her scrutiny with their own as she sat with the Abbess, the wide-eyed keeper of the temple, and two others at the head table. Ling was trying to involve her in a conversation about the various needs of the temple. Wan'er occasionally nodded to give the impression she was listening. She heard Ling's voice as if from a distance, on the other side of a fast-flowing stream. The sea of bare, unadorned faces unsettled her enormously; it was the sheer force of the nuns' lively presences that swirled through her and bore her along. Their collective will could overcome her identity as Imperial Secretary, possibly even transform her into a nun.

On the mattress that's too thin for comfort, Wan'er fidgets, further remembering her strange fear. Why would such a ridiculous idea even cross her mind? Nuns are so much the opposite of women in the Inner Palace, with their vast array of grooming needs—hair in rolled buns, face powders, rouge, lip colour, cheek and forehead decorations, fine gowns, and embroidered fabrics. What a contrast these Daoist nuns are, without any traces of seduction and camouflage. Their combined plainness was so arresting that she eventually looked closely at each face, wondering what she could discover, whether there were any clues to be found as to each woman's character.

Returning to her guest room after the evening meal, she looks at her own face in the mirror. The walking boy thought she was a man because she didn't have her face covered in white powder or wear lip colour. Was that it? He had been deceived by the clothes she wore. She was dressed contrary to her gender. She sits down at the desk and tries to do some reading, but all she can see in her mind is the Abbess's intense gaze, those strange mismatched eyes, and her entirely mysterious face. What had she said earlier, when they met alone in the study? *Where secrets abound, mysteries also exist. Where there are mysteries, there may not be secrets.* Something like that.

Indeed, Ling's face holds intrigue—it makes Wan'er want to know what exactly is hidden beneath appearances. A face that seems so open yet resembles a mask. Those eyes: why are they two different colours? What about her name? Is it the character for "bell"? Or the character for "inspiration"? Or maybe it refers to that supernatural part of the spirit shen that she had spoken about, the part of the spirit that enables one to break free of the cycle of rebirth.

The restless sensation in her legs and shoulders becomes unbearable, so she jumps up and wraps the light robe around her body. The coals are still glowing in the brazier in the corner, imparting a slight warmth to the cool night air. Its embers allow her just enough light to pace across the room several times. If she can't sleep, she might as well try to write. She lights the candle on the table, sits down, and unrolls the silk pouch containing three calligraphy brushes. A small container of ink has been left out for her. She unties the silk wrapping that protects the ancient, tattered, hand-sewn book.

She has read through Cai Yan's *Eighteen Songs of a Nomad Flute* many times over. How many times has she already imagined writing replies to these poems by the Han Dynasty woman poet? She has composed many lines in her head, yet an acute anxiety has held her back from writing them down. She's only too well aware that one of her primary duties is to write poetry in keeping with Nü Huang's reign and her wishes, and that the tone of her replies to Cai Yan's songs could be easily construed as treasonous. She dreams of the possibility of writing replies not only to Cai Yan but also to many poets whose work she can access with complete ease in the Imperial library. No one need suspect. She mustn't be so fearful, she chides herself. How could anyone discover her poems if she keeps them safely locked away?

That's why Ling's confidence as she did that calligraphic piece impressed yet disturbed her. Emboldened by that recollection, Wan'er opens the book as if for the very first time, her face slightly flushed.

In my early years, equity still governed,
But later in my life, the Han throne fell into decay.
Heaven inhumane, sending down chaos,
Earth too, causing me to be caught in such a time.
War gear commonplace, travel by road dangerous,
The common people fled, all plunged in wretchedness.
Smoke and dust darkened the land, overrun by barbarians:
They ignored my widow's vows, my chastity lost.
Their strange customs utterly foreign to me—
Can I possibly speak of my calamity, shame, and grief?
One measure for the nomad flute, a stanza for the qin,
Who can understand my heart's agony and anger?

Wan'er knows a few things about Cai Yan from the historical accounts. She was the daughter of eminent poet and statesman Cai Yong, who died in prison for colluding against the Han Dynasty. Cai Yan was captured by a raiding party of barbarian mercenaries. They forced her to become the wife of the chieftain of the southern Xiongnu. After a life with him, during which she bore him two sons, she was ransomed by Cao Cao, the new ruler, and forced to return to the capital when he established the Wei Dynasty. He needed her return to placate the ancestral spirits of her family for he wanted to ensure that his reign wouldn't be troubled by them. She, the last surviving member of a prominent clan, was caught up in the power struggles of men, used as a pawn, yet ostracized once she returned to the court.

Did Cai Yan have to struggle against fear in order to write? Was she writing as the tragic events in her life unfolded? Or did she have to wait for years until she was free to express herself? Wan'er sighs. She's not sure she would have been able to endure such dreadful circumstances. She takes up the smallest brush and dips it into the plate of poured ink.

You refused consolation, saw no merit in quiet forbearance,
A woman's plight is subject to a dynasty's whims.
What gave you courage to dare accuse
Heaven and Earth of inhumanity?
Seeing yourself caught in their conflicts
You say: a woman belongs to the chaos of her time
Yet is disappeared by war's wretched devastation.
Although yourself uncommon,
How could you have escaped the ravages of destruction?
A prisoner has no recourse, a slave no justice,
Yet gestures must be made, however humble,
Acts that hint at the most elusive of echoes.

At the last word completed, Wan'er takes a long, slow breath. The walls of the room are suddenly too close to her, far too threatening, even as silent witnesses to what she has done. She rests the brush on the rim of the lacquered bowl. How tired she is. She rests her head in her hands. How can she bear it, serving the woman who killed her father and grandfather? Servitude—that is all she has known her whole life. Is it because she has no other choices, she asks herself, that she has learned to bear the unbearable? Fear alone would be understandable, even hatred, but what can she do with the persistent yearning to be loved by the one she should consider her enemy? Tears trickle out of her eyes onto the palms of her hands, cupped to receive them. She cries so rarely, and it disturbs her, this sad and useless longing.

Exhausted, she returns to bed. If only she could escape, flee on her horse, Nomad, to some secluded place where she would no longer be enslaved by anyone. But this is an impossible fantasy. She strokes her cheek with the back of one hand. Her mother used to do the same thing to comfort her when she was a child. Even if she could escape, she couldn't abandon her mother to Nü Huang's punishment. Or leave her poems behind, abandon her commitment to the Imperial library, filled with the writings of her predecessors and contemporaries. What kind of freedom would that be, if she had to forsake what she has been passionately devoted to?

The silence is penetrated by a faint sound—distant at first, then louder and louder. She wipes her tears away quickly, walks over to the door, and opens it out into the quadrangle. The candle in her room casts some light on the otherwise dark courtyard. She sees a figure sitting on the stone bench.

"Who's there?"

The figure moves out of the shadow, and Wan'er sees that it's Ling.

"Why are you sitting there in the dark?"

"I saw that your candle was lit, so I decided I would come here with my pet cricket to see if I could entice you to open the door."

Wan'er laughs, despite her cautiousness. "For an Abbess, you are indeed very unusual in your ways."

"Does that bother you?"

"I don't know what to say."

"You seemed very distracted at the evening meal, somewhat preoccupied."

"Oh? Was that your impression?"

"Perhaps I'm being far too forward. My apologies. I shall leave now and let you rest." Ling stands up and starts to head back toward her private chambers when Wan'er calls out, "Ling, wait … Come back, please."

Ling walks toward Wan'er slowly, at an unhurried pace. Her face, as she draws closer, is barely illuminated by the candle flame from inside the room, her skin emanating an otherworldly quality in its pale, shadowed expression. When she is face to face with Wan'er, the tiny gourd vessel between them, the cricket begins to chirp even more excitedly.

"It responds, you see, to the heat of human bodies," explains Ling, as she leans her face very close to Wan'er's and caresses her cheek with her own.

Wan'er shivers, feeling a thrill travel down to her feet, its force threatening to topple her. "I would like you to come inside with me, and explain what you said about mysteries and secrets this afternoon."

"Only if you allow me one thing."

"Which is?"

"That you would let me touch your scar."

Without answering, Wan'er takes Ling's hand and leads her in.

Myriad Springs Hall
The Outer Palace at Taijigong
North Central Chang'an

In the dim light of a single lamp, the desires and fears on their faces are heightened by shadows. Sansi has arranged for this late-night meeting in a rarely used antechamber adjoining the Myriad Springs Hall. He leans back into his chair, watching First Minister Wei, Minister Su, and Princess Wei with a touch of amusement as they confer at the round marble table.

First Minister Wei begins. "Those two favourites of Nü Huang are obstacles. If not for their interfering presence, the succession of the Crown Prince to the throne would occur imminently without any concerns for our lives. I am of the opinion that removal from their position of influence may be necessary."

His unwavering voice, albeit kept to a near-whisper, shows no signs of fear. He hasn't changed. His boldness makes the rest of them confident that they can succeed in this venture. They remember that he had been the one who refused to sign a false confession while being tortured by Lai Juanchen's henchmen years ago, and such fortitude engenders their trust.

"It's outrageous, the extent to which our sovereign indulges those half-brothers. This is surely not the same woman who would not tolerate the slightest hint of ingratitude or insubordination?" Princess Wei's voice trembles with rage.

Sansi pours himself another cup of plum wine and gulps it down quickly. He can see the hatred in the consort's eyes—that she can't forgive Nü Huang for killing her children, especially Zhongjun, her flesh and blood. He quips, "The one who told Taizong she would tame the horse with an iron whip and an iron mace, failing which she would use a dagger to cut its throat?"

"How our sovereign has changed! These past five years, ever since the brothers became her lovers, Her Majesty seems determined not to recognize the blatant corruptions, the briberies, the selling of coveted positions to members of the Zhang family," whispers Minister Su.

First Minister Wei glances around at everyone. "Remember the extent to which she indulged that lover of hers, the fake monk Xue Huaiyi?"

They are silent for quite a while, pondering the consequences of their ruler's carnal indulgences. This sovereign of theirs, so fiercely powerful yet so malleable in her lovers' hands.

Princess Wei's eyes gleam fiercely in the lamplight. "How long is she going to drag on before she steps down from the throne? She relishes torturing us with her slow, declining health. Simply outrageous, dragging us away from important affairs in the Eastern Capital. She knows the Crown Prince must ascend the throne in Luoyang. I fear for my own life with each day we languish here in Chang'an. If she could execute her own grandchildren for merely gossiping against Changzong and Yizhi, she also could decide on a whim to do away with any one of us. Every moment those foolish boys are in her bed, we are in grave danger."

First Minister Wei taps the edge of the marble table, as if following the rhythm of his private thoughts. "Most definitely, we must take action soon, yet not rush into anything before the time is ripe."

"We must strip the brothers of their influence on her," Minister Su concludes, in a resolute and louder tone now.

"How do you propose we do that?" asks Sansi.

"Keep presenting evidence of their misdeeds until she can't ignore it," replies Su.

"She has been ignoring the evidence so far," counters Sansi.

Princess Wei asks, "What if the Zhang brothers manage to forge an edict? Calling for the ending of our lives? They have access to her so much more than any of the senior ministers."

"I have the Imperial Secretary's assurance that she'll be able to intercept any false edicts. She's prepared to do whatever is in her power to block the brothers," reassures Sansi.

"Should we trust a slave?" Princess Wei asks.

Sansi detects a hint of jealousy in her voice. He knows that she doesn't believe his claim that he no longer sleeps with Wan'er. He replies, "Lady Shangguan wants to continue her work well beyond this reign. We all know this. This means she's a trustworthy ally. She would have been here tonight, but she's away on some business for Nü Huang."

Sansi drinks another cup of wine and smiles with contentment. Princess Wei still avidly desires him. It doesn't matter if it's Li Zhe who succeeds to the throne rather than him. Such things are merely appearances. Princess Wei will be the one who rules the Crown Prince, and if she's in his sway, then he'll be the one in power.

After some thought, he offers, "Nü Huang is always keen to appear fair following some unreasonable concession on her part. I can imagine this scenario: the next time some charge of corruption comes up against the Zhang brothers, Nü Huang will likely dismiss the charge as she has done so far. We already know that it won't take long before the brothers commit some transgression. When this happens, she'll be eager to placate her ministers, and that's when we should seize the opportunity to request a return to Luoyang. I'm also guessing that she'll agree to the reinstatement of Zhang Jianzhi, the Tang loyalist, at court."

"A brilliant strategy! At the Eastern Capital, Jianzhi can marshal the support of the Yülin palace guards. And that," First Minister Wei pauses for dramatic effect, "will be the end of those despicable Zhang brothers."

"Let's not tell the Crown Prince anything until we need him to lead the rebellion and rally the soldiers to our side. You know how panicky he gets," says Princess Wei.

Sansi interjects, "I don't think it will be at all necessary to hurt Her Majesty. Are we all in accord over this?"

More nods or grunts in agreement, except Princess Wei. The meeting disperses at the sound of the drums signalling the Hour of the Rat.

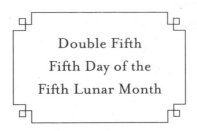

Double Fifth
Fifth Day of the
Fifth Lunar Month

The Inner Palace at Taijigong
North Central Chang'an

The ladies-in-waiting move through the corridors in pairs, carrying baskets filled with an assortment of objects: peachwood charms six cun long and three cun square, carved and inscribed with sayings to ward off the evil vapours; red silken cords; strands of artemisia and garlic, as well the leaves of sweet flag, all to be hung above doors and gates throughout the Inner Palace. The greyish-green leaves of gingko trees flutter in the light breeze overhead, casting flickering shadows below.

They can't feel too serious about the ritual. After all, what evil influences do they need to be afraid of, other than the unwelcome overtures of infatuated eunuchs or ugly, ancient men? Some can't believe their poor misfortune, having to serve a Female Emperor, depriving them of significant sexual attention, while others are relieved for the very same reason. All the ladies-in-waiting, whatever their views of palace life, require levity to sustain themselves through this mundane task. "Not another ritual," they moan, and then proceed to happily distract themselves with gossip.

The women take turns hanging the charms. But the chatter doesn't cease. They whisper stories about liaisons in the Inner Palace. Apart from their outrage at Her Majesty's indulgences with the Zhang half-brothers, they trade suspicions about His Excellency Wu Sansi and his visits to Lady Shangguan and Princess Wei. What will become of Taijigong, they wonder. Does the Crown Prince know about his wife's affair? What will Nü Huang do about appointing a successor? Will it be the Crown Prince, Li Zhe, or will she surprise everyone by appointing his younger brother, Li Dan, instead? It is one thing for His Excellency to have an affair with the Princess in the Outer Palace, but to cross into the Inner Palace and carry on with the Imperial Secretary as well! How unfair that the Zhang brothers and Minister Wu have such easy access to their lovers. "Should we even consider the Zhang brothers real men?" quips one of them, fuelling a flurry of barely suppressed giggles. "But of course," retorts the other. "Have you forgotten how they like to smuggle people from outside into the palace?" Blushes and nods ensue, since many of them are guilty of having enjoyed the infamous midnight parties.

Ah Pu watches the ladies-in-waiting pass by Nü Huang's chambers. Now that the days and nights are warm enough, the translucent rice paper has been removed from the windows and doors so that she can look through the gaps between the latticework into the walkways and garden outside. She's sure of what the ladies-in-waiting are saying. Their eyes, darting back and forth furtively, betray them. The two who help dress Nü Huang for special occasions and do her hair, Silver and Windchime, are the worst. She can tell from the naughty looks they give each other while rolling up Her Majesty's hair or putting on her face powder. They are disdainful of Nü Huang's sallow complexion, her quivering chin, and the dark circles under her eyes. *Wait until they get old*, she huffs. She turns away from the window and busies herself with tidying up the bedroom.

Ah Pu nods with delight at hearing peals of laughter from the adjoining dining room. Princess Taiping always brings joy to her mother, with her sparkling wit and conversational skills. Ah Pu leans close to the entrance and tries to pick up what they are saying.

"But, Mother, you must find a way to ignore these pressures from the Tang loyalists. Why are they so impatient?"

"Indeed, quite ridiculous. I've already promised that Li Zhe will be my successor. Thank you, my dear, I know you are always looking out for my happiness. I have much to be appreciative of—all the fine stallions you have selflessly passed on to me over the years."

More laughter. Ah Pu nods knowingly, thinking how shrewd the Princess is. For one thing, she was the one who introduced the peddler Xue Huaiyi to her mother sixteen years ago and recommended Zhang Changzong five years ago, after sampling his bedroom skills. *Has it been five years already?* Ah Pu shakes her head now in annoyance as she whips the dirty sheets off the bed. *Those half-brothers. Full of themselves.* Now they're even attempting to take over her ministering duties. Elbowing her, the most intimate of Her Majesty's maids, out of nighttime rituals, especially if they awaken first. How they snore, especially Changzong! Disturbing her precious sleep. They should stay in their own quarters more often.

She straightens up midway in her task of putting on the new silk sheets, aware that Nü Huang's and the Princess's voices have suddenly sunk to whispers. Ah Pu feels a touch of hurt—why do they need to hide anything from her?

The eunuch guard's voice announces loudly from outside the apartment, "Your Majesty, the Imperial Secretary has arrived."

"Good," replies Nü Huang. "Send her in."

"I must not linger then, since you and Wan'er have business to tend to," chimes Princess Taiping, her breezy voice pretty as birdsong, yet she doesn't rise from her seat.

"You're curious about your old friend's adventures on my behalf, aren't you? What has she told you?"

"Nothing at all, Mother. Surely you know that Wan'er is loyal to you and would never divulge your secrets?" she replies.

Ah Pu slips the muslin pouches containing dried iris leaves under the pillows and pokes her head out of the bedroom to look down the corridor. She manages to catch sight of Lady Shangguan's profile as she enters the reception hall. She hasn't seen the Imperial Secretary for days. She's slightly nervous around that woman, who keeps her words to a bare minimum, choosing instead to nod and stay quiet. *So different from the Princess.* Ah Pu has never understood why a slave would be that aloof when Nü Huang's own daughter is so warm and friendly, even to the servants. *The Imperial Secretary, fancy title or not, doesn't know her proper place.*

Wan'er stands waiting in the reception hall, listening as the voices of Nü Huang and Princess Taiping trickle in from the dining room. She wonders if Nü Huang will ask why she took longer than planned at Da Fa Temple. She places the gold-plated box on the low table underneath the window, next to a pot of exotic speckled orchids in bloom. A maidservant enters with a tray bearing a teapot, two cups, two pairs of silver chopsticks, and five peeled, pitted lychees gleaming in a silver bowl of chilled water. She places the tray on the side table between two chairs and curtsies to Wan'er. "Lady Shangguan, Her Majesty invites you to enjoy these treats while you await her arrival."

Wan'er smiles with pleasure. A special treat, one of Nü Huang's favourites at this time of year, using water gathered in the mountains and kept cool in the cellar of the Imperial kitchen. No doubt she's being rewarded with them today for her mission. She sits down in one of the chairs. With a pair of chopsticks, she plucks up a plump lychee. She closes her eyes to better savour the fruit. The cool, sweet taste of the lychee flesh sends a shiver of pleasure through her.

Nü Huang enters the hall, aided by Ah Pu on one side and the Princess on the other. "So, my dear, you have returned. I trust your stay at Da Fa Temple was pleasant and successful?"

Wan'er rises from her chair and bows. She's relieved. Judging from the sovereign's tone, she's in a good mood and not likely to question her about the delay. The Princess looks at Wan'er with a mix of pity and consternation. Her mother allows such informalities from Wan'er— partial bows, neither kneeling nor full prostrations, even sitting at the same level, side by side—rather outrageous. These liberties should be granted only to a true member of the Imperial family, not a slave. She and Wan'er haven't spent much time together since their childhood days. She feels sorry for Wan'er. Being Nü Huang's slave must be horrible. She notices the shiny box on the table under the window. Her mouth instantly drops open. She looks at her mother, who seems oblivious to Taiping's curiosity.

The Princess contains herself. She tilts her head down for a moment in acknowledgment of Wan'er's arrival and reluctantly takes her leave of them. Wan'er has guessed at what Taiping's facial expressions mean, and stifles her annoyance. She hasn't forgiven Taiping for introducing the Zhang brothers to Nü Huang.

"What have you to report?"

Wan'er retrieves the box and kneels in front of Nü Huang. "The Jin Dan elixir, Your Majesty." With head lowered, she raises the box toward her sovereign with both hands.

"At last! What a relief." Nü Huang reaches out to receive the box and places it in her lap. She caresses the box while the other shaky hand reaches out with a pair of chopsticks. They slip from her grasp before even touching a lychee and drop to the marble floor. The maidservant rushes forward from her waiting position to retrieve the chopsticks. She soon returns with a second pair.

"Allow me, Your Majesty," offers Wan'er, rising from her kneeling position. She uses the chopsticks to swiftly pick up a lychee and pops it into Nü Huang's eager mouth.

"What of the other task?" Nü Huang mumbles, moving the lychee around in her mouth to enjoy its cool textures before biting into it.

"The Abbess understands that these zhesi jisheng demon souls are extremely difficult to exorcise. Success of the ritual depends on careful observations and preparations tailored to the particular characteristics of these presences. The Abbess suggested that she be summoned immediately when the next incident occurs. She will tend to the problem as it arises."

Wan'er opens the leather purse on her belt and unwraps the amulet from the purple silk. "The Abbess suggests that you wear this or keep it near you at night when you retire to bed."

Nü Huang chews her lychee slowly, considering what Wan'er is saying. Wan'er places the object into Nü Huang's open palm. She is rather pleased at the Abbess's provision of an amulet. She eyes the gift with curiosity and closes her hand around it. With one hand still resting on the gold-plated box, the other contemplating this gift of an exquisite jade piece, Nü Huang nods, filled with immense pleasure. The Abbess has a remarkable reputation. Perhaps she can accomplish what her predecessor couldn't. Why, the former abbess didn't even provide her with such a protective device.

"They come and go so quickly. She must know that? I am assuming that the Abbess had heard from her predecessor about my troubles in the days shortly after I became Empress, but then again, she may not have heard about what was tried and what failed."

"Yes, Your Majesty, the Abbess mentioned she is aware of those earlier attempts."

"Let us proceed to the study now. I have another Palace Diary entry to dictate. I have been eagerly awaiting your return, so that we may resume our work."

The ladies-in-waiting pass by again, now with their baskets empty. All the doors and gates of the north wing have been hung with peachwood charms and red cords, the garlic and sweet flag. They have to replenish their baskets and proceed to the other wings of the Inner Palace.

Nü Huang's Study
The Inner Palace at Taijigong
North Central Chang'an

PALACE DIARY: MY WORST ENEMIES

Every Emperor has his enemies. Even more so when the Emperor is a clever and wise phoenix who has outsmarted enough competitors to ascend the throne and stay there. Now, in my definition of "enemy," let me be clear in saying that those who had spoken forthrightly, even against my judgment or ruling in court, those who had been motivated by their sense of integrity, by a sense of moral compunction—those I do not consider my enemies. Quite the contrary. I shed tears for losing those fine men; how rare they have been in my reign.

When I reflect on the most critical moments in my rise to possess the throne, I must say that the enemies I have the strongest bile about, the ones who had plagued me the most and brought me the greatest suffering, were those two women who held forth such vehement hatred against me early on in my life at the palace—Gaozong's Empress Wang and the Pure Concubine Xiao Liangde.

It was especially troubling to me that the former Empress eventually ended up becoming allies with the concubine Xiao against me. In the first place, it was the Empress who gave Gaozong the brilliant idea of bringing me back from Kan Yeh convent after I was exiled there along with the rest of Taizong's concubines when he died. She thought my return would assist in toppling the Pure Concubine from her favoured position with Gaozong, and I suppose she hoped I would happily defer to her.

While I was at Kan Yeh convent, I was confronted with my deepest fears and doubts. I began to doubt myself, to doubt the prophecy I had believed all those years prior to Taizong's death. Was the fortune teller Yuan completely mistaken? Had I been a fool, sacrificing my childhood and womanhood to an empty ambition? I saw how one of Taizong's favourite concubines, Xu Hui, wasted away. All those exquisite poems she had dedicated to him while he was alive. She was so grief-stricken at his death that she never recovered. Sorrow killed her.

In those dark months, I lived with a poisonous dread. I feared that my whole life was in vain. Watching Xu Hui die, I learned that love and adulation could destroy you if you succumbed to such sentiments. I felt anguish for my mother, who must have been devastated by the news that her daughter was now confined to a Buddhist convent.

That was not what I had envisioned my fate to be, when Taizong summoned me to the Inner Palace. My mother had begun to hope, and with that, she and I seemed to increase in affection for each other. But when I faced the humiliating solitude of being one more shaved head among many at Kan Yeh convent, the shame of my downfall consumed me. What was my mother thinking now? Was she disappointed in me? Would my brief encounter with the Crown Prince as his father lay dying carry any import with him now that he was Emperor? I was on the brink of losing my mind when I received the summons from Gaozong.

The oppressive shadow of fear miraculously lifted from me. When I returned to the Inner Palace as Gaozong's concubine, I vowed I never would let either fear or love rule me. It was as if my rescue from the convent changed me irrevocably, purged me of my previous insecurities, and strengthened my resolve.

Back in the Inner Palace, I saw how the former Empress Wang and concubine Xiao were scornful of other women. They looked down on me. How painful to feel the cold stabs of disdain from their haughty glances! I often cried myself to sleep, finding their rude rejection utterly despicable.

They underestimated me. They could not believe it when I gained Gaozong's highest favours and bent his will to mine. Most wicked, those two. They schemed to get rid of me. They had underrated the degree to which they were unpopular, disliked by both guards and ladies-in-waiting for their condescending ways. Through my informers, I learned of their alliance with each other. I was informed of their intent to discredit me. Did they not understand? Of course not. They had not been there at Kan Yeh convent with me, so how could they know anything of such dark, terrible isolations? Neither were they women who had lived through childhood and womanhood with prophecies of greatness etched into them.

They could not possibly understand my aspirations. So I had them confined to a side apartment east of Sun Splendour Gate, but they persisted in being foolish. They would whine and whine to Gaozong whenever he happened to pass by their quarters. What was he doing there, anyway? He knew I was thoroughly displeased by his weakness for them. He knew that I would be told of his visits by my informers. How dare those women request him to rename the apartment in their honour! When I heard of his attempt to call their prison "Court of Remembrance," I was aghast. After all that had happened—my success at returning to the Inner Palace, deposing the former Empress Wang, and taking her position as Gaozong's consort—those women still did not take me seriously! If they had appealed to me instead, who knows how their fates would have been different?

A woman should never whine, especially to the wrong person. I resolved to punish them. No more would these women scoff at me. Their suffering would set an example for what could happen to those who would take me lightly or treat me with less than the utmost respect.

I summoned the head of the eunuch guards. "Go," I said to him, "give those wayward vixens a good whipping. Tame them slowly. Ignorant ones must be given a lot more time to learn. Do you understand?"

For the first time, I could smell the palpable presence of revenge. An animal smell, frightful but exciting. After I dispatched the eunuch, just past the Hour of the Sheep, I could not think of anything else for hours. Merely sat in my chambers, listening to the silence, then to the sound of the drums as the passing time was signalled. By the time the head guard returned, the drums had just sounded the Hour of the Chicken. Almost four small hours. What an excruciating wait. I was ever so agitated. I had even refused my evening meal.

The eunuch entered the room and bowed low, head touching the ground. He asked, "Does Your Highness wish to hear everything that has happened?"

"Of course," I replied, rising out of my seat, taut with anticipation. "An Empress must be informed of every detail. Spare me nothing. Start from the very beginning. Tell me how they looked when you pronounced my sentence on them. Tell me what they said, how they showed their fear—everything."

So the guard raised his head from the ground and, still kneeling, smiled at me and licked his lips. "Your Highness, the former Empress's face was instantly drained of colour. In hushed, tremulous tones, she said, 'Long live Her Highness! I concede that Wu Zhao has won.'" At this point, the guard paused abruptly.

"Come now. Has your tongue been cut?" At which point, this guard's dark, swarthy face turned an unhealthy green, but he recovered quickly and said, "Your Highness possesses an uncanny ability to intuit things!" He bowed once again to me.

"Do not stray from your story, soldier. What next? What did the Pure Concubine tell you?"

"She was utterly delirious. She spat at my face, and ..." At this point, the eunuch drew a deep breath before he continued. "Her eyes took on a faraway look. She stared past me, then she exclaimed, 'Ah Wu, you treacherous fox!' Then she quickly looked at me, stretched her neck to get closer to my face and said, 'Tell her I'll return as a cat and she will merely be a rodent, a small helpless victim whose throat I'll rip to shreds.' She was screaming hysterically." He paused once again. "Your Highness, many of us have become weary of those women bullying their way through the palace. We have resented them for years. My guards and I had the pleasure of tearing off their clothes, tying them up, and whipping them, one hundred lashes each, until their skin peeled off in thin, red strips."

At this point, I raised my hand to signal a pause. Some fresh sensation was passing through me. I needed a few moments to digest the news, to understand what was happening inside me.

I thought to myself, as I stared down at the kneeling eunuch, that I must never hesitate to exercise power from now on, for absolute power, unlike love or fear, overrides one's dependencies on others. Never again would I need to rely on the goodwill of those I could not stand. When that insight came to me, I motioned to the eunuch to continue his account.

"Your Highness, even as we speak, they are undergoing the slow punishment you requested for them." My curiosity was piqued by such a suggestive remark.

He launched into the final portion of his account. "I had expended *a great deal of energy whipping them, and I was thirsty. I recalled that there was wine to be had, in close proximity. Near the side apartment where they were trussed up were storage rooms where brewing vats were kept. I ordered one of my guards to fetch wine from the vat. The women by now had fainted from the whipping. When the guard returned from the storage room with a large flask of wine, he reported that it stank in there, what with that rotting going on in the vats, and all for the sake of intoxicating us. It was then that the ingenious idea came to me. I laughed until I was choking and threw my head back to imbibe without restraint. When I had drunk my fill, I splashed the wine onto the women's faces and bodies. The stinging pain of the wine on their open wounds must have been great, for they revived with ear-shattering screams. I made them drink the wine until I could tell they were quite intoxicated. At this point, splashing any more wine on them did not evoke the same intensity of response. All they did was moan incomprehensibly. I next ordered the guards to sever the women's hands and feet from their bodies. They took down the bodies and, along with the severed parts, carried them to the storage room. I removed the lid from a brewing vat. I almost retched. I ordered my guards to dump those despicable objects, now barely alive, into the stinking, fermenting mass of plums. 'Quickly, quickly!' I shouted, covering my nose and mouth. They threw in the hands and feet, and propped up the women's torsos so that their heads were kept just above the level of the liquid. I've made sure that the lid is left slightly ajar so that there's enough air for the women to breathe."*

Breathe? When I heard that, I was seized with an uncontrollable urge to chortle, so I did. Breathe? A mix of feelings passed through me—delight and rage.

I was no longer an innocent in the rare pleasures of inflicting revenge. Those men who grow up being groomed for high positions take certain things for granted. They never would question their power to punish wrongdoers! Even Gaozong, who was weak in the kidneys and lacked the gall to face up to the nasty deeds his minions performed on his behalf, even he took it for granted, and though he closed his eyes and pinched his nostrils in detached squeamishness, nevertheless he was still waving his commanding hands this way and that.

I stood there contemplating these insights while the guard remained firmly on his knees. Enough veneration. I dismissed the eunuch, ordering that a constant vigil be kept over the vat and the deterioration of the women. I wanted to know what would ensue when the effects of the wine wore off.

The guard reported to me at every subsequent night watch. At the Hour of the Dog, he reported that their screams amplified as the wine seeped into them. On his visit to me at the Hour of the Pig, the guard's face was ashen as he announced the old Empress's death. I wondered, Where has the guard's initial look of pleasure disappeared to? It was near bedtime, but I still could not sleep. I ordered my maid to have the chief cook roused to prepare me a sumptuous meal from the Imperial kitchen.

At the eunuch's next visit, he told me he could not fathom how it was possible that the Pure Concubine hung on, screaming and swearing until the last breath departed from her body, just as the Hour of the Rat approached. What venom was in her that kept her alive for more than six small hours?

"What is your wish, Your Highness? Shall we dispose of the bodies now?"

"Yes, of course. But first …" I thought of the Pure Concubine's curse—that she would return as a cat to hunt me down. If she died such a violent, bitter death, perhaps it would fuel her return as the animal she chose? I shuddered at the thought. What if she sought me in my later years when I would be frail as a rodent and an easy prey for her?

Could that be possible? That was why I told the guard to decapitate the women—to decrease the chances they could reincarnate with memories of what had happened to them. I took other precautions. I gave each a new animal name: the former Empress I called Snake, cold and dry and low to the ground; and the Pure Concubine I called Owl, with her wide-eyed look of feigned innocence. Names of animals that belonged in the wild, far away from life in the Inner Palace.

I was not pleased with the change in demeanour of the guard at the end. He had started out being quite gleeful, but he appeared moody and even bewildered at the end, his face ashen, his voice strained. The head of my guards cannot afford to become guilt-ridden or shocked at his victims' suffering. He was supposed to provide a strong, clear example to his underlings. Showing that he was upset betrayed an absolute failure to be wholeheartedly devoted to his sovereign. Whatever the eunuch's preoccupations, they were no concern of mine. He was simply too weak. I dismissed him from his position and saw to it that he was assigned other tasks in the Inner Palace.

How could I have possibly foreseen what would happen soon after?

Unable to sleep for night after night, I thought of the women's bodies writhing in pain. What had I done? The question repeated itself endlessly. I oscillated between worry and delight. My forehead burned with a fever. Every minute sound outside my bedchamber startled me. I insisted that my maid sit up close to the bed and remain awake to watch over me. Even the flicker of a candle became a sign that there was some uneasy presence stirring around me. Whenever I slept, the nightmares began.

They hounded me, wilder and more savage than when they had been alive. Creatures with heads and appendages clumsily reattached, dripping with blood and reeking of fermenting plums; dishevelled hair barely concealed their faces, yet their intense eyes gazed past those veils of hair to penetrate me.

I have lost count of the number of hours I suffered, shivering, dreaming, then waking up with desperate cries, soaked in sweat. I shouted at them to leave me alone. I consulted with those knowledgeable in these matters, but what could they do? It seemed that nothing would deter those women.

I hated to admit it, but finally, it was too unbearable. Going to bed at night became a thing to be feared. Oh, those dreadful enemies of mine! The worst I have ever experienced. I do believe it was because they were women, a certain kind of women.

I seized every opportunity I could to spend time outside of Chang'an. Finally, I was able to persuade Gaozong we should move the court and palace to Luoyang. I told him it always had been a nuisance dealing with the troubling deliveries of tribute grain to Chang'an, what with the canal system stopping slightly short of the city. Besides, he knew of my suffering, and I suppose he had some pity on me, his beloved Empress.

I remember one afternoon, after the decision was finalized. It was shortly after Lichun Jieqi, Start of Spring, in the first lunar month. The pond at the Elegant Willow Pavilion was a placid, opaque mirror, still frozen in some places. The bare, bright yellow branches of the willow trees all along the circumference were starkly beautiful. I sat in the fan-shaped pavilion, dressed in a long coat lined with mink, wearing my mother's Tartar hat, staring at the pond and the garden around me. I wore that hat to remind myself how much I had achieved since I entered Taijigong as a young concubine of the Fifth Grade. There was a chill in the air, but the sun was strong, casting definite, dramatic shadows. I saw my reflection on the pond's surface. Then I cast my eyes longingly at the naked branches of the plum blossom trees, their buds just starting to form. I felt a glimmer of hope. Surely those demon souls would not follow me from Chang'an to Luoyang.

In the garden, surrounded by hints of spring's imminent beauty, I also thought, with a melancholic weariness too burdensome for someone barely thirty sui, that demon souls, more so than humans, have no mercy. I had become so taunted by them in the nights that I grew to worry that they perhaps also could inhabit the daylight hours, absorbed temporarily into other presences, other forms of life. I noticed a gaunt crow up on the roof of the covered arcade on my right. It strutted about boldly and then disappeared through a gap between the tiles of the roof. I could not take my eyes off that spot. I waited and waited, all the details of how the women died racing through my mind. As if to confirm my worst fears, the crow reappeared just at the very moment my mind recalled the memory of the Pure Concubine's curse. This conjunction startled me.

There was definitely something odd about the way that crow moved its body—a certain intelligence in its turns and pauses. Was such a creature capable of reflection and wilfulness like a human being? I wondered if a slight animal like that was capable of harming a human. At the very moment the question passed through my mind, the crow flew off, landed briefly on the dwarf pine across the pond, then shifted quickly to the weeping willow next to it. Was it merely another coincidence? I took no chances and ordered a guard to shoot the creature down with his bow. The crow plummeted through the thin ice on the pond and disappeared from sight.

I forced myself to look away. I steeled myself and vowed that my life was going to change for the better. I would escape those women with a move to Luoyang.

How I despised them. If they had marked graves, I would have gone there often to fling my most bitter curses and spittle upon the ground that covered their bones. Better still, I would have conserved my precious energy and had my eunuchs waste their common spittle instead. But those enemies of mine never deserved marked graves, and I do not even remember now what I had the guards do with their bodies.

What a horrible curse. If I had known then what I know now, would I have been so eager to make them suffer so while they were alive? Is this the justice of the unseen realms?

Wan'er places her brush down on the porcelain rest and folds her hands together in her lap. Throbbing pain presses against both of her temples. She looks up to see something that disturbs her even further.

Her Majesty's face is contorted with tears. Has she ever seen Nü Huang cry before? She's sure she has, but she can't recall when that was. A tiny itch in her throat makes her cough with discomfort. Wan'er wants to be either angry or afraid. Instead, she feels both currents swirling in her, hot and cold eddies entangled, pushing for some brazen gesture at one moment, insisting on retreat at another. *Why can't it be simple?* she asks herself.

"Do you think this Palace Diary is a wasted venture? Tell me what you really think." Nü Huang's voice is quieter now, as if she were talking to herself.

"Your Majesty, you show an ardent dedication to this Palace Diary. You are most urgently invested in communicating your thoughts. Few individuals possess this determination to re-examine historical events and to retell them from such an intimate perspective."

"It is not just for myself that I am doing this. You might be my slave, but you too are an unconventional woman. Surely you appreciate the worth of this document of mine. The men will be writing their own version of my reign in the Veritable Record when I am gone. It matters greatly to me that this Palace Diary exists as a statement in support of women like us, women who face immense obstacles against gaining power in the world of men."

Wan'er bites hard into her lower lip. She can barely breathe. How can Nü Huang make such a comment, especially after describing how she had those women tortured?

"Speak!" Nü Huang's voice is now firm, as she wipes her face clean of tears.

"Your Majesty understands that even unconventional women fall prey to the demands of their familial obligations and are not able to realize their dreams. They are unfortunate enough to be ruined by such ties in one way or another. Is that not usually the case? Your Majesty demonstrates an intractable and unswerving will to fulfil her wishes. You are exceptional, even among unconventional women. Nothing has deterred you. This record is clearly evidence of that will and stamina."

A slight smile crosses Nü Huang's face. She leans into the cushions behind her aching back and sighs in relief.

"You may go now, my dear."

Mount Hua

Harelip looks out to the swirling mist. Last night, he was sorely tempted to risk the climb up to this wondrous northern peak after drinking too much millet wine. It never ceases to amuse him how deluded he can become under the sway of intoxication. What was he singing? He forgets.

He inhales, taking in a full, slow breath, then falls quickly into a slumped posture, shifting his gaze inward. Since Baoshi's departure, he has twice detected traces of blood in his phlegm. He places his hand on his wrist. The pulse is floating. *All right,* he admits to himself, *the condition remains troubling.*

He can't pretend. Chronic, unexpressed grief has depressed the circulation of qi and blood. Is this irreversible? At his age, he can't be overly optimistic, yet he mustn't surrender to despair. It's too early to tell. At least he must endure long enough to see Baoshi return with Ardhanari, for only then will his restless spirit depart this world placated and satisfied. The debt must be settled, a debt that has embedded itself deeply within his lungs.

He must enlist Qian's help. He's no longer a sprightly young man. He must ask him to forage for some roots in the forest closest to the eastern peak. Licorice roots he has plenty of, as well as Danggui and Maidong roots. But he needs Beimu, and this is the right time to dig up the yellowish-white corms. As well, Qian could find him more of the orange Dihuang tubers and the long, brownish Xuanshen roots.

The thought of the sheer cliffs and forest areas where Qian must go in search of those medicinal roots sends a shiver through Harelip. He straightens up from his crestfallen posture to look at the view.

Just moments after sunrise, the dragon emerges in all its glory. While the air is still cool, the vast mystery moves and changes shape before his eyes, conquering the cliffs and masking the world below.

Last night he had fallen into bed mirthful with the effects of the wine and began to dream almost immediately. A contingent followed Nü Huang up a mountain. Loud blaring horns, the thumping of double-barrelled drums, the squeaking and pining of flutes battled with clashing cymbals and gongs. A young boy wasn't sure which group to associate with. At times, he walked with the Daoists, whose colourful yellow and orange banners and glittering outfits excited him. Later in the dream, the boy grew inordinately restless. The noisy chanting was giving him a headache. He found himself gravitating toward the Buddhist retinue. At certain moments in the dream, Harelip himself was a distant spectator, while at other moments he was shaking with anxiety, feeling as if he himself was the boy. The Buddhist monks were also chanting, albeit more softly than the Daoists. Finally, the boy chanced upon a handful of monks who didn't chant. They were rather decrepit, their robes mere rags. These monks' features ranged from unseemly to ugly, and they hobbled along with walking canes. The boy joined them, but before the whole retinue reached the summit, he turned away and fled down the mountain.

Harelip woke up well before dawn, his heart thumping hard and his throat feeling exceptionally parched. Who was that boy? Was it him or Baoshi? Perhaps the boy was no one in particular, merely someone in his imagination. Whoever that boy was, he had the sense to flee and not wait around long enough for a wicked sovereign to punish him. Perhaps Harelip was now able to finally banish fears spurred by that first dream thirty-six years ago. Despite the encouraging thought, his head still pounded painfully from the night's drunken indulgence. He looked in the direction of the window. Still dark.

The dream prompted him to take the short but steep hike up to the peak from the shack this morning. He needed to look out to this expansive ever-changing landscape, to rescue his mind from the clutches of its own inner confusion. He mustn't forget that he is a mere human in the midst of great mysteries. How many more times will he be allowed to witness this swirling splendour?

Harelip laughs at the irony. He had acquired no small amount of learning as an acolyte, his nose buried deep in the wisdom of religious texts. Yet today, as an old man, dreams continue to have the power to bind him.

Not all dreams are prophetic. Last night's dream is likely a reflection of his own fears, not of Baoshi's safety in the city. Even if he were strong enough to venture into Chang'an, what would he say to Baoshi and Ardhanari? *Forgive me, but a foolish man has come to undo his foolishness.* What is happening with Baoshi? Has he found Ardhanari yet?

He mustn't strive against the unknown. He must trust. He coaxes himself to release his mind from these assailing worries.

> *Without intuiting the sublime,*
> *You will not experience freedom.*

He has recited these last two lines countless times. The whole poem is a puzzle of sorts, meant to challenge us to examine the paths taken by our minds. Harelip wonders if his mind mostly travels with intent and discrimination, toward freedom, or if it veers too much, reckless and wayward. Nagarjuna has left behind the precious legacy of his writings, and Harelip feels as if he is often abiding in the mysteries of this poem in particular.

He touches his lips and caresses them, deep in thought. Then he rests his index finger against the sharp dent in his upper lip. He stretches his other hand out in front of him. The enveloping dragon claims it, almost causing it to disappear from view. *Do not believe you exist apart from the great mystery,* a voice reminds him. *Yield to me,* the voice persists. "Will you have me fall over the edge, then," he retorts, "over the edge of reality into the Void?" *Reality is swirling contradiction and clarity,* answers the calm, assertive voice. *The Void is not empty, and emptiness is not void.*

Foreign Quarter
West Central Chang'an

Baoshi wakes up before sunrise, when the quiet air is sweetened with the singing of larks and the chirping of chickadees.

He lies awake listening to this dawn chorus, rapt with attention.

They sing differently here than the birds on Mount Hua, but he can't quite describe what the differences are. Is it that their voices don't carry the echo of high mountain air? Or is it that these, far from the forests, have voices that don't remember the wild?

He sits up and reaches for his clothes. Eighteen days since he left Harelip. So much has happened. The first four days of his pilgrimage were spent at the village, then the long walk to Chang'an that took five days, and now this waiting at the jogappas' place. Nine days in the city so far. Now he knows that the Bronze Urn will be open next on Xiaoshu 小暑 Jieqi, less than three weeks away. *Is this pilgrimage going to consist mostly of waiting?* he wonders. A wait that feels all the more impossible with each passing day. He touches the jade pendant, remembering his Master's conviction that he will meet Ardhanari. The pendant's cool, solid presence against his skin reassures him.

Sounds of awakening from the jogappas' room. He catches a whiff of fragrance. The scent makes him think of those scent-exuding trees on Mount Hua, with secrets that would not be surrendered no matter how close he placed his face to their trunks, waiting. Other kinds of secrets, like that mysterious presence he encountered there. He closes his eyes. *You have the soft lips of a woman.*

He pushes aside the cushions that have fallen over him in the night and gets up from the straw mat. While retying his antariya, he hears footsteps going down the stairs to the kitchen. He puts on a tunic, after wrapping a bright orange breastband across his chest. After that awkward encounter with Sita and Lakshmi the first night, he resolved that he would not be ashamed anymore, at least not with the jogappas. Now he dresses like them, especially now that the days are warmer. The jogappas have been happy at his increasing ease with them, yet no one has asked him any questions. Maybe they haven't noticed, and why should they, when the left breast is still small?

He runs his hand lightly over the fine fuzz of hair on his scalp. He has decided to let it grow, inspired by the lush locks of the jogappas, although he hasn't decided whether he will let his hair grow that long. Surely Ardhanari will be back before his hair reaches his ears.

The roosters start their crowing slightly ahead of the drums. The Hour of the Dragon. The colours in the room are slowly coming alive with the sun's appearance above the horizon. He looks out the window to the backyard below. Sita is at the water pump with two buckets. As she works the pump, she adjusts her breastband into place with one hand while the other hand keeps to its steady pumping.

The water rushes into the wooden buckets in loud spurts and gushes. His ear attunes itself to the variations in rhythms, a continuous hypnotic sound consisting of stops and starts in the flow of water and the creaking of the pump. Every morning, he leans out the window and watches Sita fill the buckets, letting the sound of the water soothe his mind. He also recites the parable of the water in the pond each time, running through the whole parable quickly, half thinking through, half voicing the lines. For Baoshi, it seems a fitting way to greet Harelip as soon as he awakes.

"Each person's essences ... compared to the waters ... body to the embankments ... good deeds the water's source ... if the heart does not focus on goodness ... pond lacks embankments ... fails to accumulate good deeds ... water will dry up ... breaches the dike to water the fields ... original flow will leak off ..."

He has accompanied Lakshmi to the market for the past five mornings. Baoshi observed a fluttering sensation in his chest as he scanned the crowds, hoping to catch sight of the handsome stranger. One morning, Laskhmi noticed and asked, "Why are your eyes wandering as if your soul is travelling?" Baoshi turned his attention back to Lakshmi and smiled bashfully. That pleased the vivacious jogappa.

Seeing that Sita has finished at the water pump, he quickly puts on his pants underneath the antariya and runs downstairs.

"You must be hungry," Sita says when she meets him in the kitchen.

"How did you know? Was my belly growling so loudly this morning you could hear it in the next room?"

Sita laughs. "No, not at all."

He looks out the kitchen doorway to the chicken coop at the back, still thinking about that parable. Sita notices Baoshi's distracted look. She wonders about him. Ever since that first night he stayed with them, awakened by his frightened shouts, a question has been nagging at her. Was it merely shyness, or was there another reason he would not let them help with his clothes? She thought she sensed something different as she brushed her hand over his torso.

She sits on a stool at the door and watches him wash his face, turning over that question in her mind. She should be starting to make food for the tea shop. When he's wiping his face with a towel, she plucks up the courage to ask. "Baoshi, I wonder ... if you would mind ... uh ... if I ask you something quite ... what's the word ...?" It's rare for her to feel this awkward. The Chinese words are eluding her. She tries again, "You've been with us for eight or nine days? Maybe I can ask you now. That first night, remember? While we were trying to help you change out of your damp clothes ... I thought I felt ... I can't quite say what, but there's something rather unusual about you. Your body."

A stinging blush covers his face and he turns away abruptly.

"Oh, no, sorry. It's my Chinese ... making it more difficult ..." She holds Baoshi's shoulders gently and urges him to turn back to face her.

Baoshi slowly lifts his head and looks at Sita. Are her eyes not the eyes of a doe tenderly gazing at him? Was Sita really born male? That bump on her throat doesn't mean the same thing as those bumps on other men's throats. Harelip was right. Words are merely sounds until we grant them our meanings.

"Sita, I don't quite know how to tell you."

"Tell me a story then. What about it? Soon?"

Baoshi starts to cry, the flood of tears bursting out of him. "I know that my Master, Harelip, would be tremendously grateful to you for taking me in."

"But I've made you cry!"

"I'm crying out of happiness."

He hears the sounds of the other jogappas moving about upstairs. Baoshi quickly wipes his tears on the towel and helps Sita remove the shutters at the front of the tea shop, then puts out the chairs, which have been stacked away in the corner.

Sita returns to the kitchen to stoke the fire and boil water. Together they collect eggs from the chickens before starting to chop vegetables. When Devi arrives in the kitchen, she takes over and begins to order the others around.

Their first customers are three men who arrive together, all ordering black spice tea with three orders of roti with curry. *Their smooth skins are like the barks of some trees after rain,* thinks Baoshi. How he loves the smell of wet bark. He inhales the precious memory. These men also wear antariyas, except theirs are white, a contrast against their skin. He feels a mild rush of pleasure through his body as his eyes gaze at their muscular calves. Their antariyas are worn differently, with the endpiece looped from front to back between their legs and tucked in at the back. Their heads are covered in loose turbans made of the same white muslin.

Another table is soon taken by two men dressed in flowing red robes. They ask for eggs fried with green onions and a serving of millet gruel.

Baoshi runs back and forth between the dining room and the kitchen, serving food and removing plates and bowls and spoons before washing dishes in the kitchen.

Most of the customers don't need to look at the menu. Written in Hindi, Arabic, and Chinese, the menu is as diverse as the clientele, though it is primarily vegetarian and features the hot flaming curries of southern India. Catching snatches of conversation between Devi and the others, he learns that for the midday meal, there will be extra items offered: couscous spiced Devi's way, rendering it something quite different from the original, and dolmahs and hummus brought in by local Turkish women who enjoy making a little extra money selling food to the tea shop.

While doing his chores, Baoshi listens to the chatter. Most of the conversations are in other languages. He pays attention to the sounds and inflections as if he were listening to animals calling to one another in the wooded areas, across cliffs or trees.

Sita whispers in his ear that the three men who sit together eating their rotis with their right hands have been shamelessly comparing notes about their failing body parts. They always do, she adds. He himself overhears the other two customers earnestly discussing the rising prices of salted sea bream and the superior quality of one kind of dried seaweed over another. Their Chinese is different from his, gurgling in their throats with inflections from some other language. They are likely traders or merchants. They certainly don't dress the way his father did and enjoy punctuating their conversation by slapping the table sporadically with their hands. He wonders if his father ever visits the tea shop when he comes into the city to do business. But he quickly realizes that this is unlikely.

He has learned that most of the customers are bachelors, while a few are widowers. The customers are a mix of Hindu and Muslim, with a few Nestorian Christians, Turkish traders, and a handful of Buddhists. Some of the older ones have been frequenting the tea shop for years. He has begun to recognize the regulars, who usually come twice a day, first for the morning meal, then for the late afternoon tea. Once a week, the afternoon crowd is larger when the jogappas perform.

What do they have in common, if anything? This is the question that occurs to Baoshi as he observes the customers. They are all certainly much older than him. *Will I get more energetic and bolder as I age?* he wonders as he wipes his sweaty brow before clearing another table of plates.

MOGAO CAVES NEAR DUNHUANG

"Are you sure?" asks Old Gecko, "You really don't want to go with us?" The old man's eyes squint in suspicion.

"Yes. There's a lot I can be doing here. I don't need the rest in Dunhuang. Really. I assure you." Ardhanari tries to sound as calm as he can, even though he hears his own heart pounding loudly inside his chest.

Old Gecko can't quite find the words to describe his puzzlement, even to himself. He sees a handsome, middle-aged nephew whose grey hairs are surprisingly few, scattered across the thick mass of curls tied back in a ponytail. His nephew is indeed a pillar of secrets. No mention of whether he has a wife or family in Chang'an. Doesn't talk to the others about anything except work. A strange one altogether.

Old Gecko, Ram, Arun, Alopen, and the two young assistants jump into the rickety cart. Arun flicks the reins impatiently. The men nod and smile amiably at Ardhanari and he waves back, trying not to look too happy. He stands in the hot sun, shielding his eyes with his hand, as he watches them leave in the haze of dust stirred up by the cart.

He wipes his neck and forehead roughly with his kerchief, wrings it out before tying it back around his head.

Whether it's because of the desert or the odd companionship of the murals and sculptures or the absence of true friendship, Ardhanari really couldn't name the one decisive thing that has changed his attitude toward his sculpting. He reckons it must be everything about the atmosphere in the Mogao Caves that's having an effect on him. In Chang'an, he would work on figures one at a time, starting with the face, then work on the rest of the body, beginning the next sculpture only when he had completed the one before. That was the way he was taught to sculpt, the convention he's supposed to adhere to. But now he has chosen to work on all seven bodies, leaving their faces to the last. He wants to break the old rules, to invent a fresh way to proceed.

As he makes the finishing touches to one figure's robes, he sings softly to himself. With their faces yet to be formed, he still can tell them apart because each body is slightly different from the others. How will he make Buddha's face different from his six bodhisattvas? He also wants people to feel that these seven belong together, while still being distinguishable from one another. That is his intention at least. He imagines waves, the swirl of water, as he uses an iron file to shape curves into the front folds of the robe. Water, so essential, so desperately precious in this desert region. It makes sense that water needs to be evoked in these bodies.

He pauses to survey his accomplishments. Seven bodies waiting for their facial features. The faces are the most difficult. How long will it take? A month? Two? Then there's the entirely different issue of how much longer he's willing to stay at the caves. Now that he has seen enough to be reassured that Old Gecko isn't ailing, his urge to return to Chang'an is all the greater.

Ardhanari takes a deep breath and plunges both his hands into the bucket, starting to lift the mix of clay and straw onto the armature for the head of a bodhisattva. He'll start with a bodhisattva and work up to Sakyamuni. *Think of someone you know, whose face you're fond of,* he coaxes himself, and breathing deeply, he lets his hands take over.

WAN'ER'S APARTMENT
THE INNER PALACE AT TAIJIGONG
NORTH CENTRAL CHANG'AN

W an'er looks up from her desk, startled from her reverie. A moth has flown inside the lantern, and his wings flutter against the paper sides as he attempts to escape. She tries to coax the moth out using a dry ink brush.

Just when she has given up, the moth escapes. Now flying free, he crashes against the sides of the lantern, trying once again to reach the flame.

"Can you stop doing that?" asks Wan'er in exasperation, tempted to kill the moth and be rid of the constant distraction, but he flies away, eluding her swipe.

Even at the sound of the drums, one small hour short of midnight, she's not the least bit sleepy. It's hot and the air too humid for any sense of ease. Her mind keeps returning to that first night with Ling. Has it been almost two weeks since that encounter? Wan'er closes her eyes and her breathing slows down as she's drawn back into the memory. She surprised herself, leading Ling into her room. Not protesting when the nun caressed her face. Ling slowly moved her fingers up Wan'er's cheek, along her left temple to reach the scar at the centre of her forehead. While she lingered over the raised mark, Wan'er felt a startling sensation, as if the scar was awakened from dormancy, sending a rapid jolt of energy through her body.

As she and Ling kissed, tears welled up and she saw Ling through a misty distortion as if caught under water. She couldn't account for all of it—an extreme shyness that had rapidly given way to an uncensored instinct. It was as if Ling touching her scar awakened not only the scar but her whole person. She took Ling with such force that she sometimes shivered, frightened by her own wild need. But Ling didn't recoil. Instead, she became a soft, brooding presence that sank deeper into Wan'er with every touch.

Extending her stay at the temple for one more day and night did not do enough to staunch her thirst. When Wan'er left Da Fa Temple, she rode Nomad hard, briefly stopping at the market before departing from the western sector. She wanted to see if she could find the walking boy and that old man with the sign, but neither of them was there.

Wan'er presses the palms of her hands hard against her closed eyes. She is tired yet disquieted by her longing. Dull rhythmic sounds cause her to lift her head up to check. The moth is back, fluttering against the sides of the lantern. Being with Ling has awakened her need for mystery and she has become like this moth, relentlessly drawn to an inevitability.

I long to dishevel you. The memory of Ling's voice hot in her ear. She looks down at the blank page in her journal, while the book of Cai Yan's poems is open to her left. She should turn her mind to this work.

The bowl of plum pits sits on the floor next to her bare feet. The plum wine was cool, not chilled as well as she likes it, but the fruits were delicious and aromatic.

She lifts up the booklet of Cai Yan's poems and reads aloud to herself.

> *Not a day, not a night passes when I do not long for home;*
> *Of all who live and breathe, none can be as bitter as me.*
> *Heaven unleashed calamity upon an empire,*
> *Leaving our people without a leader,*
> *But only I have this fate, to be lost among barbarians.*
> *Customs different, minds dissimilar, how can I survive?*

With whom can I converse?
I brood on my trials, how adverse my fate,
My fourth song finishes, my suffering more intense.

Did Cai Yan believe that only she alone suffered a miserable fate? Or was she merely using such exaggerations for literary effect? Perhaps Cai Yan had thought of her fate as unique, that she alone was captured and "lost among barbarians." Wan'er pours herself another cup of plum wine and downs it quickly. If she had met Cai Yan then, if she herself had belonged to that barbarian tribe, would she have felt empathy for the woman? *Who feels pity for me in the Inner Palace?* she asks herself. *And what is pity worth when you're a slave?* Her cheeks are flushed as she writes.

Did each poem relieve your torment?
A captive lotus, voicing crisis of dislocation,
Bitterness rooted you.
With brooding breath, the gamble of anguish,
Pain's hard, fragile carapace insisted
You alone were dealt a unique fate,
Embattled, sheltered.
Questions separate us, disjunction of meanings.

Wan'er pours herself another cup of wine. She fishes out another plum from the slender bottle with a pair of chopsticks. Her head is starting to spin from drinking the wine too quickly. From underneath the jewellery box, she recovers a key and unlocks the camphor cabinet. In the front are the scrolls of the Palace Diary. She moves them to the top of the cabinet first, peering in while reaching for the secret compartment farther back. She places Cai

Yan's poems and her own inside, slides the inner door shut, and then replaces the scrolls before locking the outer doors and hiding the key once again.

She blows out the flame in the lantern, ambles over to the bed, takes off her robe, and climbs under the silk sheet, lying on her back. Her eyes make out the veils along the sides of her bed stirring from the slight breeze coming in from the windows. She touches her forehead. Damp with sweat. She feels the outlines of her scar.

Cai Yan wrote in order to resist and to protest, refusing to surrender her spirit and her voice. That these eighteen songs have survived is a rare miracle. Hers is a record quite unlike Nü Huang's Palace Diary. One woman only too aware of her captivity, while the other refuses to admit much else other than self-justification and sovereign power, yet they do share one thing in common. Their words resound with bitterness.

Wan'er turns onto her side, curling up with her arms wrapped around her breasts. How hard it is to fall asleep tonight. She turns again to lie on her back and pulls her hair away from her neck. She shifts her head around on the square pillow, trying to find a comfortable spot before falling asleep.

Ling appears, but her face is concealed by shadows. Wan'er tries to call out, but no sound escapes from her mouth. She wakes up with a shout, breathing hard. She struggles, but feels herself dragged back into dreaming.

This time she walks west toward the apartments housing the ladies-in-waiting. She hears the sounds of singing to the accompaniment of the qin. How exquisite! Her tears flow as she runs toward their rooms and pushes the doors open. She keeps opening doors, only to encounter empty rooms. In the last room she walks into, Ling waits for her, looking much younger, the wrinkles on her face gone. Ling's hair is loose, and seems to be growing rapidly so that by the time Wan'er reaches Ling's side, her hair is down to her waist.

"How did you manage to do this?" she marvels, stroking the soft, luxuriant blackness.

"The Great Way is the Immense Weapon, don't you know? But why have you taken so long to come to me?" Ling asks.

Wan'er is roused by a sudden chill. Goose pimples erupt all over her arms and the back of her shoulders. An image enters her mind of her mother, pale and terrified, lying in bed with her eyes wide open.

She jumps out of bed and throws on a blue skirt and a short-sleeved top. Taking a lantern with her, she pads down the corridors and the covered arcades in her soft-soled shoes. When she reaches the pond of the Elegant Willow Pavilion, she stops for a moment to listen to the bullfrog chorus. She gazes at the moon, almost full. She acutely feels her own need for light. Reluctantly, she moves away from the pond but keeps listening as the frogs' singing fades until there is a hush of silence. A slight breeze stirs through the back of her hair, teasing and playful.

She hesitates at the main doors of her mother's apartment. There doesn't seem to be any sign of disturbance. It was only her mind deceiving her, she decides.

She turns back. When she nears the pond this time, she takes the zigzag stone bridge toward the fan-shaped pavilion. Raising her lantern to hang it on the hook under the pavilion roof, she sits on the inside ledge, rests her head on the balustrade, and looks down at the pond. The moon's reflection is clear and still. Lotus blossoms rise up, magical and eerie, crowding around the moon in the pond. She wonders for what or whom do the bullfrogs call. A concert of lonely sounds.

The wind stirs, carrying the scent of jasmine blossoms. The drooping branches of the willow trees on the south side of the pond start to sway slightly. She looks down at the water again. It ripples slightly. A small dark head pokes out. A turtle. Before long, it disappears beneath the surface. The lantern's twin in the water wavers with the turtle's movement. She touches her forehead. Clammy. She shivers, noticing how the air has cooled.

Ever since Nü Huang's most recent entry in the Palace Diary, she can hardly concentrate on any task before her mind returns to the words that her sovereign uttered. *I must never hesitate to exercise power from now on, for absolute power, unlike love or fear, overrides one's dependencies on others.* And then, the very last sentence in that entry: *If I had known then what I know now, would I have been so eager to make them suffer so while they were alive? Is this the justice of the unseen realms?*

The justice of the unseen realms. She remembers how sickened she had felt while transcribing that account of torture. Will Ling be able to do something about these virulent demon souls? If her predecessor could not succeed, how will she be able to?

Of all the willows across the pond, only one is a particularly small tree, with curiously twisted, contorted branches. She stares at it. What is this kind of willow called? While trying to remember, she keeps staring at the tree and notices that its branches are moving much more than those of the other trees, as if compelled by more than the slight wind. She shivers, this time from fear. On the far side of the pond, the corridor behind the willow will take her to the forbidden part of the east wing. She has never dared to venture there before, but she feels tempted tonight, unable to shake off those descriptions of the torture of the two women.

The moths swarm around her raised lantern. She removes the lantern from the hook, leaves the pavilion, and walks around the edge of the pond until she approaches the willow. It stops moving the moment Wan'er reaches it.

Dazed, she enters the corridor. The air is musty, stale with the years of neglect. The lantern light reveals the large leaves of a banana tree in the corner of an inner courtyard. She reaches the doors of a storage room on her left, then hurries past it, feeling a great uneasiness come over her, but she continues to walk until she reaches the end of the corridor. Wan'er turns right and keeps walking until she comes to another set of doors to her left. The doors are barred with a padlock. Her heart is pounding fiercely. She sets her lantern down so that she can draw close to the doors. A gust of wind rushes down the corridor and extinguishes the candle in her lantern. She gasps and turns around, just in time to glimpse a stooped figure hobbling away. Abandoning the lantern, she runs back along the corridor, giving chase. But the figure has disappeared, nowhere to be found. She keeps running, gasping for air but not relaxing her pace until she reaches her apartment.

At her doors, she feels a hand grip her shoulder firmly from behind and she shouts, but another hand comes over her mouth to stop her from making any more noise.

"Where have you been?" Sansi turns her around.

"You frightened me!" she exclaims.

"Well?"

"I couldn't sleep. I had to take a stroll."

"Where have you been?"

"Just walking through the east wing."

"How queer. I came to see you. We've not seen each other since your return. Anything the matter?" inquires Sansi. "You look rather pale. And your skin is cold to the touch. You should be more careful."

Wan'er doesn't say anything in response but pushes open the doors to her apartment.

"Still mad at me, aren't you?"

She smiles at him with a tinge of sadness. "I'm merely a little preoccupied, Sansi."

"I see." He casts a look of longing at Wan'er. She makes no gesture to welcome him in. Aware of this, Sansi turns away, heading to his own residence in the Outer Palace.

Nü Huang's Aparment
The Inner Palace at Taijigong
North Central Chang'an

"Your Majesty," coos Changzong to Nü Huang as they lie with their bodies intertwined, while Yizhi sleeps on the other side of the bed, his back turned to them. "There's the matter of First Minister Wei Yuanzhong. You know he's not the least bit fond of my brother and me."

Nü Huang strokes Changzong's smooth chest. "Mmm? That's true, my boy. Obviously. You've been rude to him. I would be cross at you too if I were him."

"I was wondering if there's anything you could do to dissuade Wei from his bullying. He is tiresome. Vexatious."

"Not a thing, Changzong. I may be very fond of you and Yizhi, but the First Minister is one of my most excellent and upright zaixiang who went through the most trying of times with me, and I won't be persuaded to subject him to any more difficulties, not if I can help it."

"But he wants us dead!"

"I doubt it. Don't worry, my boy. You're letting your fears get the better of you."

"Your Majesty, surely you understand how that can happen! How about your fears of the demon souls?"

Nü Huang stops stroking Changzong's chest. That was a nasty move.

She will not put up with that. Too vain for his own good. She turns her back on him and reaches over to the small table on Yizhi's side. The last of the Jin Dan elixir. With a porcelain spoon, she scoops it up from the small bowl where it has been mixed with honey and tea and swallows it. When the unpleasant taste completely leaves her mouth, she blows out the lantern and wraps her trembling body around Yizhi.

Yizhi smirks while pretending to be asleep. Nü Huang's arm rests along his, the amulet on her wrist cool against his knuckles as she wraps her fingers around his hand. His vain brother—see how his arrogance trips him up. *You just wait,* he thinks as he feels Nü Huang's body warm against his back, *I'll find a way to outstrip you.*

FOREIGN QUARTER
WEST CENTRAL CHANG'AN

"I'm ready to tell you a story," begins Baoshi. A constant rain has been falling since sunset, and the bamboo blinds, stirred by a breeze, beat a gentle, hypnotic rhythm against the window.

The jogappas turn to look at the boy. His features are even more striking in the candlelight. They admire the arching eyebrows and bright eyes, but mostly his full lips.

"Once upon a time, there was a man who became sorely afraid of punishment. He knew he would get into trouble because he didn't want to pretend he was like everyone else. He couldn't live his former life anymore. He had to choose. Either stay and pretend, or leave and endure all the losses that came with that decision.

"He left. For many years, he lived as a hermit, helping those who sought him out. He resigned himself to his new life. He sang songs, recited poetry, and learned about the plants and animals that lived around his shack. He didn't anticipate that one day, he would be visited by a man who was terribly angry. The man didn't come in search of a cure. He wanted to stay angry at what fate had dealt him. He had been given a son who wasn't enough of a son. The man wanted to get rid of this odd creature. He wanted the hermit to take him."

Baoshi pauses, hearing the tremor in his voice. He drinks some more tea and considers what to say next.

"That son was me. One of the first things the hermit Harelip taught me is that I am a miracle of Heaven, that I must embrace my Two-in-Oneness. In his wisdom, he taught me that words are merely sounds, that everyone means different things by them. Since I was called a boy for eight years, he would still call me that, even though we both made new meanings for the word 'boy.'"

He pauses again, looking at the faces of the jogappas to check their reactions. They're all showing varying degrees of surprise on their faces.

"I'm a boy like no other I know of. One with a body of both male and female parts. I've survived the shame of my father's rejection thanks to love from Harelip, my true father and teacher. When I started out on my pilgrimage to Chang'an, I was walking away from that secure love into a world of unknowns. Since being in Chang'an, I've struggled once again with fears of being shamed and rejected. This city is another kind of wilderness, as my Master has put it. Rather than surrender to my fears, I've decided to trust those who love me. That's why I'm telling you now."

Xiazhi 夏至 Jieqi
Summer Solstice
Fifth Lunar Month
Full Moon

The Inner Palace at Taijigong
Chang'an

Nü Huang's Private Scroll : Guarding against Yin

The longest day. The yin and yang contend with each other. Decay begins to set in from this day forth, while growth and vigour attempt to maintain their weakening hold.

The Hour of the Pig has just commenced and it is still light out. The day has been fraught with exhausting events. Even though my eyes are heavy with sleep, I feel an urge to make this entry.

Wan'er came down with a fever yesterday and could not be present at the ritual this morning. She hardly falls ill. I am concerned for more than one reason. My mind races with all the possible reasons. Could her visit to the Abbess on my behalf have affected her? She has been somewhat unfocused since her return to the palace. My physician has just tended to her and reports that she is resting well. I have not forgotten Lady Zhen's prophetic dream. Indeed, at this time of the year during the Han Dynasty, they had practised the ritual of weighing earth and charcoal against one another. If my slave was prophesied to measure out the affairs of the world, and she was too sick to attend today's court ritual, should I be concerned?

From the Hour of the Chicken the night before, for the whole twelve double hours until earlier today, I have fasted and observed all the ordinances prescribed for a Son of Heaven. This morning, at the Hour of the Snake, I proceeded to the Ceremonial Space between Taiji Gate and Chengtian Gate. While members of the court and the Imperial household looked on, the old fire was extinguished and a smaller one kindled with a bronze mirror by the Keeper of the Fire. I thought back wistfully to the ritual at Spring Equinox, Chunfen Jieqi, and sighed quietly to myself. Then, I had celebrated the start of yang energies outstripping the yin. But today, as I bowed to my ancestors, I shuddered at the imminent dangers as we approach the Day of Concealment three weeks hence. As the yin ethers arise, one must be increasingly vigilant, for there are always problems when the slowly increasing yin struggles and may become hidden or trapped during the heat of summer. We must be careful during such vulnerable days when the vapours are poisonous and people's spirits are vexed.

I burned incense to my ancestors in the smaller adjoining hall and appeased them with offerings of buns and fish. My father and mother, then Taizong and Gaozong. I asked all of them to have mercy, to protect me from the evils of this season. As I paid my respects, I could not help but feel painfully aware that Wan'er was not present.

I am reminded on this occasion not to indulge in frivolity, that I must refrain from all manner of excess. Even though the injunction to abstain sexually was lifted four small hours ago, at the Hour of the Chicken, I have informed Yizhi and Changzong that they are not to bother me tonight, and to sleep in their own apartment. I can tell that they are restless. Every year at the Summer Solstice, they complain about my abandonment. How they fuss and frown at my insistence that they join me in remaining subdued and suspend their carousing with others!

I must reassure myself. My mind is probably unnecessarily stirred up, fretting over Wan'er's illness. There have been no incidents with the demon souls ever since she returned and I began to wear the Abbess's amulet. Could it be that I finally will be free from their influence?

SHANGGUAN WAN'ER'S APARTMENT
THE INNER PALACE AT TAIJIGONG
NORTH CENTRAL CHANG'AN

The fever has subsided. Wan'er feels her mother's cool, reassuring hand touch her forehead lightly before applying another poultice. The pungent, sharp smell of the medicinal concoction is familiar to Wan'er from her childhood.

"My dear, you mustn't strain yourself! Can't you appoint someone else to take over so that you can rest a few more days?"

"No, Mother, there are some duties only I can do. Her Majesty wouldn't trust anyone else with the dictation of the Palace Diary, for instance. I simply can't stay away another day. You know how serious it was to have missed the Summer Solstice ritual. I must resume my duties tomorrow."

"Daughter, at least make sure you eat well and drink lots of tea, as well as have the servants brew a cleansing soup for you."

"I will, Mother. Thank you. Your medicine has been working far better than the Imperial physician's."

Lady Zhen laughs, glad to be so appreciated. But her expression changes to one of concern. "Wan'er, you seem rather troubled lately, ever since you returned from your errand for Her Majesty outside Taijigong. What is it? Can't you tell me?"

Wan'er furrows her brows and remains silent for quite a while. "Mother, it's just ... about how we, I mean all of us, are haunted by the past and can't entirely rid ourselves of painful legacies."

"We never completely escape, do we?"

"You haven't spoken with me about my grandfather and father all these years. You've told me about how we were spared from death, about your prophetic dream, but not much else. I've had to read the historical records to gain some idea of what happened. But as you and I know, many truths exist outside of those records."

Lady Zhen's face acquires a grave expression. "Why talk about such tragedies, Daughter? There's nothing that will bring them back to us."

"But I want to know."

"What do you want to know? And why?"

"I want to know ... to know ..." Wan'er pauses, suddenly uncertain of what exactly she needs to find out, "what motivated my grandfather to be so opposed to Wu Zhao. Didn't Father talk to you about this at the time? He must have."

Lady Zhen sighs. "Father-in-law did it for the sake of ideals. Beliefs that cost him and my beloved husband their lives. Zhi was innocent; his only crime was that he was the son of the Vice President of the Secretariat." She removes the poultice from Wan'er's forehead, disposes of it in the small ceramic urn outside the main doors, then returns to the bedchamber to pour water over her hands at the basin and wipe them dry.

Returning to Wan'er's side on the bed, she continues. "You ask me why Shangguan Yi opposed Wu Zhao. He believed that Li Zhong, one of Gaozong's sons by a concubine, should succeed him, instead of having Li Hong, Wu Zhao's own son, become the Crown Prince at that time."

"Yes, I know that. But why did he believe that?"

"Your grandfather's sense of the order of the universe and the affairs of men, I would guess. Li Zhong was Gaozong's oldest son. Very Confucian of your grandfather. Daughter, we women have had to watch while men throw themselves into dangerous ventures, ignoring our needs for them to remain safe. But who am I to speak thus? I can't understand it, my dear. And now look, my dream-come-true. One who measures out the weight of the world—you are the Imperial Secretary to the woman who killed our men. Is there some kind of unseen balance that must occur across the span of history? But I hold no bitterness, as you can tell. It is my selfish concern, however, that you not risk your life. You remind me too much of your grandfather. It's that burning ambition of yours. Wan'er, are you going to risk your life the way Shangguan Yi did? Is that why you are asking me these questions?"

Wan'er doesn't want to answer. Instead, she reaches out for her mother's hand and, taking it in her own, raises it to her cheek.

Xiaoshu 小暑 Jieqi
Slight Heat
Sixth Lunar Month
New Moon

CENTRAL CHANG'AN

The Bronze Urn rests on a three-tiered marble platform. Even from a distance, its presence throbs with promise. Along the perimeter of the stone courtyard runs a corridor, with the main entrance on the south side. From the four corners of the square courtyard rise watchtowers in which sentinels are housed, alert for any kind of mischief. Between the watchtowers, yellow banners flap loudly in the robust summer wind. Behind the Urn stands a wooden hall five bays wide, with all its doors shut. Two guards flank the Urn, arms by their sides, their swords sheathed.

A box within a box within a box, thinks Baoshi of this modest compound set within the fang to the northeast of the Foreign Quarter. Chang'an started as an idea created by someone's mind, before that box became realized as physical reality. He recalls his first day here, when he was confronted with the city's semblance of neatness, but he soon discovered a wealth of chaos thriving within its walls.

Baoshi is dressed today in his own clothes, aware of himself as a walking boy once again. He joins the long line winding its way toward the Bronze Urn. Who knows how long this will take? He told Sita not to wait and urged her to return to the tea shop. From the conversations around him, he learns that some have come quite a distance, from places as far away as the lush hilly areas in Sichuan, the river deltas of Lingnan, or the dusty outposts in the Gansu corridor. "Only the Son of Heaven can help us," a man behind him whispers. The others around him complain that the Urn should be open more times in the year, for how else can the common person reach the Emperor?

As Baoshi draws closer to the gate, he notices the official who sits at a table to the left of the large red doors—he's asking questions of everyone who wishes to approach the Urn. When Baoshi's turn comes, the semi-bald official with the wispy trails of grey hair behind his ears regards him coldly.

"What's the purpose of your visit?" He leans back on his creaky chair.

"I'm here to present an appeal on behalf of a village at the foot of Mount Hua. The villagers have recently suffered a calamity and wish to appeal to the Emperor for assistance."

The man groans. "Everyone who comes here has suffered a calamity of one sort or another. What business is it of yours, this village's predicament? Are you from the village?" His voice is loud, his throat hoarse. Baoshi studies the man's face carefully. A most unhealthy redness to his skin. Probably his liver, excess yang.

"No, but I'm from Mount Hua, and I know of the villagers' plight. That's why they asked me to present this letter on their behalf." He feels inside his satchel, the other hemp pouch of herbs still there. He pulls out the letter, folded in two.

"Do you know which mouth of the Bronze Urn this letter should be dropped into?" asks the official.

Baoshi is puzzled and shakes his head. He had no idea there was more than one part to the Urn.

The official takes the letter reluctantly. His oily hands grasp the piece of parchment roughly, crumpling it at the edges. He begins to read aloud from the letter, so that those standing near him can hear. "The villagers appeal to the goodness and mercy of the Son of Heaven, she who has graced the throne with her wisdom. O Great and Venerable Ruler, hear the cries of your most miserable and humble servants who have suffered countless sorrows. We ask of Your Majesty that she extend her thoughtfulness to our predicament ..."

He can't finish the letter. The man is laughing so much that tears stream down his cheeks. The people in the line regard the man with drawn and serious faces, unable to see the humour of the situation. When his laughing subsides, he hurriedly wipes his tears away and rises from his chair.

"All right, all right. You can go ahead. When you reach the Urn, ask for the Fifth Young Master. He's the important man from Taijigong overseeing the activities today. He'll have to decide for you which section of the Urn is appropriate for this letter."

The line now moves quickly. The Bronze Urn, with phoenix bodies encircling the vessel, looms directly ahead of him.

"The birds look like they're about to fly away at any moment," the woman ahead of him observes.

When Baoshi's turn arrives, he steps onto the top platform and studies the vessel, which stands an imposing two heads taller than him, and is the width of three or even four people combined. The guards stand stiffly at attention, never seeming to respond to anyone in the line. The Urn has three openings shaped like the mouths of fishes, level with his face. Above one opening is engraved "Exposure of corrupt officials." Above the second opening is "Suggestions for government policy." The last mouth bears the phrase "Injustices against the populace."

"I see why there's a dilemma for many people!" Baoshi exclaims. He crosses his arms in front of his chest, deep in deliberation. Which one of the three openings should he drop the letter into? He looks at the letter, reading it for perhaps the hundredth time since Qian and Ke entrusted it to him. There's no explicit mention of corrupt officials in the letter, but he remembers Qian and Ke's expressions when they spoke of their need to be protected from the anger of the local officials. They didn't say what sacrifices they would have to make if Nü Huang doesn't intervene on their behalf, but he sensed that they would wish to do their utmost to avoid that possibility. He turns his attention to the second opening, "Suggestions for government policy." The issue of having to pay tribute grain regardless of what natural calamities have befallen the villagers surely reflects the rigidity of government policy, unjust since it doesn't allow for compassionate treatment of people made helpless against their will. The villagers continue to live under such dreadful and vulnerable conditions. Why hadn't the local officials sent any help to the villagers to build up the crumbling embankment at the Yellow River? It's also unfair that they would have to endure more suffering after losses they had no control over. These are clearly injustices against the populace. Perhaps the third mouth is the most appropriate, then. While spending time nursing the injured, he heard what Qian had to say about the history of their village. The elders remembered a time about twenty years ago when Nü Huang lowered taxes and released grain from storage when there were famines and droughts. If she could do it then, the elders argued, she has the capacity and the heart to respond yet again in the same way.

With a sense of renewed hope for the villagers, Baoshi positions the letter outside the fish mouth for "Injustices against the populace" and is about to release it when he remembers that he's supposed to speak to some dignitary from the palace. He calls out to one of the guards. "Please, I was asked to consult the man from Taijigong."

Without saying anything, the guard marches up to the wooden hall behind the Urn. In a few moments, the middle two doors are flung open. A man strides out, following the guard. He's dressed in a pristine white hu fu outfit trimmed with a lower hem of gold thread. His riding boots are cut from pony hide. A column of silver moons flash down the outside of each boot.

"Hurry up now, you mustn't slow down the procession. What is it you want?" The sides of his mouth are turned down in annoyance. Should he have stayed at the palace today? He regrets coming out to the city in this heat. So many inconveniences supervising the activities at the Bronze Urn.

Zhang Yizhi stops abruptly, gasping with delight when he finally takes a good look at Baoshi. Who is this Heaven-sent beauty? *Why,* he thinks, bedazzled, *this boy's beauty exceeds my brother's.*

"What brings you here?" inquires Yizhi, making sure his tone is authoritative yet friendly.

Baoshi bows deeply at the waist. "I am Baoshi, a walking boy. I'm here to deposit a letter on behalf of some villagers."

"Show me, my boy." Yizhi stretches out his hand and, opening the letter, scans it quickly with an impassive expression.

"It appears you have a very serious matter to present to the Emperor. Are you aware of the implications of submitting this letter?"

"If you would pardon my humble ignorance ..." Baoshi bows again, his heart fluttering with anxiety. Why is the man suddenly sounding harsh?

"You are accusing Nü Huang of neglect! Of not caring enough for her people! That she could abandon them to such misery! How dare you?" Yizhi flings the letter down on the ground. Baoshi bends down to pick it up and, in that instant, Yizhi spits at Baoshi's face.

Baoshi grimaces and wipes his face with a sleeve, recoiling from Yizhi. No one, not even his father, has ever spat on him.

"What do you have to say for yourself? You've gotten yourself into a dangerous predicament, haven't you? Risking the ire of our Beloved Emperor!" *I have him at my mercy now,* Yizhi thinks with glee.

"If I could gain an audience with Her Majesty, I shall be most honoured to explain myself and this letter fully. I mean no disrespect."

"Well … what a smart young man you are!" Yizhi is taken with Baoshi's bold request. What if he could persuade Nü Huang to see this fellow for just a few moments? Surely the boy will have to repay him with any favours that he, Fifth Young Master, deems suitable. Even if there isn't an opportunity for an audience with her, he can always convince the boy that he'll deliver the letter to her. What a delicious plan. He angles his body slightly away from Baoshi and smiles slyly to himself as an idea occurs to him. He hurries back into the wooden hall and emerges with another guard.

"Arrest this boy!"

The people in the line are now murmuring disconcertedly, concerned at what is occurring. Someone shouts, "What's going on?"

Yizhi yells back to the crowd. "Look here! I'm merely making sure this boy is aware of the seriousness of the matter. Pay heed to what I'm saying. You can't make any false claims or submissions. That just won't be tolerated. It's my job to make sure no one takes Nü Huang's generosity lightly."

A voice from the crowd booms out, "No more lies! No more Lai Juanchen and his henchmen. Good riddance. And may you and your brother get what you deserve!"

"Who said that?" Yizhi is most annoyed. How dare some commoner compare him and his brother to that evil man Lai in the same breath!

Yizhi strides proudly ahead while Baoshi is being pushed along by the guard. The gatekeeper rises from his rickety chair, taken aback by this ruckus, as Yizhi, the guard, and Baoshi pass by.

As he settles into the carriage, Yizhi is pleased at his newfound sense of accomplishment. He's slightly nervous about the brave venture, yet thrilled by his ingenious plan. Baoshi is forced by the guard to sit facing Yizhi, his hands tied together in front of him with leather straps. The guard shuts the door and proceeds to drive the carriage toward Taijigong. Yizhi smiles wistfully. Time to return to the finer distractions—music, plum wine, and a few lighthearted games of Go with the palace ladies. And now there's this special catch from his hunt. He must plan his next steps carefully. He would like to be seen as doing something outstanding, something that even his brother has never dared to attempt. If he discloses his ruse to Nü Huang, will that impress her? Yes, most certainly. Nü Huang has turned a blind eye to the smuggling of outsiders into Taijigong for their midnight parties. So what's wrong with one more guest? This would be an exceptional gesture, though, since no one so beautiful has been found before.

The carriage races east along the large central lane, then turns north, heading toward Taijigong. After a long silence, Baoshi speaks up. "Surely you don't do this to everyone who seeks help from Nü Huang? Why should you bind my hands? Have you forgotten that I had requested to see Nü Huang?"

Yizhi squints at Baoshi with unconcealed skepticism. This boy is too clever for his own good. He snarls, "Do you take me for a fool? I have to put you under arrest. This will be the only way I can convince the guards that I'm bringing you into Taijigong under official business. You can't possibly understand. Besides, it's not as if you're entering the Inner Palace as part of any retinue that Nü Huang may sanction occasionally for big parties and banquets. I mean—would the guards believe you're a singing boy or a courtesan, dressed in those old clothes? Of course not!"

Baoshi blinks quickly, several times in succession. Something terribly odd is happening to his captor's face. Sharp slivers of light are erupting from the man's head, especially around his eyes and forehead. *What is it?* He ponders for a while before the answer comes to him. *This is a person in great distress and rage, a person whose body shen has become poisoned. Or is it that other shen, his spirit?* That too, Baoshi decides. He retreats inward to protect himself, falling back into silence. Since he left Mount Hua, at various times he has felt confused, fatigued, impatient, even worried about Harelip, but today, fear for his own safety grips him.

He tries to soothe himself with a silent recitation of the parable of the water in the pond. In his mind, he hears Harelip recite the parable in that unmistakable voice of his. It was easy to learn texts from Harelip because his voice was so reassuring and warm, inviting him to enjoy the sounds of words and the textures of ideas. His voice imparted a belief that everything was possible, as long as one possessed the curiosity and the motivation to go in search. An ache of longing for Harelip spreads painfully through Baoshi down to his toes. He looks down at the floor of the carriage and ponders his situation.

This stranger is full of hate. Whom does he hate? His mind is not stable, his behaviours dramatic and excessive. His situation is like that of the water that has been diverted into the fields. He has leaked out practically all his precious essence. From his few words to me, I know that his mind is caught up in fanciful ideas. That may be the reason for the sharp glints around his face.

Baoshi looks out of the window of the carriage, averting Yizhi's attempts to engage his gaze. As the grand south gate of Taijigong looms ahead, he remembers once again how lost he had felt that first day in Chang'an. He takes a slow, deep breath and reminds himself to stay calm.

MOUNT HUA

Harelip stands outside, watching clouds trail over the crescent moon. A chill runs down his spine even though it isn't the least bit cold tonight. He has been plagued by worries about Baoshi. *Has he found Ardhanari yet?* It's been nearly seven weeks since the boy left. He learned about Baoshi's delay at the village, but that was only four or five days. *What can be the matter?*

He holds an image of Baoshi in his mind, but the image keeps wavering and fading. He tries to send him words of encouragement, as if he were talking to him. Short, smooth phrases replete with patience and regard. He imagines that Baoshi is also talking to him. But it doesn't work; his mind is wracked with worry.

He is seized with another spasm of coughing. His arms encircle his body as he bends over and feels the waves of pain pass through him. The coughing subsides before too long. He breathes a sigh of relief. He can't be imagining that he has felt better ever since drinking the new brews—fewer traces of blood. He is grateful to Qian, who spent many hours searching for those special roots over the past few weeks. But the improvement is only slight and not permanent, he reminds himself. He must make sure he has as much rest as possible. He must stretch his breath out, as if rationing it carefully. *But what if Baoshi doesn't return soon enough?*

He winces at the question as he reaches for the jade pendant. When his fingers can't find it but land instead on his chest, he's startled by his absentminded gesture.

The Forbidden Apartment
The Inner Palace at Taijigong
North Central Chang'an

Baoshi sits upright on the floor in the centre of an empty room. Not a single piece of furniture except the chamber pot covered up in a corner. He was left alone for much of yesterday and last night, with only a modest flask of water. He decided to sit in meditation and attempt to still his mind, which has been racing with anxieties. He hears the sound of the key in the padlock and opens his eyes to see his kidnapper approaching him with a confident swagger.

"Phew! Have you stunk up this vacant apartment so quickly already?" Yizhi stands over Baoshi, gloating. "How's my lovely doing? Suffering from my absence? Are you now sufficiently miserable and desperate for my kindness?"

Once again, Baoshi studies Yizhi's face. The broken shards of light around the man's face now pierce his neck. *How painful,* thinks Baoshi as he winces. He would rather not talk to this man. Yet what choice does he have? What would Harelip advise him to do? Would his Master have agreed with the way he dealt with the conflict at the Bronze Urn? He might have successfully fought off the two guards, but that would have meant that the villagers' letter stood no chance of ever reaching Nü Huang. That would have been terrible. Besides, fighting might have ultimately compromised the safety and welfare of his jogappa friends, if trouble at the Bronze Urn led the guards to search them out. He turns his attention to his kidnapper.

"When may I see Her Majesty?"

"I'll keep my word, I assure you. But first, you must indulge me."

Yizhi squats down and leans toward the boy, placing a hand on Baoshi's chest. With a quick movement, Baoshi lifts his arm to push Yizhi's hand away and with two fingers of his other hand, strikes at Yizhi's neck.

Yizhi gags, his throat seizing up from the sharp strike. Losing his balance, he reels backward and falls on the floor, stirring up a cloud of dust. He coughs and chokes, rubbing at his neck.

"You insolent ingrate!" Yizhi sneers as he gets back on his feet and spits down at Baoshi's head. But Baoshi shifts his body sideways and the gob misses, landing on the floor. *What kind of a man is this,* Baoshi wonders, *who uses his saliva like a weapon?*

"What is it you want from me in exchange for an audience with Her Majesty?" asks Baoshi, now rising up to his feet, his fists ready at his sides.

"You know what I want," Yizhi purrs. This beauty is an unreasonable, wild creature after all. The throb of pain at his throat is duller now, but his bowels are feeling rather distressed. He considers summoning the guard to beat this wretched boy up. Then it dawns on him that it might be possible that the boy would defeat the guard, which might mean worse things for him. Exposure of his foolish actions, disgrace in Taijigong, and who knows what else, perhaps rejection from Nü Huang. His guts churn even more. He throws a furtive glance at the chamber pot. He will have to try a different approach.

"You ... you're not going to hurt me, are you? I only want to be friends with you," Yizhi says, making his voice sound as entreating as he can.

"I'll strike back only to protect myself. Treat me with honour and I won't hurt you." Suddenly his belly emits a flurry of loud gurgling sounds.

"Oh, you must be starving! All right, I realize my behaviours have been far from courteous. I've neglected to be hospitable. More than a whole day without food! How inconsiderate of me. Can't have you see Nü Huang on an empty stomach, and such a noisy one at that!" As Yizhi heads toward the door, he turns back abruptly. "You realize that if I agree to your request, you'll have to repay me according to my stipulations?"

"We haven't come to such an agreement. It was you who offered to take me to the Emperor, yet you had me bound. Now you keep me locked up in this room. For you to extricate something from me under such circumstances is most unfair." Baoshi keeps his voice low, but his body quakes with a ferocity he never thought he was capable of. He could lash out at Yizhi now, strike him down and render him unconscious, even kill him. He could do it without the guard outside hearing anything. But he restrains himself.

"Guard," Yizhi pauses at the entrance, as he opens the door, "take the chamber pot away, will you?" He steals another glance at Baoshi. *Too delectable to be ignored. I must be shrewd with this one.*

Late at night, when Baoshi's belly is growling even more miserably from hunger, the guard brings him a generous tray of food and leaves a lantern lit in the far corner. Baoshi draws his knees close to his body, trying to ignore his hunger pangs. After staring at the tray for quite a while, he finally lifts the lid of a clay pot and his mouth waters from inhaling the fragrance of its contents: slices of fish, barely cooked greens, large scallops that look firm and juicy. He tentatively tries a spoonful of broth. Delicious. A side dish of prawns fried in rock salt, with a sauce on the side. He dips a finger into the sauce and licks. Not too sweet but with just the right hint of tanginess. A big bowl of rice cooked so perfectly Baoshi is able to savour the textures of each grain as he stuffs his mouth with food. He doesn't bother to peel the shell off the prawns. Everything tastes wonderful.

He eats every morsel on the tray and straightens up to burp three times, very loudly and deliberately. He smiles. What a relief to eat. Sweat drips onto the tray from his face and neck. He's thirsty. The food was good but a bit too salty. He sniffs at the flask on the tray. Smells a bit like the wine Harelip drinks. He pours a little into the cup, downs it in one gulp, and makes a face at the slightly bitter aftertaste. Then he walks up to the window quietly and peers over the rice paper border. The guard slouches against the wall outside. He's rather chubby, a big belly on him. Like the bun seller in the market. But this guard's face is much smoother, almost as smooth as his own. *I wonder if I can get some water to drink. This wine is too strong for me.* He walks back to the middle of the room and plops down, dizzy all of a sudden. The room begins to move around him. The lantern's shape wavers and dissolves quickly.

Nü Huang's Apartment
The Inner Palace at Taijigong
North Central Chang'an

Ah Pu places a calming hand on Nü Huang's shaking hand as the two ladies-in-waiting, Silver and Windchime, remove the white face powder. Once again, Ah Pu notes, the two women stifle their giggles.

Nü Huang has the sensation that her skin is being suffocated under all that whiteness. It's always worse during the height of summer. At the end of the day, she feels relieved when the white mask is removed. She reaches out for the amulet on the cabinet top, trying to keep her face still while the women are working on it. Feeling along the surface, her hands can't find the amulet. Didn't she leave it here this morning as she always does? She stares hard into the mirror as the women fuss over her hair.

"Hurry up! What's the problem with removing the hairpins?" complains Nü Huang, who can't believe that her maids are having a difficult time with such a simple task.

"Your Majesty, I'm having the hardest time with my fingers. How stiff they are suddenly!" exclaims Silver. Windchime looks at her in surprise and nods in agreement. "So am I!"

Nü Huang looks into the mirror again and catches a glimpse of two shadowy figures behind the maids, moving slightly.

"Who's there? Who?" she calls out, her voice strained.

The figures show themselves, with the all too familiar dishevelled hair in front of their bloodied faces, but this time they raise their wrists to expose the stumps where their hands had been removed. Then they disappear as rapidly as they appeared.

"You're intent on tormenting me, aren't you? Well, you shall not succeed, I tell you!" hisses Nü Huang into the mirror. Her hands tremble dramatically as she lifts them up to cover the mirror.

"What is it, Your Majesty?" asks Ah Pu.

"Nothing, nothing. Soon ..." Nü Huang's voice drifts off.

THE FORBIDDEN APARTMENT
THE INNER PALACE AT TAIJIGONG
NORTH CENTRAL CHANG'AN

When Yizhi sneaks into the room at dawn, he's delighted to find Baoshi slumped unconscious on the floor. He sends the guard away and closes the doors. He tiptoes toward Baoshi and leans his ear close to the boy's face. The barest trace of breathing. The drug has worked wonderfully. Any more of that poison, and it would have permanently debilitated him. Now the boy can't lift even a finger to defend himself. Yizhi imagines all the lovely moments he will savour. It's been a long time. But it was different back then. *This will awaken old memories,* the uncomfortable thought occurs to him, and he brushes it away immediately. *Don't be silly,* he scolds himself.

He's going to initiate this boy the way he was initiated a long time ago. He reminds himself yet again, *That was quite different.* He should be grateful to his uncle for having helped him. Taught him how to use his body to gain favour. Power, that's what his bedroom skills have enabled him to attain. With this thought, his jade member stirs, a pleasurable tension.

He squats next to Baoshi and strokes the nape of his neck, shivering with anticipation. How fragile innocence is! Didn't his uncle thrill at the privilege of deflowering him? Never before today has he been lucky enough to be in the same position. His eyes moisten with tears. Isn't he fortunate? His fingers trace the slope of Baoshi's neck down to the throat, flitting down to his chest. *Dangerous boy, now you can't hurt me.* He discovers the jade pendant and fingers it with curiosity. He sneers, considers the pendant crude. His tears fall easily, spotting Baoshi's jacket as well as the floor. So many tears that he begins to feel confused. Isn't he happy? Or could he be sad? He chides himself, *Fool, what are you doing?* He blows his nose and turns his attention back to his task. He strokes Baoshi's cold lips with a single excited finger. *What a luscious one.* Now completely helpless against him. He brings his own face close to Baoshi's and his breath quickens, his excitement increasing. He would like to take those lips in with his own desiring mouth, but not now. Some inexplicable hesitation causes him to pull away from that temptation. As he loosens the sash of Baoshi's jacket, his right cheek starts to twitch, as if a centipede were dragging its tiny legs across his skin. His guts churn with the old discomforts. "Cursed problem," he swears under his breath.

With awkward fumbling, he removes the jacket, struggling with Baoshi's heavy, limp arms. When Baoshi moans, the effects of the drug starting to wear off, Yizhi panics, thinking he had better hurry up. He rips Baoshi's tunic apart.

He can't believe what he sees there, the swelling left breast so markedly larger than the right. Yizhi gasps with shock. *Freak,* he thinks, *a freak of nature.* He wants to examine the rest of Baoshi's body. With trembling hands, he begins to untie the sash around Baoshi's pants. He is slipping the pants off Baoshi's legs when a chill descends on his shoulders.

What are you doing? A voice echoes in his head. Or could it be coming from outside of him? Faint yet distinctly female. A burning itchiness eats through the back of his head. He turns to look. A piercing scream escapes from his throat, and his legs buckle under him as he struggles up. He throws opens the door, letting out another penetrating scream.

"Fifth Young Master! Traipsing around so early in the morning?" exclaims Wan'er.

Yizhi, shaking still from fright, stares at Wan'er blankly. He stammers, "Horrible, horrible! Something ugly back there." He waves a hand behind him as he lifts the other sleeve to cover his mouth, and breaks down into sobs, gasping for air.

"What is it? Tell me!"

"A woman. Headless. Another woman in the corner, crouched down. At the forbidden apartment," he sputters out. He's sure they will finish off that boy. He's lucky he escaped. He shows Wan'er the back of his neck. "Look here, she dug her fingers into me."

"I don't see anything. What were you doing there?"

Yizhi, still sobbing, doesn't answer. He avoids Wan'er's stare and rushes off. Wan'er hurries toward the forbidden apartment, her heart thumping loudly, her mind filled with all kinds of questions. What has Yizhi done that prompted the demon souls to appear?

Wan'er hesitates at the Elegant Willow Pavilion. She should dispatch a messenger to Nü Huang first. Or look for a guard to accompany her. But by that time, it may be too late. She must go see for herself. She clasps her hands together in a gesture of resolve, then crosses over to the other side of the pond.

Striding down the musty hallway, Wan'er tries to calm down by telling herself that, in their long history as demon souls, these women have plagued Nü Huang, but that has been the extent of their harmfulness. To her knowledge, they have not troubled anyone else. Until now. For some mysterious reason, they've shown themselves to Yizhi.

The doors to the forbidden apartment are wide open. She slows down as she nears the entrance. Inside, a body is slumped on the floor, his clothes in disarray. He's stirring and moans as if in pain. She glances around the room. No one else in there. When she flips the body over, she gasps with shock. Despite the short fuzz of hair on his head, she instantly recognizes the face. The sweet boy she met in the market weeks ago! What is he doing in Taijigong? His eyes are half open. She spies the tray of empty bowls and the flask of wine. She shakes him by the shoulders and he grimaces, a deep frown furrowing his forehead, unable to fully come to. She realizes he's been drugged.

His tunic is torn. She notices his left breast, exposed. She quickly covers him up, drawing the jacket over him and retying his pants. How odd—she had been convinced that he was a boy. Yet he's not a girl the way most are. With some effort, she drags his body up and he leans on her, mumbling incoherently. His eyes dart about while his eyelids remain half-closed. As she's helping him out of the room, he manages to mutter, "The letter," pointing back at his satchel. She leans him against the door and fetches it, slinging it across her body.

What is she to do with him? She decides to take him to her mother's apartment. As she's guiding him down the corridor, she catches sight of a gardener bent down near the pond's edge, weeding around the clumps of bamboo, his back to them. He doesn't seem to hear them, continuing at his task as they move past him. Something about the figure seems familiar, but she can't quite place him. She's drenched in sweat by the time she stumbles into her mother's apartment and calls for help.

Mogao Caves near Dunhuang

Arun shouts out a clear warning from his vantage point at the top of the cliff. "A sandstorm approaching fast!" Old Gecko and Ardhanari are balanced on the outer scaffolding, while Ram, Alopen, and the two apprentices are inside the new cave one level below, working on the mural of Guanyin. As the storm gains in momentum toward the cliff, its turbulence escalates into a high-pitched whine. Old Gecko and Ardhanari untie the kerchiefs around their necks and wrap them over their noses and mouths. The sand tumbles down over the top of the cliff face in a rapid swirl. Arun scurries down and, along with the other two, heads toward the cave where the others are.

Ram rushes forward as Old Gecko and Ardhanari stumble through the mouth of the cave. "Where's Arun?"

Ardhanari clears his eyes of sand and is about to go out again when he is pushed to the ground.

"No! Father, no!" Ram's protest doesn't have the slightest effect on Old Gecko, whose silhouette fades behind the veil of sand.

Old Gecko can't see Arun for a long time. He clambers up to the second level and, holding tightly onto the top horizontal pole, moves slowly, his body struggling against the force of the storm. He finally makes out Arun's vague outline, arms barely holding onto a pole that has broken off while his legs dangle in mid-air. Arun sways back and forth, trying to reach the intact scaffolding. Old Gecko draws near enough to stretch out his arm. When Arun grabs it, Old Gecko shouts, "Swing over!" With phenomenal strength, Old Gecko pulls Arun over until he reaches Old Gecko's side moments before the broken pole is whisked away by the sandstorm.

They both collapse to the ground when they reach the inside of the cave. Arun's breathing is laboured, and he cries out in gratitude and distress. He looks at Old Gecko, whose arm hangs, detached from the shoulder. Old Gecko says nothing, his eyes shut tightly and his face caught in a deep grimace of pain. Alopen lifts Old Gecko up into his arms and carries him farther into the cave.

The sand is accumulating fast at the mouth of the cave. If nothing is done soon, they'll be completely sealed off. Ardhanari rushes to the niche at the back of the cavern, summoning the two apprentices to help him. He leaves Sakyamuni Buddha on his lotus throne but decides to rip the remaining six from their bases. Together, the three men drag the sculptures, some with barely any facial features, to the entrance. They form a barricade with two rows of statues.

Alopen grabs Old Gecko's arm and resets the bone before the old man has any time to think about it. Old Gecko lets out an immense yelp that echoes through the antechamber, and his body relaxes into a faint. The men sit stunned in the quickly diminishing light. Ardhanari takes off his kerchief and wipes his uncle's face. He strokes the old man's forehead and begins to sing in a gentle, coaxing whisper a few lines from his grandmother's favourite song.

> While you still have a voice,
> Should you not chant the name of Krishna?
> In happiness or distress,
> Should you not chant his name?
> To cast off the influence of troubled stars,
> Should you not chant for Krishna?

"What should we do now?" asks Ram.

Old Gecko moans as he comes to. "That really hurt, Alopen. I'm sure you enjoyed doing that."

"True, boss. I actually enjoyed helping you. How could one not be impressed by your courage?"

"If you hadn't come for me when you did, Father, I don't know what would have happened to me," Arun says, still shaken.

"You would have fallen, my son. Fallen from the sky, like an apsara robbed of its powers." Old Gecko groans. "An old man like me should have quit doing this work a long time ago. Look where it's gotten me."

"Father ..." Arun sobs, terrified. He buries his hands into the folds of his antariya. "You're going to die, aren't you?"

"None of that gibberish. It's only my arm. Don't jump to conclusions." He looks at the entrance, studying Ardhanari's barricade for a very long time.

"Nephew, a brilliant idea. Later, when you reassemble and repair them, the statues will glow with their extraordinary courage. These bodhisattvas have truly intervened on our behalf. They have saved us."

Alopen quips, "We paint murals and make sculptures, and they come back to assist us? Sometimes, you have the strangest ideas, boss."

Old Gecko closes his eyes and sighs. "Is this not home enough for you, Ardhanari? Do you really have to go back to the city?"

"Uncle, I belong in Chang'an. Neither Khotan nor here is my home anymore. You know that."

Old Gecko snorts in disapproval. In all these months of working with Ardhanari, he still has no idea what his nephew really is about, his likes and dislikes. He has learned, though, that Ardhanari doesn't like to do what everyone else is supposed to be doing. It seems to Old Gecko that Ardhanari spends a lot of time living in his imagination.

One of the apprentices has gathered some twigs and strikes flints to make a small fire, but Ram stops him, saying, "No, we have to conserve the air. Who knows how much longer we'll be here."

Ardhanari touches Old Gecko's leg lightly. "Uncle, I returned to these caves because you wrote to me—the only time I've received a letter from you since I decided to remain in Chang'an. Can you imagine my shock when I heard from you? What was I to think? You made it sound as if you were close to death!"

"No one's motives are simple." Old Gecko opens his eyes. "Your mother and father entrusted you and Meru to me. Meru was married off soon after your parents' deaths, so she was easily taken care of. I had plans that you would be under my apprenticeship, but instead, you took off all those years ago and didn't return. Do you know that I never felt at ease with you leading a life of mystery in Chang'an? Why didn't you return? It took a great deal of effort from me, and no small amount of swallowing my pride, to locate you through people who travelled to the city. And finally you came, but only after my letter. Do you have any idea how difficult it was for me to be the one who broke the silence?"

"Uncle, I was shocked but happy to have heard from you!" Ardhanari's voice cracks with emotion. *What does it matter,* he thinks, *even if Uncle wrote the letter because of pressure from the Cui family?* He senses a hint of genuine tenderness in the old man.

"It wasn't as if I completely lied, Nephew. One never knows how long one is allowed to live, especially at my age."

"How long do you think this sandstorm will last?" asks Alopen, interrupting.

Old Gecko answers, "Hard to tell. Sometimes, it has lasted a mere fraction of a small hour. Other times, a lot longer."

"And how long could that be? Or am I asking yet another stupid question?" questions Alopen.

Old Gecko laughs. "You're all doing a fine job distracting me from my pain."

Appearances have been deceiving, Ardhanari realizes. In the darkness, talking with his uncle, he begins to shed his former view of Old Gecko as a prickly soul, disdainful of others. Ardhanari wishes that a purifying stream of water could rush through his body to cleanse him of sadness. He resumes singing. His voice resounds in the hollow space while, outside, the storm continues to howl.

Nü Huang's Study
The Inner Palace at Taijigong
North Central Chang'an

"Your Majesty, I must apologize for being late. I had to tend to an emergency. I was on my way here for our appointment when I encountered Fifth Young Master in a state of utmost distress. He told me the cause of his upset and then ran off before I could ask him more questions." Nü Huang registers her surprise by raising one eyebrow and waits for Wan'er to continue. "He smuggled someone into Taijigong and kept him in the forbidden apartment in the east wing. As a consequence, Fifth Young Master met the ire of the demon souls. I encountered him on my way here, and he told me that he saw a woman with no head and another crouching in the forbidden apartment. I went to the apartment to investigate and discovered a young man semi-conscious from having been drugged."

"He has disturbed the demon souls? Kept an outsider in the forbidden apartment? That means he removed the lock and entered the room. The idiot!" The muscles in Nü Huang's jaw twitch in annoyance. "Where is this person now?"

"He is recovering in my quarters. His name is Baoshi."

Nü Huang's face loses its usual tough demeanour, exposing her panic. She whacks her sandalwood fan hard against the leg of her throne chair. "Great offence! He has disturbed them in their territory, and they are enraged. And just two days away from the Day of Concealment. A travesty!"

"When I reached the apartment, the doors were wide open. I found the young man sprawled on the floor, but I saw nothing else. I searched his leather satchel and found a letter addressed to you from a village at the foot of Mount Hua. They have suffered a flood disaster, and the letter calls for your merciful intervention. I am deducing that this person must have gone to the Bronze Urn two days ago when it was Fifth Young Master's turn to supervise. I don't know the full story yet, since the young man is still recovering."

"Bring him to me when he has recovered. I will question him myself." With a flick of her wrist, she opens the fan and beats the air near her face furiously.

Eavesdropping outside the study, Yizhi overhears what Wan'er says. He hides himself when Wan'er exits, heading east. He must seize this opportunity to tell his story to Her Majesty quickly before anyone defames him.

He enters the study and flings himself onto the floor at Nü Huang's feet, crying out, "Your Majesty, I have something of utmost urgency to report to you!"

"You! How dare you intrude into the forbidden apartment? Now look what has happened! An utter disaster!" Her voice is hoarse with annoyance.

"Your Majesty, did the Imperial Secretary tell you why I smuggled him in? Of course not, because I didn't tell her. You see, there's something very special about this boy," he lets his voice caress that last word suggestively.

"Oh, is that so?" Nü Huang calms down, sufficiently intrigued.

"The truth is, he's not just a boy. He's ... he's a freak of nature. Some strange, exotic creature. Priceless find! His left breast is like a woman's, while his right breast is nothing special to speak of. And I was about to check the rest of his body when the demon souls ..." He pauses, shuddering with the recollection of the horrible sight.

"A freak?"

"You know, like some creature from *The Classic of Mountains and Seas*."

"Fascinating." Nü Huang taps her closed fan quietly against the edge of the table, considering what Yizhi has said.

LADY ZHEN'S APARTMENT
THE INNER PALACE AT TAIJIGONG
NORTH CENTRAL CHANG'AN

Baoshi recuperates on the daybed in the study, drinking a foul-tasting medicinal brew.

"Feeling better? What a fortunate thing you had those herbs in your satchel. Saved me from the fuss of getting medicine from the Imperial physician. I could see that those herbs are more suitable for dealing with poisons from snakes and insects, but the brew works well enough to purge the poison from your body. I'm sure you'll recover completely."

"My head hurts terribly. Who was that who saved me?"

"My daughter."

"Oh?" Baoshi tries to recall her face. He was barely able to stand up and his eyes couldn't focus very well, yet she had looked familiar for some reason.

Wisteria enters with a tray of food. A bowl of steamed rice and some fish cooked with ginger and green onions.

Lady Zhen encourages Baoshi. "Eat. The food will help you to recover strength."

The sight of food, unfortunately, makes him feel queasy. The smell of steamed rice is pleasant enough, but the fish smells too strong. He takes some tentative bites of the fish with scoops of rice.

"You're fortunate. What if my daughter hadn't found you? The poison might have worked a more lingering effect." Lady Zhen sighs.

Later in the day, Wan'er arrives at her mother's apartment to discover Baoshi reading some scrolls left on the rosewood trunk. He's sitting up, dressed in a silk gown, while his tunic is draped over the changing screen, already carefully mended by Wisteria. He looks up and blinks several times as he puzzles over the scar on Wan'er's forehead. Why is this woman so familiar? He stares hard at the scar and at Wan'er, intrigued by this inexplicable feeling of being drawn to her. *It would be impudent of me to ask about the scar.* He tries to get up to bow.

"No need for that, please."

"I am most grateful."

"I must apologize for looking in your satchel. I needed to check what your letter said before I reported to Nü Huang. She wants to see you."

He beams at her. "How wonderful!"

She stares at him, stunned by his warmth. An image of his left breast flashes through her mind. What a queer young man. Or woman. She realizes that he doesn't remember her from the market.

"You've forgotten who I am, Baoshi. I was that stranger who spoke to you and the old man at the Western Market."

He hadn't spoken to any woman. Old man, why yes, the one with the sign. When he realizes what Wan'er is saying, his mouth drops open, and his eyes widen with incredulity. *So that's why the face looks familiar.* But that handsome stranger had an easy boldness that he hasn't sensed so far in this woman dressed in the stunning green robe. His face reddens in a blush. *How embarrassing.* He looks down at the poems he has been reading, wanting to direct her attention elsewhere. "These are elegant. I like them. They're such vivid descriptions of the palace and the city."

She grimaces at Baoshi, pained by the reminder. They are poems by her grandfather. What can she possibly say? Nothing will change the past.

Baoshi smiles shyly at Wan'er, adjusting himself to seeing the stranger now in this different disguise. She's rather subdued, compared to how she was in the market, he observes.

Nü Huang's Study
The Inner Palace at Taijigong
North Central Chang'an

"Tell me, what brought you to the Bronze Urn?" Nü Huang asks Baoshi.

"Your Majesty, I wanted to submit a letter to you at the Urn, and there was this man who told me I was very presumptuous in my desire to do that. I heard someone refer to him as Zhang Yizhi. So I asked to be given an audience with you to defend myself to you directly, and he agreed. He had me tied up and brought me here. He said he would make sure I obtained an audience with you if I let him touch me, but I refused. Some time after that, a tray of delicious food was brought to me. I felt very dizzy after drinking the wine. I shouldn't have been so careless. The next thing I knew, he was back in the room, trying to remove my clothing." At this point, Baoshi's throat tenses up. He's sure of that memory. Submerged, as if under water, as if in a bad dream, his limbs heavy and useless. He couldn't defend himself. The memory of his temporary incapacitation upsets him.

"Then he suddenly screamed, said something—I don't recall what—and he ran off. The next thing I remember is that this kind woman here came to my rescue." He finishes his account, careful to respect Lady Shangguan's request not to mention her mother. He produces the letter, warm from being tucked inside his jacket. His hands shake with nervousness as he presents the letter to Nü Huang.

Nü Huang purses her lips. *Merely a boy,* she observes. *What a nice complexion.*

"Please, Your Majesty, you are the only hope for these villagers."

"My eyes are not very good. Wan'er, please read this to me."

After Wan'er has finished reading the letter aloud, Nü Huang resumes her questioning. "Where have you come from? This village?"

"I ... I ... lived on Mount Hua with my Master. Your Majesty, will you help the villagers? They cannot pay their tribute grain. The officials will descend upon them at the end of the summer."

"For the trouble that Fifth Young Master has put you through, and for your earnest willingness to help these villagers, I shall grant you this request, Baoshi, but I have a stipulation—that you make no mention to anyone of the kidnapping. Not a word."

Baoshi nods his head in solemn agreement. "I promise, Your Majesty."

Nü Huang addresses Wan'er. "Draft a decree on behalf of this village and any surrounding ones affected by the disaster. Have a messenger send my decree to the local officials. Order them to desist from requesting any tribute grain this year and, in addition, to provide sufficient grain to allow the affected villages to survive the winter."

Wan'er bows, nursing her private delight for Baoshi, and leaves the study with the letter.

"Thank you, Your Majesty." Baoshi touches his head to the ground.

Nü Huang fixes her gaze back on Baoshi. "Precious Stone, isn't it?"

"Yes, Your Majesty."

"A precious stone, a rare gem. How appropriate a name." She pauses, watching for any reaction from Baoshi. Nothing she can discern. "Now I want to ask you about a secret Fifth Young Master shared with me moments earlier. Yizhi told me you have a peculiar body. Tell me more about this."

Baoshi frowns in consternation as his heart pounds faster. Had the man seen more than what was beneath his tunic? He can't be sure. He coaxes himself to bring his thoughts back to the present challenge facing him. He brings his hands together in front of his chest in a show of reverence and lowers his eyes before speaking. "Your Majesty, our cosmic universe is indeed filled with myriad wonders. I am honoured that my body serves as a tribute to our universe's infinite range of miracles. My Master calls it my Two-in-Oneness."

"Who is this Master you speak of?"

Baoshi's heart now pounds at a furious pace. If he says Harelip's name, Nü Huang will know who it is, surely. But that was so long ago. Still, it would be too risky to speak his name.

"What is the matter, boy? Speak up, answer me."

"His name is ... Master. That is what I call him."

"You mean to tell me he doesn't have a name? Impossible!"

Baoshi, still on his knees, quakes with fear. He cannot stall any longer. He looks past Nü Huang at the wall behind. Two long silk scrolls hang side by side. He swiftly scans the couplets written on them. "His name is Shen Dao, Your Majesty." The concocted name spills out of his mouth. He bows so that his head touches the ground once again.

"What an auspicious name. Come over here." She gestures to Baoshi to sit on the footstool in front of her throne.

Up close, Baoshi can smell her breath. It's a striking, foul smell. Not as straightforward as the bun seller's but more complex in its origin. He studies the colour of her skin. An unearthly and eerie grey. *Poison,* he ascertains, *much more potent than the kind I was given. There's a lot inside, enough to show up like this on her skin and breath. That means it has been accumulating in her body for years.*

"A name is everything. It is absolutely crucial, is it not?" Saying this, she thinks of how she had taken such pains to come up with just the right character to brand Wan'er with.

"That is most true, Your Majesty. My Master also taught me that the power of a name comes from the meaning we impart to it."

"Well spoken, walking boy. Now—about your Two-in-Oneness. I can see how useful you could be to me. There could be a variety of possibilities." It occurs to her that an examination of his body by the Imperial physician would be the beginning of some fruitful venture. Perhaps this might eventually lead to some refinement of the immortality elixir? And, if necessary, he might need to sacrifice his life.

"We could learn a lot from your body, Baoshi." She regards him with a sombre expression on her face.

Baoshi shudders, a chill passing over him. He realizes from Nü Huang's tone of voice that his life is in danger.

"Your Majesty, I request an opportunity to speak at some length, in order to respond adequately to your interest in my Two-in-Oneness."

"Permission granted."

"Your Majesty, let me begin by reciting a poem:

The dharma
Hinges on two truths:

Personal experiences of the world
And truths which are sublime.
Without knowing how they differ,
You will not know the deep;
Without relying on conventions,
You cannot discover the sublime;
Without intuiting the sublime,
You will not experience freedom."

Nü Huang smiles, impressed. He has picked a subtle, philosophical poem. A lovely recitation, in a convincing, heartfelt tone of voice. Her hands are seized by a flurry of tremors, and she grasps one with the other as they rest in her lap.

Baoshi takes a deep breath and continues. "Your Majesty appreciates that our world is filled with the most subtle energies, the most sublime truths. My Master taught me to cultivate both yang and yin energies in my body shen as well as my spirit shen. One is to be flexible and alert, open to movement in whatever direction is most suitable at any given moment. For only where there is movement is there any life to speak of.

"When I set out on this pilgrimage, out into the unknown world, I was confronted with the challenge at every moment to ask myself, where do I direct my steps? I no longer had the luxury of relying on my Master's presence and guidance. Ultimately, I cannot escape having to answer the question of what to do with my life."

"You mean your destiny?" Nü Huang interjects.

"Yes, Your Majesty. Destiny. My Master said I have a choice. Since I am an acolyte, I have yet to decide whether to take vows to become a monk. I always have wondered, does destiny mean that we cannot choose at all, or does destiny mean that we choose and fashion our paths? I cannot say

I know the pure and absolute answer that will suffice for all beings, Your Majesty. All I know is, I'm following what draws me."

With that last pronouncement, Baoshi completes his speech and takes a moment to reflect on what he has said.

Nü Huang feels a tremor spread from her hands to the rest of her body. A memory returns. Herself at thirteen sui, entering through the gates of Taijigong for the very first time. In her young, ambitious heart, she had nursed that confidence in the fortune teller's prophecy that she would become the ruler of this vast empire. The pulsating truth of that memory grips her even now. How that reassurance had emboldened her, helped her push past fears in her darkest moments! She grasps her fan from the table and clenches it tightly with both hands as her body quakes.

When the tremor subsides, she sighs audibly and speaks. "You have acquired much wisdom at such a young age." She reaches down to grasp the boy's shoulder. "I suppose I was hoping your body could be the key, my last hope, in achieving immortality."

Nü Huang turns her head to look into the courtyard. She's not looking at what's there but allows her mind to drift farther west, past the walls of Taijigong, until she sees Taizong's tomb loom in her imagination. She would prefer to be buried with him instead of Gaozong. There are already many things she will have no control over. Such is the vast, unrelenting mechanism of convention.

"Does your Master want to achieve immortality?"

"No, Your Majesty."

"Oh? And why not?"

"He's too busy meditating, teaching me, fetching water, cooking."

"How miraculously simple." *What a startling attitude,* Nü Huang thinks. Naïveté can be ridiculous. *Is that all there is for some people? Simple folk.* How different from her! She feels her chest clenched by an odd discomfort. Hermits and their disciples, living on sacred mountains. What if Yuan the fortune teller hadn't come to her father's house and given them that prophecy about her? What if she hadn't seduced Gaozong when he was Crown Prince? What if, what if? Her mind drifts away into recollections of her life. Surely everything has been predestined. She was meant to live the life she has had. Recluses like Baoshi and his Master live in an entirely different sphere of existence. Her world and theirs are most definitely irreconcilable.

"Do you want to return to your Master?" she asks.

"Yes, I do." He nods nervously.

Nü Huang lifts the bowl of pastries from the table and offers it. "Eat!"

Baoshi gingerly picks up a pastry and pops it instantly into his mouth. The lotus seed paste is sweet and smooth against his tongue.

"Do you know anything about exorcism? Did your Master teach you any tricks to get rid of evil, virulent influences like demon souls?"

"No, Your Majesty. I know nothing about exorcism."

"Surely these demon souls of my enemies can spare me now that I am old and approaching death?"

Baoshi closes his eyes to concentrate, trying to intuit the motivation behind this unanswerable question. Water appears in one image after another. The flood that overwhelmed the villagers. The pond at which the monk Nagarjuna stood before he received the divine inspiration to write his poems. The single tear that slowly trickled from Sita's eye. When he opens his eyes, he sees, in contrast, evidence of Nü Huang's drought. Vital energies are being drained out of her. Her dry and pale complexion, the lack of liveliness in her eyes. The demon souls may be distressing her, but it's the poison in her body that's the greatest cause of this ill health—yet how could he say this to her?

He replies, "Your Majesty, I hope you will find peace soon."

Nü Huang is startled by Baoshi's earnest and genuine concern. She nods approvingly. "All right, Baoshi, I will ponder all that you have shared with me. I have been impressed sufficiently by your answers to spare you."

Baoshi moves from the stool to the floor and bows deeply, touching his forehead to the ground.

"Good. You demonstrate true gratitude and respect. I like that."

Nü Huang is amused by his look of curiosity, shamelessly directed at her. When was the last time anyone was curious about her without any hint of self-interest?

Wan'er returns with the drafted decree. She unrolls the scroll and shows Nü Huang what she has written and reads it aloud to her and Baoshi. He catches a glimpse of the calligraphy. A steady hand. Very tidy and easy to read, unlike Harelip's wild scrawl. Nü Huang nods with approval as Wan'er reads. Then she affixes the Imperial seal on the decree with trembling hands.

"Go now, you are free to leave. I shall dispatch an official from our court to expedite this decree."

Wan'er now speaks up. "Your Majesty, may I arrange for Baoshi to be escorted safely out of Taijigong to where he wishes to go?"

"Yes, of course. Take care of it, Wan'er. You have acted decisively in this matter. I thank you."

Back at her apartment, Wan'er touches Baoshi lightly on both shoulders. He can scarcely bear to look directly into her eyes. He feels warmth permeate his whole body yet again.

"Baoshi, you've been remarkably fortunate in gaining an audience with Her Majesty. Tell me one thing before we part. Be honest with me. Is it true that you weren't hurt by Yizhi?"

"Oh, Lady Shangguan, the brew has purged all the badness." Baoshi smiles reassuringly at her.

Wan'er sighs with relief, feeling tenderness come over her for this most unusual person. She was right that first time she met him. Now that she knows about the secrets in his body, she wonders if that strange inheritance makes him more forgiving toward others.

"Honourable Lady," Baoshi begins, quite unsure how to tell her, "I have something urgent I must tell you."

"Oh?"

"Her Majesty, she is ... How shall I put it? She's not very well, is she?" He glances down at the ground in a show of hesitation.

Wan'er looks askance at Baoshi and coaxes him. "Tell me."

"There's poison in Nü Huang, something quite extraordinary embedded in her organs. It's been there for years. It's too late, I'm afraid. That was why I didn't tell her. Did I do the right thing?"

Wan'er drops her arms to her sides and feels a sudden chill come over her. Baoshi has no reason to lie about this, but how could he possibly know? Yet she's inclined to believe him. She has known that Nü Huang is unwell, known that she could die soon, but to hear about poisoning is truly a shock. With Imperial tasters checking every morsel before it passes into Nü Huang's mouth, who could have poisoned her?

"Thank you for telling me, Baoshi."

"I'm very sorry, Lady Shangguan." He bows deeply at the waist. He hopes she won't hold it against him for breaking the bad news to her.

"I'll summon a carriage for you. Where must you go to now? Return to Mount Hua?"

"I still have to wait for someone in Chang'an. He should be back any day now."

"Where shall I ask the carriage driver to take you?"

"The Foreign Quarter."

At a side exit next to the Moon Splendour Gate, while the driver waits with the carriage, Baoshi struggles with what to say. There are insufficient words to describe the feelings welling up in him. She has saved his life, and by doing that, she also has helped the villagers. If only she could run away with him. He blurts out, "Can't you come with me, Lady Shangguan? I mean, take the journey to the Foreign Quarter?"

Wan'er sees the look of longing in Baoshi's eyes and she understands finally. She takes his hand in hers. His hand is so pleasantly warm compared to her chilled one! She is touched to be the object of this walking boy's adoration. Some part of her wishes that she too could leave, but it is Ling whom she longs to escape to.

"No, Baoshi. I can never leave Taijigong of my own volition."

"But you were in the market! With that most stunning horse of yours."

"I was on a mission for Nü Huang."

"Oh, I see." He pouts, feeling rather unhappy. What if he never sees her again?

"Quickly now, don't delay," she encourages him, seeing his dejected expression.

"I'm grateful for meeting you, Honourable Lady. I'll ... I'll never forget you." With that farewell, Baoshi makes one final bow before entering the carriage.

Wan'er walks back to her own apartment, increasingly upset at Baoshi's remarks. Nü Huang poisoned. A suspicion about how the poisoning has happened gnaws at her. There can be no other explanation—it has to be the Jin Dan elixir. Or could it be the Eternal Spring potion? But Nü Huang has been drinking that potion once a month for at least twenty years now. No, her health only started to deteriorate after she started on the Jin Dan elixir. Have the alchemists done this deliberately? Once inside her study, she sits at her writing table, cupping her head in her hands. She must pause to think about this. Could it be that no one has deliberately set out to poison her? That all this alchemy is horribly misdirected? What can she do now? No, it's too late. The Luoyang version of the elixir was ingested two years ago. And Nü Huang told her she has finished the last bit of the Jin Dan.

There is no quick or definite way to prove poisoning. Even in the unlikely event that Nü Huang believes her, what would the sovereign do in a fit of rage? She would execute the alchemists, possibly even have Ling killed. This last possibility causes her to shiver with fear.

She must remain strong, for she can't afford to collapse under the strain. She wants to survive the uncertainty of the times and maintain her role as Imperial Secretary into the next reign. She must focus on ensuring that her plan comes to pass. Anything else is beyond her reach.

Sweet Dew Hall
The Inner Palace at Taijigong
North Central Chang'an

Nü Huang stares at the vial of Eternal Spring potion. She grabs it, downs the vial of potion in one gulp, and gags. "Bah, it always tastes so foul!"

She flings the vial down on the side table and turns her attention to the woman kneeling in front of her. The current Abbess is nothing like her predecessor. Quite the puzzle. No obvious signs of the power of her position at Da Fa Temple. The Abbess Ling is quiet and restrained, dressed in a plain brown robe. Her predecessor liked to talk about herself a lot when she appeared at Gaozong's court, like a chirpy songbird that won't stop. But this Abbess maintains a serene posture ten paces away from the throne in the Sweet Dew Hall.

"Your Majesty," begins Ling, "please describe to me what you have experienced and all else you may have heard of." Her voice resounds through the hall as clear as a bell, her tone even and composed.

Nü Huang informs the Abbess of her own experiences and also repeats what Wan'er had told her about Yizhi's encounters with the demon souls in the forbidden apartment.

After listening to Nü Huang's report, Ling responds without pause. "According to my reckoning, tomorrow is the Day of Concealment in the ancient Zhou Dynasty, a day rife with the potent influence of gu 蠱 poisonous vapours in the heat of summer. As you know, Your Majesty, great distress and evil can occur during this period of the year. Disruptions within the forbidden apartment have increased the demon souls' ire. May I have permission to seek audience with the Imperial Secretary to question her further?"

"Of course. A guard will escort you to her study. She is expecting you. Stay as long as you need at Taijigong."

"Thank you. Your Majesty, I also must request the assistance of two brave guards tomorrow evening, at the Hour of the Dog, equipped with spears, arrows, and ropes."

"This will be done as you wish. Two of my most skilled guards."

"They don't have to be the most skilled, but they must be brave and have steady nerves."

"I see. Courage before skill. I will command the head eunuch to select the guards according to your needs. What do you plan to do, Abbess?"

"I am not sure yet, Your Majesty. I will go to the forbidden apartment myself tonight and see what I discover. I must draw the demon souls out, experience their ways, before I know what needs to be done."

Indeed, reflects Nü Huang, *this Abbess makes no grand promises, unlike her predecessor.* And it doesn't appear that she'll rely on any fixed rituals. No blaring trumpets and drums? No incense? No chanting? Unbelievable. All departures from convention. Astonishing and a touch worrisome. Yet the Abbess has acquired a tremendous reputation for being an effective exorcist. The previous fangxiang shi she hired forty years ago relied on ostentatious ceremonies. Perhaps she need not worry then. *Perhaps this one will succeed.*

Shangguan Wan'er's Study
The Inner Palace at Taijigong
North Central Chang'an

"It's my turn to visit you in your domain," whispers Ling into Wan'er's ear.

Shivers course down Wan'er's spine, all the way to her toes. She doesn't turn to face Ling but waits, breathless. She can't believe it. Her face flushes with immense pleasure.

The cricket calls, familiar yet wholly unexpected, so she thinks she must be dreaming. She laughs with delight and turns around to see Ling holding out the gourd container, once again between their warm bodies.

Ling sets the container down on Wan'er's desk. "I'm going to the forbidden apartment by myself tonight, and I've told Nü Huang I need two guards to accompany me tomorrow night."

"I want to go with you."

"I must go alone tonight. Tomorrow, you may watch from a distance, but you mustn't let whatever you see compel you to interfere. No matter what. Things may not be exactly as they appear at any moment."

"All right."

"I want you to tell me of other incidents that you might know about, that you didn't disclose to Nü Huang. Have there been others?"

Wan'er looks askance at Ling. How can a mind be so direct yet entertain devious possibilities? She tells Ling about her mother's experiences, and about the night she ventured to the storage room and the forbidden apartment.

"A stooped figure, you say? Could you tell whether it was a man or a woman?"

"A man. I don't know why I would say that. Possibly an old man, definitely someone with a limp, but one who could still move rather swiftly."

"Of course this complicates the situation. Could the person be an accomplice to these demon souls?"

Wan'er shakes her head. "Who could it be? Someone who wants to wreak revenge on Her Majesty? There are too many who could be suspect, but most of them are outside the Inner Palace. They couldn't be wandering alone at night here. The guards would never let outsiders pass through." Saying this, Wan'er knows this isn't entirely true. There are enemies residing in the Outer Palace who move with ease into the Inner Palace.

Ling paces back and forth in Wan'er's study, fingers of both hands interlocked in front of her belly. "This mysterious figure may not be interested in revenge toward Nü Huang. Just because we suspect that the zhesi jisheng require some kind of revenge or vindication doesn't mean this accomplice shares the demon souls' motives. In which case, what would his motive be? Is it sympathy or guilt? His own feelings rendered him vulnerable. This is always the case with humans susceptible to the influence of demon souls."

"Impossible."

"You're thinking only of the present, my love. Think, some forty years ago, around the time Empress Wang and the Pure Concubine were imprisoned in the apartment. Who was implicated or had some role in their deaths? Or did those women have lovers or allies who are still alive? Family members?"

"All gone or banished," replies Wan'er, to Ling's last two questions. She has no idea what to say to the first question. The story about the women's deaths comes back to her, the way Nü Huang told it. Such a good storyteller Nü Huang is. Wan'er can still hear the sovereign's voice as she dictated that entry in the Palace Diary.

"Wu Zhao would have relied on eunuch guards to carry out her orders. What happened to them?"

Wan'er marvels at the way Ling's mind sifts through the possibilities. She's seduced by the nun's quirky turns of logic. She walks to the window and looks out. The modest courtyard contains little—a dwarf pine in a green glazed urn, a maple tree, and some small shrubs.

Her eyes rest on the dwarf pine. It may be twisted and low to the ground, but she can see that it has weathered much and remains strong. She thinks about that night she ventured out to the forbidden apartment. There was that odd moment with the small willow near the forbidden apartment. The willow swayed by mysterious forces. The eerie sensation as she walked down that corridor. The extinguished lantern. Then the stooped figure. What had Ling said before? Where there are secrets, there are mysteries?

Days later, she had fallen ill with fever. Then early yesterday morning, she had bumped into Yizhi and rushed into the forbidden apartment and discovered Baoshi.

She wheels around to face Ling the moment an image returns to her. "There was a gardener bent over at the pond's edge. He looked like he was weeding. I passed by him yesterday morning when I helped Baoshi out of the apartment."

"It's probably not a coincidence. The gardener, the stooped figure— one and the same. Watching out for the demon souls, present when there are intrusions in the forbidden area. He has some reason to remain close by. Why should he be sympathetic to their presence?"

Wan'er's forehead wrinkles as she ponders what Ling has said. Sansi would consider the nun's deductions quite ridiculous. He has always believed that his aunt is suffering from the products of her fanciful imagination. "We have a need to frighten ourselves," he said to her. She herself is torn, not sure what to believe. Had she imagined how she felt that night when she went to the forbidden apartment? It couldn't have been her fear playing tricks on her. She hadn't imagined the sight of the stooped figure hobbling away from her. And Yizhi was truly terrified yesterday, enough to abandon his attempts to molest Baoshi.

"I'll leave you now, my dear. I need to prepare myself for this evening," Ling announces, touching Wan'er's arm lightly before walking toward the doors.

"Wait, there's something I want to ask you."

"Yes?" Ling turns back to face Wan'er.

"I have some concern about the Jin Dan elixir. It's merely a suspicion, I will admit, but is it possible that there's something amiss about it, that it could have some harmful effects?"

"I've wondered the same myself."

"You have? Why would you continue to have the alchemists at the temple if you doubted their abilities?"

"I didn't say I doubted their abilities. Isn't Nü Huang served in many ways by her collaboration with them in the pursuit of immortality?"

"I see what you are saying. But don't you care that she could be harmed by their elixirs and potions?"

"It is not my place to question Nü Huang's wishes, Wan'er. You must know that. I've made room at the temple for the alchemists because it is our sovereign's wish. My own opinion about the worthiness of their pursuits I've left completely unexpressed."

Uttering this, Ling draws Wan'er to her and embraces her firmly. Wan'er responds initially with a flinch, but then relaxes her body, surrendering to Ling's warmth.

Ling steps out into the corridor and follows the guard to the guest apartment, tucking the cricket container inside her robe. Wan'er stares through the lattice window, following Ling down the corridor with her eyes. She's agitated by their conversation about the Jin Dan elixir. But more than that, she worries what her lover's solo visit to the forbidden apartment will yield.

FOREIGN QUARTER
WEST CENTRAL CHANG'AN

Baoshi is mesmerized by the arc of water. Ever since the first time he saw the fountain, he has marvelled at how water is forced to perform like this, day after day, trapped and limited to an unnatural existence. How unlike the streams and waterfalls on Mount Hua.

He's glad to be back in the Foreign Quarter. When he returned to the tea shop two days ago, the jogappas were relieved to see him and of course plied him with questions, but he refused to disclose any details of the kidnapping. He only told them he had gained an audience with Nü Huang, impressing them to no end.

He can't stop thinking of Lady Shangguan. She looked very beautiful in her green gown. He's sure he'll never see her again, or that handsome stranger she once was. Never.

How can someone seem so different from one encounter to the next? In the market, she was radiating warmth, no sense of fear about her. Yet in the Inner Palace her face was overshadowed by severely sombre expressions. She was like the brilliant moon obscured by clouds, especially in Nü Huang's presence.

He nods. Sometimes a person can be shockingly different, depending on the circumstances. The Imperial Secretary is like the chameleon stick insect that disguises itself as bark sometimes but turns dramatically showy at other times. He supposes he understands when he thinks of the stick insect. It's often a matter of survival.

Baoshi remembers the cautionary words Harelip uttered to him moments before their parting. *Liken this journey to your first exploration of the creatures that inhabit the forest areas on this mountain. Appearances don't define character. You'll experience a wilderness of meanings out there in the city. Choose only those interpretations that unfetter your mind.*

A wilderness of meanings. And words are only sounds until we give meaning to them. No, he hasn't forgotten his Master's eloquence. He closes his eyes as his mind returns to the memory of Harelip delivering the very first lesson in the forest. He can summon the sound of that twig being scratched against the earth as Harelip wrote out the characters for sun and moon. The hard brilliance of yang contrasted with the more elusive necessities of yin energies. The skills of fighting or of healing. The skill of manifesting force or the skill of concealment. Does Lady Shangguan know how to fight and defend herself? Or does she know only the yin skills of concealment and nurturance?

He wipes the tears from his face with the edge of his sleeve. He mustn't linger in this sadness. One of the neighbourhood dogs scampers up to him. She wags her tail and sniffs with great interest, catching the new scents. Baoshi peers inside the tea shop. The copper pot is on Lakshmi's head once again as she performs her dance routine.

The Storage Room and Forbidden Apartment
The Inner Palace at Taijigong
North Central Chang'an

When the Hour of the Pig approaches, Ling makes her way to the corridor leading up to the east wing, where the storage room and forbidden apartment are. Looking down that long tunnel of darkness, she sighs at the onset of a memory. The first time she spoke to Wan'er in her study at the Da Fa Temple, she had felt that same sensation rise up in her. Now she knows even better what she must do. *The Great Way Is the Ultimate Weapon.* It was Abbess Si who had arranged for that sign to be erected at the entrance of the temple in loving memory of Qilan, the one who had recognized Ling's unusual gifts. Losing Qilan was a rupture that caused her to experience life as encompassing more chaos than she had dared imagine.

At first she didn't want to admit that her abilities had deepened following Qilan's death. How did that come about, exactly? A mystery. A secret. How else can she explain the sudden knack since then for finding the places where distressed presences hide out? For knowing how to communicate in her mind with them? Where there are secrets, there are mysteries.

When she's ready, Ling strides down the corridor, entering the dank darkness. She approaches the locked doors of the storage room, repeating in her mind, *The Great Way Is the Ultimate Weapon.* She draws near to the thin gap between the padlocked doors and listens to the silence within. From inside the folds of her plain brown robe she pulls out the gourd vessel, removes the ivory lid, and inverts the container. The cricket falls out and scampers in through the crack between the doors.

Very quickly, the cricket starts to call out, his pitch altering as he moves across the room. His sounds tonight are dissimilar to the ones he usually makes—much slower and at a lower frequency. Ling closes her eyes and listens. When it's time, she takes a few long breaths and grasps the padlock in both hands, crushing it open.

The doors swing open, pushed apart by a sudden wind. The stench of rotting plums assaults Ling's nostrils. She closes her hand over her mouth and nose and scans the room.

Two dark forms loom across from her. They are huge round vats resembling the one at the Repository at Da Fa Temple. But these are empty, and the smell, a lingering illusion from long ago.

Once again, the cricket's sounds fluctuate, prompting Ling to ask in her mind, *Where are you?*

Here.

Where?

The voice guides Ling to one of the vats. She looks in. What she sees causes her to convulse violently, shot through with a horror that won't let go. The energy courses through Ling, all the sensations and emotions of the women dying slowly in the vats.

Ling collapses to the floor, still gripped by convulsions. Only when her hand closes around the talisman necklace is she able to feel the waves of sensation fade away, rippling out further and further away until she's finally left alone, breathing hard, her body drained by the momentary possession.

I see, Ling whispers through her mind. *You have much you won't forgive.* She takes a few deep breaths, pausing to collect her thoughts. *You're still in the depths of misery. Don't you wish to be released?*

After a considerable silence, the answer arrives. *Perhaps.*

She retrieves the cricket and returns him to the safety of his container, then steps out and closes the doors of the storage room. She's about to proceed to the forbidden apartment when she senses someone in the shadows behind her.

"Who's there?"

The figure tries to escape, but Ling is swiftly upon him and wraps her arms tightly around his neck. He sputters and chokes, begs her to release her grip.

She drags him out into the open area next to the pond. Although the moon is not quite half-full, Ling can see that the old man's eyes are filled with terror. His face is gaunt, his cheekbones prominent, and his collarbone protrudes from his emaciated frame underneath the tattered shirt.

"Who are you?"

The man sobs one moment and laughs the next. "What a long time it has been, what a long time! Who are you that you've been sly enough to accomplish this tonight? No one has ever been able to approach them as much as you have. I may be breathing, but I've been without vitality all these years. Who am I? I don't know. But once I was the head of the eunuch guards. The one who had to carry out Nü Huang's commands to torture the old Empress Wang and the concubine Xiao. How could I have suspected I would become enslaved by my own deeds? Nü Huang saw how I had been changed by that night of torturing them. She didn't like that, not at all. I lost my position as the head guard, but I've remained here in the Inner Palace, working as a lowly gardener."

"What is your relationship to the demon souls?"

"They've held me captive all this time, compelling me to serve their wishes."

"They couldn't have done this if there hadn't been some vulnerability in you," declares Ling.

"I've changed. How did it happen? I had been only too glad to fuel my anger at their arrogant ways while the women were alive. They were unreasonably mean toward the eunuchs! I had begun torturing them with the greatest relish. Such a release. If only it had been that simple. Toward the end of their demise, something very odd started to happen—I began to feel the stinging sensations of their bodies in the fermenting wine. I wasn't just feeling sympathy. My body throbbed and stung as if I had become fused with them. I tried to resist such feelings, but I failed in the end. After they expired, I had to look after the final decapitations and dispose of their dismembered bodies. I couldn't sleep for many nights. Guilt gnawed at me. I began to recall their dying screams, the call for vengeance. I became obsessed with those moments—how their rage kept them hanging on, particularly the concubine Xiao.

"It was uncanny. It seemed to me that as their life force was departing, they became even more menacing. After the women's deaths, their souls were transformed horrifically. The women, the demon souls—they aren't identical, you know. I had hated the women, but I was entranced by the ugliness of the demon souls. I couldn't stay away. Night after night, I came to the boarded-up storage room and the forbidden apartment. The demon souls appeared to me, showing me how they could put their bodies together and then pull them apart. They laughed at me, and I shivered with dread. The more time I spent with them, the more I felt life drain out of me toward them.

"It was as if my imagination became progressively detached from the rest of my mind, drifting far away from me, lost to my own will. No, I didn't change. It was they who changed me."

Ling studies the ghastly shell of a man for more clues. That's right, he hadn't understood the power of hatred to chain him to the very targets of his hate. There was simply no answer that would be adequate for such a man after all these years.

Mogao Caves near Dunhuang

Ardhanari stands at the apex of a sand dune and looks out at Crescent Lake below. He feels grateful for this moment of beauty. Tomorrow, at the break of dawn, he'll be going to Dunhuang with Alopen to spend a few days there while Alopen's merchant friend stocks up on supplies before they travel with the caravan to Chang'an.

The lake is placid, its surface unruffled by any breeze. How serene the atmosphere in contrast to the sandstorm. The water in the lake must have been extremely choppy then. But now the moon is reflected calmly on the crescent-shaped body of water.

He glances back at the Mogao Caves behind him. Old Gecko isn't happy that he's leaving so soon. He told his uncle that he isn't going to rush completion of these sculptures, and he promised he'll return to the caves next spring to finish the work. *That will have to do,* thinks Ardhanari as he crosses his arms in front of his chest. *I'll let my uncle worry about how to explain the delay to the Cui family.*

His mind turns once more to the pilgrim monks who first discovered the cliff face. They believed that their prayers for water were answered when they found the stream. *Gratitude endures,* thinks Ardhanari as his eyes take in the rows of caves in the moonlight. The numbers of havens have multiplied over hundreds of years. From a distance, the caves resemble the burrows of animals, entrances to other worlds.

He breathes in the cool night air, glad for the quiet moments alone, and gazes out once again at the magnificence of the dunes. Here is a fickle, eternally changing landscape, a contrast to what lies within the caves, where art has been created to last. There's no telling how many murals and sculptures will remain preserved into the far-flung future, what visitors in five hundred or even a thousand years' time will think when they make their pilgrimages to view the caves.

But that's his vanity speaking. Surely the first pilgrim monks didn't carve out those havens for posterity's sake. They were grateful for water, grateful for life's replenishments. That must have been why they created those niches in the cliff. Why should anyone forget the fearful trials she or he has encountered? Without the memory of such suffering, the pilgrims most certainly would forget the rare, gentle touch of grace that kept them from obliteration.

He came to the caves in search of a lost vitality. What has he learned? That he had forgotten about the beauty of imperfections. Over the years, especially since he felt his body declining into the vagaries of middle age, he has been increasingly caught up in expressing beauty through idealized features and smooth contours.

He has changed his mind. Or perhaps it has been changed for him. What had happened to his treasured works during the sandstorm taught him an invaluable lesson. When he returns next spring to help his uncle and cousins, he will not cover up all the damage to the bodhisattva statues. Some flaws he'll want to preserve, not conceal. He recalls how Old Gecko had put it—that the sculptures had saved them. Not merely that they had acted as a physical barricade. Those figures bear the marks of the sandstorm. Marvelling at their maimed condition when he first surveyed the damage, the answer to his dilemma came to him. Now he wants to make sculptures that, rather than distance people from harsh realities, inspire them to be transformed by chaotic onslaughts.

One bodhisattva bears a slight gash on his lip. Not at all like Harelip's mouth, but it was enough to evoke old feelings. Why are such losses so endearingly poignant? He watches the dunes gently shift in front of him under the moonlight. As the wind moves across the surface, the sands begin to sing a soft lilting lullaby. He stretches out on his side and props his head up on one arm, fighting off that heavy pull of sleep. He must stay awake a little longer to enjoy this final night at the Mogao Caves.

THE DAY OF CONCEALMENT
ELEGANT WILLOW PAVILION
THE INNER PALACE AT TAIJIGONG
NORTH CENTRAL CHANG'AN

The half moon is a burnished orange. Wan'er waits under the roof of the fan-shaped Elegant Willow Pavilion. Ling hasn't told her anything about her visit to the forbidden apartment last night, but she doesn't mind. She suspects that Ling doesn't want to frighten or burden her with details. *This is the safest place to be,* she decides.

When the drums sound out the Hour of the Dog, Ling appears at the far end of the pond, dressed in her yellow ritual robe and a star hat. She wears a large mirror pendant, which catches the reflection of the torches carried by the two guards. One guard holds a spear while the other has a bow slung across his torso and a quiver of arrows on his back. Each guard also wears a bundle of rope suspended from a large belt. Wan'er watches as Ling pauses in front of the willow tree, speaking with the two eunuchs.

One of the guards drives the torch into the earth next to the willow. Wan'er looks into the pond, entranced by the dancing reflection of the torch flame on the water surface. The willow, completely still at first, stirs slightly.

Ling senses the movement and looks up at the willow's unusual branches. She begins to sway her body in imitation, exaggerating until the tree's movements also amplify in tandem. Even from this distance, Wan'er can see that Ling's face has altered from its usual demeanour. She's shocked to witness the movement of the willow, even more pronounced than that first time. She's equally startled to see Ling respond so dramatically. *What is going to happen next?* She crosses her arms in front of her, feeling chilled despite the hot summer night.

The cicadas and the frogs call out, constant in their rhythms. Ling makes a quick turn and advances down the corridor. Now Wan'er can't see what's happening. She'll have to content herself with waiting here. Ling was right—she's too afraid and is relieved to be watching from this distance.

Ling flies down the corridor with a rapid flurry of footsteps, the guards lagging behind her. Her gown flaps loudly. She comes to a sudden halt at the doors of the forbidden apartment.

I've come for you, she thought-whispers to the demon souls. She grabs the padlock and dismantles it the way she had done the previous night with the other lock, squeezing hard until it cracks open.

The guards stand on either side of her. Ling angles her pendant so that she uses the reflected light to scan the walls, the ceiling, and finally the floor.

Ling's voice rings out forcefully. "Where are you? Show me who you are. Do not hide!"

The mirror, on a second pass around the room, illuminates one demon soul crouching in the corner, her face entirely hidden by a mass of hair. Small cries trickle out of her in a childlike, stuttering whine. She's draped in torn clothes, soiled with darkened, caked blood.

"You've suffered needlessly and caused suffering for far too long."

The demon soul's plaintive whine echoes in the room and beyond with its boundless misery. An infectious grief convulses Ling and the two guards, leading them to feel immense despair and bitterness.

"Where is your companion?" asks Ling, fighting against the powerful emotions coursing through her, trying to hold true to her own sense of reality. The demon soul retracts her body farther into the corner, not answering.

The crouching demon soul finally stops her whining and raises her head. With the stumps at the end of her arms, she pushes her hair away. Her eyes gaze out with frozen terror, her whole face wrenched by pain.

You can leave now. It's time. Offering these words with her mind, Ling senses relief emanating from the demon soul.

Finally, someone who's neither angry nor afraid. The voice enters directly into Ling's mind.

Go, you can go, Ling coaxes her further.

"Shall I shoot her down?" asks the guard, unaware that he's interrupting a private conversation.

"Do nothing of the sort. Retract your bow." Ling answers without taking her eyes off the crouching presence.

See how they're afraid of us?

Their fear is irrelevant, answers Ling.

What about our enemy's fear? The one who harmed us?

You need not suffer anymore.

Then have the guard pierce my being once again, one last time.

Ling pauses to contemplate the demon soul's request. Is this a ruse to counter the departure?

It is a gesture I ask for because it is familiar, answers the demon soul, hearing Ling's mind.

She understands now. She gives the guard the command to take aim as she keeps the spot of light trained on the demon soul. When the arrow penetrates the demon's heart, a sharp, terrifying scream reaches them from outside. Ling keeps her gaze on the demon soul, who makes a moaning sound that grows softer and softer until it can be barely heard. The spectre dissolves before their eyes, leaving an arrow lying in the corner. The veil of embittered grief lifts from Ling and the two guards.

The nun turns around without delay and runs back in the direction of the pond, the guards following at her heels. The scream is coming from the willow, which thrashes about violently, its fine green leaves making a loud flurry of sounds. As they near it, the scream stops abruptly and the willow ceases to thrash. A black liquid trickles out from its trunk, like blood leaking from a wound. Accompanying its flow onto the stone paving is a low hissing sound. Ling and the guards listen until the only sounds that remain are the rhythmic calls of cicadas and bullfrogs from the pond.

"Fetch an axe and cut the tree open," orders Ling, breathing heavily from the exertion. The tips of her fingers and the crown of her head crackle with fiery sparks.

Wan'er leans against the balustrade of the pavilion, her whole body trembling with fear. She cannot bear it. She gazes down at the pond instead. In the reflection, she watches one guard tie ropes around the trunk, while the other chops. It doesn't take long before the slim trunk is tugged loose from the remaining stump. Ling bends forward and directs her mirror pendant at the wound. She looks into the mirror. When she sees what's hidden inside the tree, she sighs with relief and releases her pendant, letting herself gaze directly into the hollowed stump.

There is a fourth figure in the reflection on the pond. Wan'er looks up in alarm. It's the stooped figure. He hobbles forward, heading toward the others, whose backs are turned to him. Wan'er shouts out a warning, "Watch out! Behind you!"

Ling whips around and the old man is startled. She grabs him by his shoulders and insists, "You must come and look."

Wan'er rushes out of the pavilion and heads toward Ling. Everyone draws close to the stump to stare down at the coiled remains of a snake. A stinking odour rises up to them, so horrible that Wan'er begins to retch.

"Put the torches to the tree," Ling orders the guards.

They stand off at a safe distance as the tree stump burns. The guards chop up the rest of the tree trunk and branches, throwing them into the fire. In the crackle of the blaze, Wan'er stares at Ling's face, which moves through different expressions, from hard and implacable to surprising tenderness.

The stooped figure stands watching too, with tears streaming down his face. He crosses his hands tightly over his chest, crying.

"It's over. You're free now," Ling tells him.

Wan'er remains silent. So many questions plague her, yet she feels subdued and tired. Can it be true that Ling has successfully exorcised those demon souls? She squints at the burning willow crackling in the engulfing flames and shields her eyes from the heat.

Shangguan Wan'er's Study
The Inner Palace at Taijigong
North Central Chang'an

"My work is finished. I must go soon," Ling tells Wan'er the next day when they meet in Wan'er's study, that wistful smile coming to her lips yet again.

"Leaving already?" Wan'er doesn't try to hide the tone of regret. They haven't had the opportunity to lie together in her private chambers.

"Not immediately. I have a meeting with Her Majesty at the next double hour. I will report to her that I've been successful, but I would like to omit all the details about the gardener. Will you agree to subscribe to my account of the events?"

Wan'er hesitates, weighing the risks. Who will talk? Will Nü Huang bother to summon the guards to question them? Unlikely. She could always make sure they would be happy to keep their mouths shut.

"All right. I won't say anything. I still don't understand why you would want to protect the man. Who is he?"

"He was the head of the guards who tortured the women," answers Ling. "Complicity—there's nothing like it to bind one to a tortured soul."

Wan'er lowers her gaze, feeling uneasy and confused. Ling is surely referring to the old gardener. So why would she think of herself as the complicit one?

Ling notices Wan'er's discomfort and raises a hand to stroke her cheek. She places two fingers lightly on Wan'er's scar and closes her eyes. She remembers the first time she touched the scar and shivered with all the unspoken emotions buried in Wan'er. Fire had burned an indelible consequence into that child and hadn't merely seared her skin but altered her spirit irrevocably. There is never any going back.

She knows about losing innocence. But then, she had someone who saved and restored her. She knew a miraculous and transformative love. Ling sighs, tenderness warming her chest.

"I couldn't recognize you last night. Everything frightened me terribly."

Ling holds Wan'er's hand gently against her lips, speaking into her fingers as she kisses them. "That's what a fangxiang shi is gifted with—the capacity to understand a malevolent influence and to absorb it momentarily. Becoming possessed in order to exorcise. That's probably what you saw in my face as I went through all those moments of possession."

"Possession? But weren't you frightened?"

"No. I'm never frightened. I've been taught how to proceed without fear. There's nothing of that other world that surprises me. Not anymore."

Wan'er feels a strong ache of longing—a mix of admiration and desire. "Was there grief? Or did I imagine it?"

"True, there was grief. But the story behind it is far too long to relate at this time. You have such a fine sensitivity, Wan'er. But you don't entirely trust it, do you?"

Wan'er stifles a gasp as tears come to her eyes. How is Ling able to see her deepest truths? She cups Ling's face in her hands and kisses her with a force fuelled by desperation and hunger, disappearing into the sustained moment as if she were someone else, no longer constrained.

"I can't bear that you're leaving so soon." Wan'er sobs without restraint, surprised by her depth of sorrow.

"Don't forget me, my love," Ling whispers into Wan'er's ear, then gazes at her with a whimsy she thought she had lost long ago.

Foreign Quarter
West Central Chang'an

It seems to Baoshi that he has watched Sita at the water pump for an infinite number of mornings since his arrival in Chang'an. Didn't Sita say that Ardhanari would come back at the end of summer? Two more weeks to Liqiu Jieqi, Start of Autumn—any day now. He wakes up each morning with a keen sense of anticipation that he'll soon meet this mystery friend of Harelip's.

The longer he stays here in the city, the more tired he seems to become. He needs to return to Harelip and the mountain. When he set off from Mount Hua, he thought that his sole purpose was to find Ardhanari and bring him back to Harelip. That seemed difficult enough, and then when the villagers needed him to deliver that letter, he felt as if his burden had been multiplied several times over.

But now that obligation to the village has been fulfilled. It's been less than two weeks since he departed from Taijigong. Nü Huang's messenger must have reached the village by now. He smiles with satisfaction as he imagines the villagers' relief when they heard Nü Huang's decree read aloud by the messenger, and the joy they felt at the gift of grain.

Ever since his return to the Foreign Quarter from Taijigong, he feels as if he has changed, no longer the same boy he was when he first strode through the city, wide-eyed and confused. Why is that? He wrinkles his forehead. He certainly hasn't wavered from his wish to fulfil the intent of his pilgrimage. Indeed, all his experiences so far have deepened his resolve to return to Mount Hua, not merely for his Master's sake but for his own life.

He thinks of his audience with the Female Emperor—Nü Huang was simply interested in his physical body's Two-in-Oneness. She wanted to use his body to serve her quest for immortality, but he had dealt with that by refusing to be caught by such a preoccupation. What a liberating moment it had been for him! He recalled how he had recited Nagarjuna's poem to Nü Huang—that's right, his Two-in-Oneness is really about a vital mix of subtle energies that animates him. *Without intuiting the sublime, you will not experience freedom.*

He has asked himself if he could be happy with the jogappas. Would he like to return to the Foreign Quarter after he brings Ardhanari to see Harelip? He feels a pang of sadness when he realizes his answer. He'll miss them, but he can't imagine leaving his life on Mount Hua for life in the city.

The only looming question, the most urgent one, remains to be answered. He listens to the sound of water rushing out of the pump into the bucket and repeats Ardhanari's name countless times under his breath, as if by this simple act alone he could summon him back sooner.

GARDEN NEAR THE EUNUCH'S QUARTERS
THE INNER PALACE AT TAIJIGONG
NORTH CENTRAL CHANG'AN

The old eunuch moves through the shadows undetected. He limps toward the back of the garden, where a stone shrine marks the beginning of a path through a thicket of black bamboo. He walks along the slim path through the grove and emerges at the other end, at an intimate corner next to the wall, graced with two stools and a table. He doesn't need a lantern to find his way, having come here so often. But this time, he has decided to do more than sit quietly on a stool, passing time aimlessly. He has come here for a specific purpose.

He can't believe it—that he's now free of the demon souls' power. He has been listless these twelve days, unused to being spared their relentless demands. Have they really gone? Hard to believe. He hasn't been at peace, wondering if they might return at any moment. He has to know something, to see this for himself.

He grips the heavy stone table firmly with his hands and rocks it back and forth, shifting the table until it has been moved enough to one side. He squats down and brushes his hand across the fine sand underneath, clearing it away with a steady, patient rhythm until his fingers reach the hard metal surface. He taps on it. Then he hesitates. He hasn't opened this case since he buried it here all those years ago.

After he had his guards cut up the women's bodies, they made a fire and burned the remains. He sent the guards away while he watched the fire rage, burning into his memory every detail of the long night. Early in the morning, when the last embers had died down, he gathered the ashes and tiny bone fragments and placed them into the iron box, hiding it under this table. He told no one, not even his guards. He knew he was doing something that would incur Empress Wu Zhao's wrath should she ever discover his treachery. But he didn't care, especially after she had stripped him of his position. He told Her Highness later that he had disposed of the ashes outside Taijigong. She had accepted it without question. The truth was that after all that he had witnessed, he simply couldn't bear to throw the remains away so callously. Their ashes and bones were the only evidence left from that tortuous night. No, he had decided, they had to stay within the Inner Palace.

He pries open the box after a bit of a struggle with the rusty lid. When the lid falls open, he looks in. He can't see too clearly, only more darkness and shadows. Even so, he peers anxiously into that hollowness. After some time, he plunges his hand inside. The soft ashes and the hard bits of bone are still there. He smiles. He half expected that even their remains would have disappeared as a result of the Abbess's exorcism. But now he knows. Yes, only he knows. He had been confused, but now it makes sense to him. He needed to come here and do this. Feel death with his hands.

Vermillion Phoenix Pavilion
The Inner Palace at Taijigong
North Central Chang'an

"Here is a question for you," begins Nü Huang. She and Wan'er sip from small bowls of a delicate broth made with figs and slices of lotus root. They're seated under the roof of the hexagonal pavilion. The days are still pleasant as the end of summer draws near.

Nü Huang, though, wears a thin cloak made of a fine gold silk, trimmed with an embroidered border of dragons and phoenixes. On a side tray next to their table are steamed buns the size of peony buds, touched with a hint of pink colouring at the tips. And a plate with a single ripe persimmon, gleaming with a bright orange hue. Wan'er puts down her bowl and spoon and clasps her hands together in her lap, readying herself.

"Why do you think those demon souls were so relentless?"

"Your Majesty, I am no expert on such things," Wan'er demurs.

"I am asking for your opinion. Speak your mind, whatever comes to you." Nü Huang's hand in mid-air starts to shake, the tremor strong enough to cause the broth in the spoon to splatter onto the napkin under her chin. Ah Pu rushes forward from her waiting position outside the pavilion to wipe Nü Huang's chin and to take over the feeding.

While Ah Pu is helping Nü Huang, Wan'er looks out at the pond. Almost all the lotus blossoms are past their flowering, the pond now mostly populated with brown seedpods, carcasses of their previous glory, while the broad lotus pads are yellowing with decay. Her heart is burdened with the thought that Nü Huang is much like one of these withered blossoms. It pains Wan'er to know that Nü Huang has brought herself closer to death by her thirst for immortality. *Is this the justice of the unseen realms?* she asks silently, recalling her sovereign's words.

Wan'er turns her mind back to answering Nü Huang's question. "Demon souls. Perhaps their persistence and virulence derive from whatever went unachieved while they were alive, as if everything becomes amplified at death." Wan'er chews slowly on the lotus root slices, cooked perfectly so as to retain a trace of crunchiness.

"The Abbess has surely destroyed them. What a talent she is! Ever since her exorcism, there have been no more incidents. Not a single one. Marvellous." Nü Huang smiles gleefully to herself. She leans close so that her breath falls moist against Wan'er's ear. "What will you choose to do once my reign is over? When I am dead and gone. Will you forget my wishes?" Nü Huang grabs Wan'er's wrist.

"Or will you promise to take care of my Palace Diary and my private scrolls and compile them? Promise me you will not forget." Then she releases Wan'er, who grabs her own wrist and strokes it.

Wan'er closes her eyes for a few moments, giving her enough time to stifle her tears. A tussle of emotions rages within. Upset mixed with yearning for the impossible. She mustn't cry. Nü Huang will interpret tears as a sign of something suspicious.

She finally meets her sovereign's questioning gaze. "I promise to take care of your writings, Your Majesty."

"I am happy to hear that. You know ..." Nü Huang's lips quiver. "I have never doubted it—that you were destined to be by my side all these years. I have never forgotten your mother's dream that you are to weigh out the affairs of my world. All these difficult years, where would I be without your loyalty? You are the kind of daughter I never had." Nü Huang's voice wavers with emotion, but she continues. "You have the power to do whatever you wish with the Palace Diary entries, and whatever else I will leave behind in my private scrolls. Yes, indeed, the prophecy will come to pass, and then you will be weighing out my world, the world I have so assiduously described these past few months in the Diary entries. I hope ... I hope you will not abuse that power I grant you, my dear."

"I promise, Your Majesty, that I will perform my duties with the greatest discretion."

"Never mind discretion, Wan'er. If I wanted discretion, I never would have started the Palace Diary in the first place."

Wan'er nods, shifting her eyes slightly away from Nü Huang's searching gaze. She stares at the carved phoenix figures on the pillar.

While Ah Pu feeds a slice of persimmon to Nü Huang, Wan'er stretches out a hand to caress the lacquered vermillion pillar. She can smell the fragrant nanmu wood. She remembers that Wu Zhao the

Empress had played hide-and-seek games with her when she was a very young girl. A haunting memory of the Empress's playful laughter echoes through her. She jolts back to the present when Nü Huang resumes talking to her.

"Wan'er, this is what I am asking of you, that you would use your conscience and wisdom to choose from some of the entries in my private scrolls and compile them together with the other entries to form a coherent Palace Diary to be bound and stored in the library here. Then have a copy made to be placed at Luoyang."

"Yes, Your Majesty. As you wish."

"I believe that there is not much else I want to include. Perhaps a few more entries left to dictate to you. After those are recorded, I will hand my private scrolls to you. But don't bother reading those until I am dead." Saying that, Nü Huang sighs with relief. She takes a tiny bite of a steamed bun, savouring the sweet lotus paste inside. "Speaking of Luoyang, it may be propitious for the court to return there next summer."

Wan'er swallows her mouthful of steamed bun in shock and almost chokes. She sips more soup until the food goes down smoothly. "I had no idea it would be so soon, Your Majesty."

"Why, yes. I've finished the Jin Dan elixir made by the alchemists at Da Fa Temple, and I'm not due for another one until two years hence. All the zaixiang are whining and screeching like monkeys, impatient to see that the Crown Prince succeed me sooner than later, aren't they?" Nü Huang casts a searching glance at Wan'er, who stays silent. "Indeed, we must head back to Luoyang and finish affairs there, so I can hand the reign over to my son."

Wan'er has a sinking feeling in her belly. She ought to be feeling excited, but all she can think of at this moment is that she may never see Ling again.

"You look unhappy, my child. What is it?"

For a few moments, Wan'er imagines confessing to Her Majesty that she would like to remain in Chang'an, write poems, compile works for the Imperial library, and be close to the Abbess, with whom she is infatuated. The thoughts gush out, but only in her mind. The fantasy passes quickly, and she focuses on what must be said to hide her true feelings.

"I am considering all the tasks that must be done to facilitate the move. The library, the court, and palace documents. Which documents to leave here and which to bring with us. I hope there will be enough time to do everything."

"Yes, of course you will have time. Twelve months should be sufficient. You must not fret about that. I can provide you with assistants, if necessary." Nü Huang finishes off a steamed bun, licking her lips with satisfaction.

"About the Immortal Crane Event ..."

"Yes, Your Majesty?"

"Arrange for all the preparations to be halted. I would like to delay this event until the court and palace return to Luoyang. There have been too many difficult things to deal with here in Taijigong. I feel it would be more auspicious to hold the celebrations there—that would be such a pleasant event to herald my return to the Eastern Capital!"

"I will tend to this, Your Majesty."

"Good, very good. I can rely on you. I have always known that, my dear." Tears come to Nü Huang's eyes.

Myriad Springs Hall
The Outer Palace at Taijigong
North Central Chang'an

They gather together just as the drums signal the Hour of the Monkey, when sunlight sneaks through the latticed windows with the soft slant of a late afternoon.

Wan'er gazes incredulously at those seated around her. It must be that she has gained illicit entry into someone else's dream. How else could it be that the conspirators have finally welcomed her into this meeting? Even Princess Wei is casting sly smiles of acknowledgment in her direction. The zaixiang ministers are now so emboldened as to meet without the concealment afforded by darkness, across from the Thousand Autumns Hall. She admires the marvellous six-fold screen behind them, a gift of the Japanese envoys to Taizong more than seventy years ago.

She moves her eyes very slowly across the ink and gold-coloured screen, which depicts an outdoor autumn festival. On the first two panels on the left are a cluster of guards, some hoisting fancy umbrellas to shield members of the Imperial court. In the midsection of the screen, male drummers prance alongside a troupe of female dancers in kimonos. The women carry leafy sprigs in their hands, their faces shielded from the sun by bamboo hats. The procession moves along the shore next to the river. In the final two panels of the screen, huddled at the river's edge, is a small group of village folk gawking at the extravagant procession.

Sansi looks sombrely at Wan'er. "Your Eminence, please tell the rest of our gathering what Nü Huang said to you only two days ago."

Wan'er nods as she replies, "Her Majesty betrayed no evidence of hesitation in her voice when she confided her distinct wish to move the court back to Luoyang next summer."

"Splendid news!" First Minister Wei punctuates his response by spitting forcefully into the spittoon.

"We must act swiftly." Princess Wei's voice sinks emphatically into that last pronouncement.

Sansi quickly speaks up. "Most definitely, Your Highness. Now is the moment to memorialize to Her Majesty for the reinstatement of our ally Zhang Jianzhi at court."

First Minister Wei continues, "And then he will undoubtedly have the Yülin guards in the Luoyang court at his ready disposal!"

"Why, this is all going to happen very quickly then!" exclaims Minister Su.

Princess Wei casts a quick glance at Wan'er. "That means, my dear, that our next Emperor will soon require your services. You must tend to him with unwavering devotion, so that we'll be assured of your loyalty."

First Minister Wei and Minister Su smile knowingly at Wan'er, nodding their heads.

Wan'er's face flushes red-hot. How brazen of the Princess! Must the future Empress remind her that her duties as Li Zhe's Imperial Secretary most likely will include serving him in his inner chambers? Such a condescending tone, clucking at her as if she were a maid. Wan'er curls her hands into fists under the table.

"I propose that we eliminate the Zhang brothers at the very first opportunity, once the court returns to Luoyang."

"A most apt suggestion, First Minister, since we've suffered enough misery pandering to them," Sansi replies.

Wan'er shudders at Sansi's cold tone of voice. No one has invited her to speak her mind, but she can't bear to let this moment pass her by. As she raises her arms, her sleeves fall away, exposing her wrists as she places one hand on top of the other on the table.

"I may not like the Zhang brothers like the rest of you, but what is the necessity of killing them when all that is required is to arrest them and raise the Crown Prince to the throne?"

"Some actions may not be necessary, Lady Shangguan, but they may be the most expedient when it comes to what swiftly advances us to power. Killing them sets an example for everyone in the court and palace." Sansi's face shows no change in expression. Wan'er sees how determined Sansi is.

Wan'er catches the gleam of approval in Princess Wei's eyes. Feeling a twinge of distress, she turns her head away and stares down at the shadowed patterns of the latticed windows, captured on the marbled floor. Sharply angled lines, made to look random, crisscrossing. Meant to reference the natural chaos of the cosmos and to suggest the opposite of the orderly structures of Taijigong. Contrived, nonetheless. These shadows remind her of the impossible conundrum of mazes built to trap adventurous yet foolish souls who wander into them, each drastic turn ending in a blocked passage.

SHANGGUAN WAN'ER'S STUDY
THE INNER PALACE AT TAIJIGONG
NORTH CENTRAL CHANG'AN

Later that same night, when Wan'er is alone in her study, she goes to the camphor cabinet. Pressing her lips firmly together, she unlocks the cabinet and once again reaches past the hidden door into the secret compartment. She takes out the bound journal that contains her replies to Cai Yan. She has written replies to all but the last of Cai Yan's eighteen songs, which she now reads silently to herself.

The flute's origin, the nomads themselves.
Matched with the qin, their music twinned.
With these eighteen stanzas, my song is finished.
Yet the tones continue, my longing without end.
Subtle strings and pipes reflect the work of creation;
In sorrow and joy they mimic men's hearts.
The nomads and Han—
Heaven and Earth separate us, my children west of me.
Bitter am I, angry spirit that floods the void,
The universe cannot contain the vastness of this feeling!

At her writing desk, Wan'er rubs the inkstick deftly against the wet stone. She inhales, taking comfort in the smell. With her calligraphy brush dipped in the fresh ink, she writes out her reply.

Trapped in eternal wandering,
Your songs are voice—
A lost pilgrim returned to her home.
Subtle is a woman's longing, stirring in sighs
While the body sits placidly, wrists still bound
Your spirit wanders beyond limits
The nomad flute travels
A wild haunting melody
My isolation joins yours.

She'll have these poems dispatched to Ling first thing tomorrow morning. There'll be so much to do to prepare for that move to Luoyang that she can't afford to keep pining for Ling. A tear escapes reluctantly from one eye and stains the purple silk that covers her parting gift.

Liqiu 立秋 Jieqi
Start of Autumn
Seventh Lunar Month
New Moon

APPROACHING CHANG'AN

The geese glare at Ardhanari. It's either from envy or boredom, he believes. After all, they've been travelling together in cramped quarters. Surrounding them are rolled-up carpets and crates filled with bronze ewers and vases, packed down with straw. He hears the muffled conversation through the walls of the carriage. Alopen is excitedly talking to his friend the merchant owner in Sogdian dialect.

Ardhanari squints through the tiny side window as they pass through the main south gates of Chang'an. At dusk, there are few travellers about and the roads are clear. Alopen opens the other window into the back of the carriage and asks Ardhanari, "You said one fang west of the market?"

"Just drop me at the entrance to that ward and I'll make my own way."

"Are you sure?" calls out Alopen.

"Definitely." He hates to impose any further, knowing that Alopen's friend is eager to return home to his family. Besides, he doesn't want Alopen to carry any gossip back to Old Gecko.

After waving goodbye, Ardhanari crosses the street and starts down the narrow winding alley. A fleeting sensation passes through him, a memory of that first day he arrived in the city almost forty years ago. In one sense, he hasn't aged at all, for the feelings of that young man still course through him—the same thrill at the frenetic rhythms and colours, the curiosity and astonishment at being in the largest city on the face of the earth. Even now he gazes at the stone pavements and the ramshackle buildings of the Foreign Quarter with renewed appreciation. He has returned after months away, surprised by the familiar made strange.

He recognizes some people walking down the street. He nods and smiles, but many of them frown at him, puzzled. Even the man who had taken over his room while he was away walks by without realizing that it's him. *Must be the beard and the dishevelled state I'm in,* he muses. That former Ardhanari he left behind was immaculate about his appearance, with nary a hair out of place.

At the fountain, he savours a few large gulps of water while crows perched on the upper tier of the fountain watch him. As the sky shifts from a blaze of crimson and mauve into a quickly encroaching darkness, the crows' silhouettes diminish from view. Ardhanari straightens up and looks at the tea shop with joy. On the second floor, both rooms are warmed from within by the glow of candlelight.

Approaching the tea shop, he's startled by the sound of footsteps from around the corner. A stranger emerges from the shadows and approaches him rather gingerly, as if walking on tiptoe.

"Are you Ardhanari?" asks the stranger, now slightly illuminated by the light from the rooms above. A Chinese boy, no less, glancing shyly at him. Pronouncing his name to sound like the phrase, "Where is the good man?" in the Chinese language. Aren't those his antariya and tunic he's wearing?

Baoshi draws near Ardhanari and pulls out the jade pendant to show him. In the flickering light cast from above, Ardhanari stares down at the carved jade with disbelief. It is unmistakable, this jade carved by his own hands, formed by the impulse of love. He gasps with recognition and staggers back.

"Harelip?" exclaims Ardhanari, confused.

"I am Baoshi, Harelip's disciple. He sent me to Chang'an to find you."

"He's still alive!" He reaches out to firmly grasp Baoshi's arms. "But why now, after such a long silence? And why did he even leave in the first place?"

"He had to flee the city. He couldn't tell anyone where he was going. He was afraid, you see, to risk anyone else being harmed."

"Who's there?" Sita's voice calls out nervously from the window above.

Ardhanari shouts out, "Sita, I'm home!"

There is the sound of footsteps down the stairs before the front doors are flung open and a cacophony of enthusiastic greetings rush toward him. The jogappas compete with one another to embrace him.

In the room upstairs, with food and drink on the table, Ardhanari lies back against the cushions along the wall and scratches the itch on his thickly bearded chin. He shakes his head in disbelief at what he hears.

"I came to Chang'an because Master had a dream that I was to meet you," Baoshi says. "He believed it was necessary that I find you." Finally being able to say this to Ardhanari, he feels overcome with emotion and begins to cry, burying his face in his hands. His Master's dream has come true.

"You must come back with me to Mount Hua. You simply must," urges Baoshi.

"But why? What's the meaning of this sudden urgency? After all this time?" As Ardhanari voices his thoughts, he hears the answer nestled somewhere in his own questions.

"How long have you been here?"

"About eight weeks? Please, will you come back with me?" asks Baoshi again. "I just don't know ..." He can't bear to say it.

"We've loved having him here!" Lakshmi chimes in, not paying attention to the serious tone of the exchange.

"Will you go?" asks Sita, with a grave expression on her face, touching Ardhanari tentatively on the wrist as she pours him some tea.

Ardhanari crosses his arms in front of his chest. Why, he has just come home after four months away, and now he's being asked to consider setting off on another journey to see a man he never expected to see again. He remains silent for quite a while, a sullen, troubled look lingering on his face.

"How can I say no to this?" His voice wavers, giving way to the rupture of emotions. "But I'm very tired. Give me a day or two to rest before we go. In the meantime, tell me everything about your life with Harelip. It's only fair after all these years of absence."

Lady Zhen's Apartment
The Inner Palace at Taijigong
North Central Chang'an

Wan'er finds her mother out in the courtyard garden tending to her chrysanthemums. Lady Zhen is thoroughly absorbed in gazing at the blossoms as she prunes away dead leaves. She's humming a tune under her breath. Wan'er pauses to listen. It's a familiar tune from childhood, about willows welcoming the onset of spring.

Wan'er is amused her mother has chosen a song not in keeping with the season. Once again, her mother is being her usual eccentric self.

"You look well, Mother."

"Daughter!" Lady Zhen turns around to see Wan'er. "It's true, ever since the heat has left us. I always feel happier in the autumn than in the summer. Don't you?"

"I love autumn as much as I adore spring. We have this same exchange every autumn, remember?"

Lady Zhen's eyes sparkle, happy at Wan'er's teasing tone. "Since those demon souls departed, I've felt so much better."

"That's good, Mother. The exorcism ritual worked. I don't understand how it happened. All I know is that the Abbess of Da Fa Temple is a kind-hearted and powerful person. Actually, I find her quite compelling."

Lady Zhen smiles, once again hearing the distinct tone of warmth in her daughter's voice.

"Her Majesty has informed me that we'll have to move back to Luoyang next year."

"Oh? But you mustn't go. Could Nü Huang allow you to remain here? The Imperial library. The rare parchments." Lady Zhen feels a surge of worry tighten her throat.

"I must go. I have no choice. I am the Imperial Secretary, after all."

"I know we're Her Majesty's slaves. We've had to live very restricted lives. But Wan'er, please consider this seriously. What about the possibility of escaping this plight once and for all? Leave Taijigong and go far away. Disappear, far away from the clutches of Nü Huang and her zaixiang ministers. Leave me here, Daughter, for no one would bother to punish me if you left."

"Mother, why are you suggesting this all of a sudden? What an outrageous notion! Where could I go? And how could I leave you? Even if I escaped, how will I manage not to get caught, with this scar marking me?" She points to her forehead, feeling exasperated. Her mother is voicing fantasies she herself has entertained. But she had thought them too foolish to ever voice aloud.

"When those demon souls came to visit me, I became more fretful. And now, this imminent move to Luoyang. I can't help but sense that there are dangerous stirrings afoot. Every time we move from one capital to the other, it's because something dreadful has happened or will happen."

Wan'er falls silent. She's disquieted by her mother's fretfulness and doesn't know what to say. She lifts a hand to caress her scar. The two wrinkled forms lie side by side, asking her if she knows what kind of transformation is possible. *Not just a mark on the skin. A sign of the burden of others.* Ling's words return to haunt her.

"Please consider what I've said." Lady Zhen pauses, her face clouded by concern. "There are too many painful memories back at the palace in Luoyang. Go there, if you must, but I won't follow you. I've achieved peace after such a long time."

Wan'er looks at her mother with consternation. She never thought her mother wouldn't follow her to the Eastern Capital. How could she bear to suggest that they be apart? They might disagree on some things, but they haven't left each other's side in all her life. Thirty-eight years is a long time. Is it unfair to expect her mother to always be near her?

"Will you seek permission for me to remain here with Wisteria? There will be others who remain, as always. I'm fortunate to be such an inconsequential member of the Imperial household, and old enough to be humoured, I think."

"I'll make the request on your behalf. As you wish." Wan'er stares at the large chrysanthemum blossoms, suddenly overwhelmed by their shocking whiteness. White—the colour of endings, and of death. Yet it is also the colour of purity and innocence. Their beauty reminds her of a poem of Tao Yuanming's. She recites two lines from it in a wistful tone:

> My dusty cup shames that emptied wine cask
> The cold flower blooms uncelebrated.

She may be the cold flower that will never acquire her full share of acknowledgment from Nü Huang, from the Crown Prince, or from anyone else at court, yet she's resolved to follow her convictions. She's willing to take the risks, go to Luoyang to participate in the next reign. There is no other choice possible. She stares, willing her eyes to discern the subtle shadows underneath the soft curves of each petal. She can't imagine abandoning this life in service to the throne and the one who sits on it. This has been all that she has known and all that she wishes for. It is not mere servitude; she has also been protected and allowed to indulge her creative imagination. To flee into anonymity—what is that compared to this?

"Wan'er, you must not let your ambition blind you. Be careful." Lady Zhen sighs and draws her eyes back to the chrysanthemums. "Aren't these exquisite?"

"You have a gift for cultivating them, Mother."

THE INNER PALACE AT TAIJIGONG
NORTH CENTRAL CHANG'AN

NÜ HUANG'S PRIVATE SCROLL: CAVERNS AND MOUNTAINS

Last night I had a dream in which the earth opened up, and I looked down an enormous cavern that plunged so deep I could not see its bottom. The wind whistled as it swirled through this dark hole in the ground, and I felt my feet teetering dangerously at its edge. Around me the landscape was miserably desolate, stretching out like a flat expanse of rock. But what rock! Red and pockmarked, like the texture of a well-cooked piece of pork tripe—it looked quite delectable. I stood there, wondering if it would taste any good. Scattered throughout this magnificent landscape were gigantic crows, their wings either ripped to shreds or entirely missing. The sky, blue at first, turned into a luminous yellow. I felt as if I were caught in a magical spell.

When I awakened this morning, I could not stop thinking of this dream, its strange yet compelling images. The opening up of the ground, and me perched at the edge, are surely signs of my imminent death. Try as I might, I cannot escape this mortal inevitability. My mind turns to thoughts of the tomb in which Gaozong lies.

At Qianling, Gaozong's wasted body waits for mine. The Imperial Way is a long path, leading up to the mountain that entombs him. Some call this final route Shen Dao, the Spirit Path.

That path is flanked by the likes of winged horses, vermillion birds, and a dignified assembly of officials and foreign dignitaries—all stone replicas, of course. At the inner precinct gates, a pair of lion sculptures crouch, waiting for me.

Finally I have come to this.

All my life, I have been driven by an insatiable need to discover, to know, and to dominate. Now I am a wrinkled ancient teetering at the edge of death's cavern, but I remain heartily and most lustfully attached to this world of sensuous distractions. Yet even the illustrious and gifted Nü Huang is visited by a dream of maimed crows, gigantic yet unable to fly.

In that dream world, desolation became oddly imbued with an eerie beauty. In a landscape so utterly devoid of embellishment, desolation was exposed for its wealth of meaning. That void waits for me. Emptied of human companionship—yet how alluring the texture and intense redness of that rock!

My mind flashes to that walking boy's face now as I write this, struggling with the tremor in my hands. How uncanny that his Master's name would be Shen Dao. That encounter must have been fated; I grow even more certain as I write this. Why do I feel more shrunken and hollowed out ever since he left Taijigong? With my love of shiny surfaces, of gold and silver and ornate decorations, I was confronted with this ridiculously simple boy who did not try in the least to impress me the way most people seek to do so. But rather, he sought to impress upon me certain ideas that he holds dear in his heart. I wonder, will he continue to abide by such beliefs and strictures as he matures into an adult, or will he become corrupted by life's innumerable temptations?

Dreams, they do not lie. Are they not like oracle bones? Except that the fissures in our dreaming moments do not stay immutable but beckon us to seek answers just beyond our waking grasp.

LEAVING CHANG'AN

They set out well before sunrise, when the streets in the Foreign Quarter are still empty and many people are fast asleep inside their homes. Ardhanari and Baoshi hardly speak as they walk through the quiet streets. Around them, the watchtowers of the city loom, silent witnesses.

Once they're beyond the city walls, they begin to talk freely.

Baoshi has to fight his own impatience, wanting to hurry back to Harelip. He must remain steady in his resolve—focus on moving his body with deliberate mindfulness, away from the colourful, seductive pace of Chang'an and toward a life back on Mount Hua. When he thinks of that first trip up Mount Hua at eight sui, forced out of his life with his mother and father, and he compares that frightened boy with the person he has become, he's filled with a sense of amazement. There isn't any taint of bitterness, his father's cruelty long surpassed by Harelip's love.

Late in the afternoon on the third day, they near the village. Baoshi chooses a route that allows them to avoid being detected. One or two dogs bark anyway, sensing their presence from a distance.

They reach the first plateau of the mountain just at sunset and decide to stop for the night. A rock crevice provides some protection from the wind. They crawl into the crevice, just wide enough for Ardhanari to make a small fire for them. They unfurl the blankets that the jogappas gave them, cover their bodies, and drift quickly into sleep. Sleeping and waking throughout the night, Baoshi is pulled through different dreams, filled with the faces of those he met on the pilgrimage. He dreams of chasing after the mysterious stranger in the market, running until he is breathless. Then he sees himself dancing with Ardhanari and the jogappas. They unravel his breastband as they twirl around him. Nü Huang's wrinkled face changes into the lecherous Yizhi, whom he fends off easily. He wakes up at the end of this last image, mumbling that no one is going to entrap him ever again. Looking around, he's relieved to find Ardhanari snoring gently next to him.

Baoshi stares at the dark expanse of sky overhead, then turns his face in the direction of the shack. *How is Harelip?* So many times during this pilgrimage he has posed this question, waiting for some sense of his Master to come to him. Tonight, he feels certain that his Master too must feel that they are close.

He looks at Ardhanari again. If he feels impatient because of several months' separation from Harelip, how has the thirty-six-year separation affected Ardhanari? And Harelip? Now that he has learned more about his Master's life in Chang'an, he feels a soft ache of empathy for him, guessing at the particular kind of anguish he must have felt at having to leave his beloved behind.

Far too restless to return to sleep, he rouses his travelling companion in the bluish shadows before dawn. They continue their ascent in the dim light. Ardhanari yawns and yawns, as if he has been asleep for a long time. The air thickens with fog. Baoshi's mind is keenly focused on the movement of his body, where to plant his foot on the next step ahead of him. The sound of his walking stick, a light tapping rhythm, relaxes him while Ardhanari lags behind, panting from the exertion.

Baoshi recalls that last conversation with Harelip just before he left Mount Hua. Harelip asked him to recite the parable of the water in the pond. Now, as he ascends, he recites it again.

"Each person's essences might be compared to the waters of a pond and the body to the embankments along the sides of a pond. Good deeds are like the water's source. If these three things are complete, the pond will be sturdy. But if the heart does not focus on goodness, the pond lacks embankments and water runs out. If a person fails to accumulate sufficient good deeds, the pond is cut off at its source and the water will dry up. If one breaches the dike to water fields as if the pond were a river or stream, then, even though the embankments hold, the original flow will leak off and the pond will eventually empty."

This was the place in the parable where he had stopped, unable to recall the rest. As he climbs the last few steps of the final slope, he continues. "Then the bed of the pond becomes scorched and cracked, and that is when all kinds of sickness will emerge. If one is not cautious about such things, the pond will become an empty ditch."

Ardhanari listens intently to Baoshi. Images of his damaged sculptures come to mind. He makes a wish under his breath: "May the good deeds of my hands manifest through the figures I create. May I breathe vitality into all that I touch."

The fog conceals the surroundings as they near their destination, but Baoshi can conjure up the sights in his mind easily as he breathes deeply and strongly. He knows the meaning of intuition now. He remembers how he had answered Nü Huang: *I'm following what draws me.*

Baoshi turns to Ardhanari. "We're almost there."

Ardhanari nods, suddenly afraid. Baoshi senses this and takes Ardhanari's hand gently in his.

"Over there. Can you see?"

Ardhanari catches a glimpse of the shack through the fog. "What do we do now?"

"Don't be afraid. Come." Baoshi gently tugs at Ardhanari's hand as they walk toward the shack.

Baoshi leans his walking stick noiselessly against the outside wall of the shack. Standing at the open entrance, they wait in silence. Ardhanari chokes back his tears as he stares at the upright back of the old man sitting on his cushion. The monk's voice is a weak yet determined whisper as he recites the Heart Sutra.

"... without attainment, bodhisattvas take refuge in Prajnaparamita and live without walls of the mind. Without walls of the mind and thus without fears, they see through delusions and finally nirvana—" Harelip stops, a coughing spasm interrupting him. After it subsides, he takes a few deep and slow breaths before resuming. "The mantra of great magic, the unexcelled mantra, the mantra equal to the unequalled, which heals all suffering and is true, not false, the mantra in Prajnaparamita spoken thus: *Gate gate, paragate, parasangate, bodhi svaha.*"

Baoshi and Ardhanari are suspended in the sutra's eternity until they hear the cymbals being struck together three times. Harelip opens his eyes, rises from the tattered cushion, and bows to the altar.

"Master, look! I've returned with him."

"Harelip," Ardhanari utters cautiously.

Turning slowly toward their voices, Harelip's eyes brim with tears, elated to see the man he thought he would never see again. Like him, Ardhanari shows signs of being worn down by time and suffering, yet his eyes retain a tender familiarity. And standing next to Ardhanari, his precious and radiant Baoshi. Gone is the anguish of waiting, inconsequential at this moment.

Harelip's voice trembles with gratitude. "Welcome back, miracle of Heaven."

AUTHOR'S NOTES

This is a work of fiction. Although some characters and incidents in this book are based on actual historical figures and events, these have been altered to suit my narrative purposes.

All Chinese names are based on the Pinyin system.

The symbol 𣲷 is the original Shang Dynasty character for hua 化, which means transformation or change, as in bian hua 變化. This symbol and explanations of its origins were taken from Cecilia Lindqvist's *China: Empire of Living Symbols,* translated from the Swedish by Joan Tate (New York: Addison-Wesley, 1991).

The body shen is written as 身, whereas the spirit shen is 神.

Lines from Nagarjuna's poem "Awakening" (in epigraph and text) are adapted from *Verses from the Center: A Buddhist Vision of the Sublime,* translated by Stephen Batchelor (New York: Riverhead Books, 2000).

The term "sui" in Chinese refers to age. At birth, a person is already one sui, the time in the womb being taken into account.

The parable of the water in the pond is paraphrased from "The Xiang'er Commentary to the Laozi" in Stephen R. Brokenkamp's *Early Daoist Scriptures* (Berkeley: University of California Press, 1997), 114.

The song Baoshi sings on the way to Chang'an is my translation of "Sad Song," a Han Dynasty ballad from *Chinese Poetry: Major Modes and Genres,* edited and translated by Wai-lim Yip (Berkeley: University of California Press, 1976), 113.

Krishna's song, sung by Ardhanari, is based on "Narajanma Bandage," a bhajan song found on the CD *Krishna Lila* (San Francisco: Six Degrees Records, 2002). Translated lyrics were viewed at http://www.chebisabbah.com.

The translated poems of Cai Yan's "Eighteen Songs of a Nomad Flute" were found in *Women Writers of Traditional China,* edited by

Kang-I Sun Chang and Haun Saussy (Redwood City, CA: Stanford University Press, 1999). The initial translations in that edition were done by Dore J. Levy, but I have altered them. I wrote the poems by Shangguan Wan'er.

The Union of the Triple Equation was adapted from text in Daniel Reid's *The Tao of Sex, Health & Longevity* (New York: Fireside, 1989).

Two lines from Tao Yuanming's poem "The Double Ninth, in Retirement," recited by Shangguan Wan'er, were found in *The Poetry of T'ao Ch'ien*, translated by James Robert Hightower (Oxford: Clarendon, 1970).

Lines of the sutra recited by Harelip are from *The Heart Sutra: The Womb of Buddhas*, translated by Red Pine (Washington, DC: Shoemaker & Hoard, 2004).

I consulted *Chinese History: A Manual* by Endymion Wilkinson (Cambridge: Harvard University Press, 2000) for the Jieqi system of dividing the year according to the seasons, and for telling the time of day using the twelve double-hour classification.

I relied on Derk Bodde's *Festivals in Classical China* (Princeton: Princeton University Press, 1975) for Han Dynasty origins of festivals, and for details about exorcism and exorcists. He referred to zhesi jisheng 磔死寄生 as "those, who having suffered execution with public exposure, now cling to the living."

Other primary resource books:

Blunden, Caroline and Mark Elvin. *Cultural Atlas of China*. New York: Checkmark, 1998.

Fitzgerald, C.P. *The Empress Wu*. Vancouver: UBC Press, 1968.

Hammer, Leon. *dragon rises, red bird flies*. New York: Station Hill Press, 1990.

Thorp, Robert, and Richard Vinogard. *Chinese Art and Culture.* New York: Harry N. Abrams, 2001.

Twitchett, Denis. *The Cambridge History of China: Sui and T'ang China,* vol. 3, 589–906. Cambridge: Cambridge University Press, 1979.

Whitfield, Roderick, and Susan Whitfield. *Cave Temples of Mogao.* Los Angeles: Getty Conservation Institute and the J. Getty Museum, 2000.

ACKNOWLEDGMENTS

Thanks to Arsenal Pulp Press, *The Walking Boy* has made a reappearance in a revised form.

Thanks also to Ronnie Hill Lee Photography for the author photo and to Jo Zhou, who provided materials on ancient methods of tea preparation, tea ware, and tea culture in China.

Thanks to all my readers who read the first edition of *The Walking Boy* and waited a very long time before *Oracle Bone* appeared in 2017. May you be willing to wait for the appearance of the third novel in this series, and may I succeed in accomplishing this next creative project.

LYDIA KWA is the author of the novels *Oracle Bone* (the first in the chuanqi series), *This Place Called Absence* (shortlisted for the Books in Canada First Novel Award), and *Pulse*, as well as two books of poetry, *The Colours of Heroines* and *sinuous*. She lives and works on the traditional and unceded territories of the Coast Salish peoples as a writer and psychologist.

lydiakwa.com